'A warning: if you don't wish to become addicted to the most impressive new fantasy sequence in many a moon, you should avoid *Bodyguard of Lightning*, the first novel in Stan Nicholl's compelling *Orcs: First Blood* saga. If, however, you're in the mood for the most imaginative (and viscerally exciting) re-invention of some of the most cherished concepts in the genre, then Stan is your man' Barry Forshaw, LineOne SF site (http://www.lineone.net/)

'Excellent fantasy with a twist. Writing from the point of view of the orcs is a neat idea and Stan Nicholls pulls it off with great panache. Fast and violent . . . an all action adventurer. You'll never feel the same about *The Lord of the Rings*' *SFX*

'Nicholls tells his tale briskly and entertainingly, and doesn't pull any punches when it comes to showing the hard and unglamorous life of military men (and women). It's refreshing to see things from the orcs' point of view for once, and Nicholls has a different (often amusing) take on each of the elder races'. *Starburst*

Also by Stan Nicholls

Legion of Thunder

ORCS
FIRST BLOOD

Bodyguard of Lightning

STAN NICHOLLS

This edition published in Great Britain in 1999 by
Millennium
An imprint of Victor Gollancz Ltd
Orion House, 5 Upper St Martin's Lane,
London WC2H 9EA

To receive information on the Millennium list, e-mail us at:
smy@orionbooks.co.uk

A CIP catalogue record for this book
is available from the British Library

ISBN 1 85798 558 3

Printed in Great Britain by
Clays Ltd, St Ives plc

This is, of course, for Anne and Marianne

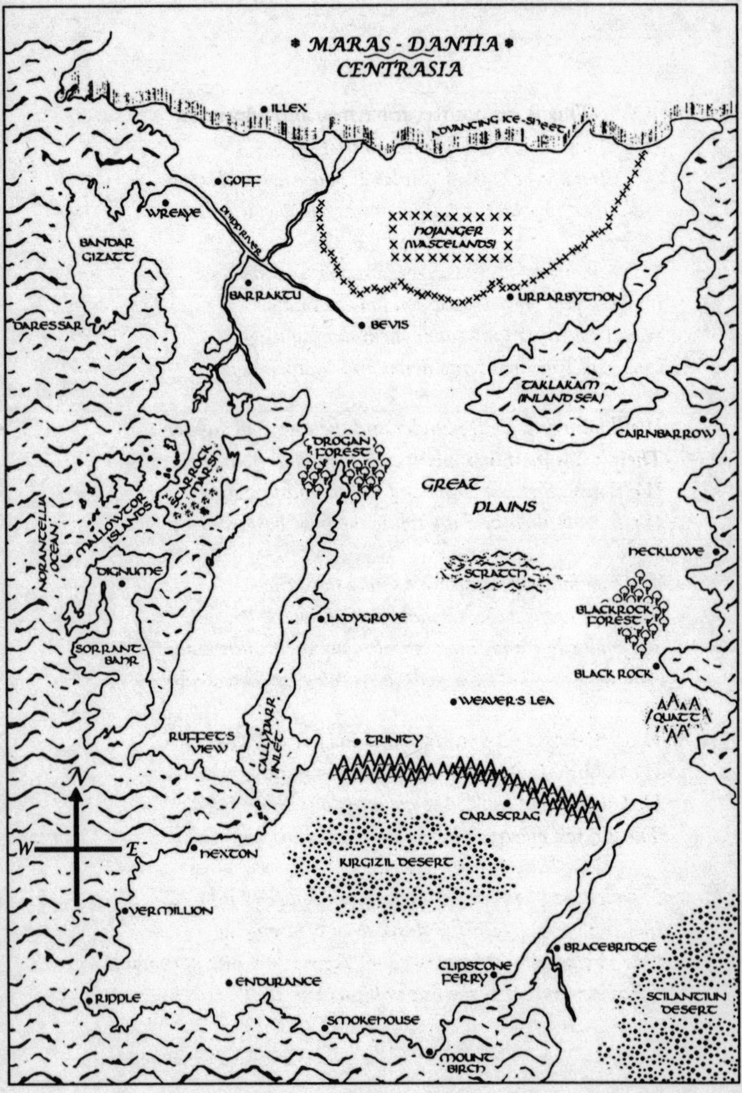
MARAS - DANTIA
CENTRASIA
ILLEX
ADVANCING ICE-SHEET
GOFF
WREAYE
BANDAR GIZATT
HOJANGER (WASTELANDS)
BARRAKTU
URRARBYTHON
BEVIS
DARESSAR
TAKLAKAM (INLAND SEA)
CAIRNBARROW
DROGAN FOREST
SCARROCK MARSH
MALLOWTOR ISLANDS
NORANTELLIA OCEAN
GREAT PLAINS
HECKLOWE
SCRATCH
DIGNUME
LADYGROVE
BLACKROCK FOREST
SORRANT-BAHR
BLACK ROCK
WEAVER'S LEA
QUATT
RUFFET'S VIEW
CALLYDARR INLET
TRINITY
N
W
E
S
CARASCRAG
HEXTON
KIRGIZIL DESERT
VERMILLION
BRACEBRIDGE
CLIPSTONE FERRY
ENDURANCE
RIPPLE
SCILANTIUN DESERT
SMOKEHOUSE
MOUNT BIRCH

Oh we'll rant and we'll roar like true orcish warriors
We'll rant and we'll roar for all that we be
We'll march back from yonder all laden with plunder
Oh what treasures, what pleasures, then you will see

Farewell and good-bye to you fair orcish ladies
Farewell and good-bye to you ladies of hame
We've taken a liking to mayhem and fighting
Our blades we will bring down and sharpen again

We'll burn and we'll plunder and then we will sunder
Their heads from their necks and their gold from their purse
We'll meet them in battle and kill them like cattle
We'll drink their beer dry while the poor bastards curse

The first land we sighted we saw a tall spire
We crept up in darkness and set it aflame
We took silver and chalice for we bore them such malice
And we hope that next year they won't be there again

We found a fat farmer, we found his fair daughter
We tickled him up with the point of a knife
He babbled and gabbled, gave us gold without haggle
The girl ran off screaming so we roasted his wife

Now let every orc warrior take up his full tankard
Now let every orc warrior drink deep of strong ale
Our Wolverines' spearpoints will skewer 'em like pork joints
Far richer and fatter the orcs will prevail!

Traditional war band marching song

1

Stryke couldn't see the ground for corpses.

He was deafened by screams and clashing steel. Despite the cold, sweat stung his eyes. His muscles burned and his body ached. Blood, mud and splashed brains flecked his jerkin. And now two more of the loathsome, soft pink creatures were moving in on him with murder in their eyes.

He savoured the joy.

His footing unsure, he stumbled and almost fell, pure instinct bringing up his sword to meet the first swinging blade. The impact jarred but checked the blow. He nimbly retreated a pace, dropped into a half crouch and lunged forward again, below his opponent's guard. The sword rammed into the enemy's stomach. Stryke quickly raked it upward, deep and hard, until it struck a rib, tumbling guts. The creature went down, a stupefied expression on its face.

There was no time to relish the kill. The second attacker was on him, clutching a two-handed broadsword, its glinting tip just beyond the limit of Stryke's reach. Mindful of its fellow's fate, this one was more cautious. Stryke went on the offensive, engaging his assailant's blade with a rain of aggressive swipes. They parried and thrusted, moving in a slow, cumbersome dance, their boots seeking purchase on bodies of friend and foe alike.

Stryke's weapon was better suited to fencing. The size and weight of the creature's broadsword made it awkward to use in close combat. Designed for hacking, it needed to be swung in a wider arc. After several passes the creature strained with effort, huffing clouds of icy breath. Stryke kept harrying from a distance, awaiting his chance.

In desperation, the creature lurched toward him, its sword slashing at his face. It missed, but came close enough for him to feel the displaced air. Momentum carried the stroke on, lifting the creature's arms high and leaving its chest unprotected. Stryke's blade found its heart, triggering a scarlet eruption. The creature spiralled into the trampling mêlée.

Glancing down the hill, Stryke could make out the Wolverines, embroiled in the greater battle on the plain below.

He returned to the slaughter.

Coilla looked up and saw Stryke on the hill above, not far from the walls of the settlement, savagely laying into a group of defenders.

She cursed his damned impatience.

But for the moment their leader would have to look after himself. The warband had some serious resistance to overcome before they could get to him.

Here in the boiling cauldron of the main battlefield, bloody conflict stretched out on every side. A crushing mob of fighting troops and shying mounts churned to pulp what had been fields of crops just hours before. The cacophonous, roaring din was endless, the tart aroma of death soured the back of her throat.

A thirty-strong flying wedge bristling with steel, the Wolverines kept in tight formation, powering through the struggling mass like some giant multi-stinged insect. Near the wedge's spearhead, Coilla helped clear their path, lashing out with her sword at enemy flesh obstructing the way.

Too fast to properly digest, a succession of hellish tableaux vivants flashed past her. A defender with a hatchet buried in its shoulder; one of her own side, gore-encrusted hands covering his eyes; another silently shrieking, a red stump in lieu of an arm; one of theirs staring down at a hole the size of a fist in its chest; a headless body, gushing crimson as it staggered. A face cut to ribbons by the slashing of her blade.

An infinity later the Wolverines arrived at the foot of the hill and began to climb as they fought.

A brief hiatus in the butchery allowed Stryke to check again the progress of his band. They were cleaving through knots of defenders about halfway up the hill.

He turned back and surveyed the massive wooden-walled stronghold topping the rise. There was a way to go before they reached its gates, and several score more of the enemy to overcome. But it seemed to Stryke that their ranks were thinning.

Filling his lungs with frigid air, he felt again the intensity of life that came when death was this close.

Coilla arrived, panting, the rest of the troop close behind.

'Took your time,' he commented drily. 'Thought I'd have to storm the place alone.'

She jabbed a thumb at the milling chaos below. 'Weren't keen on letting us through.'

They exchanged smiles that were almost crazed.

Bloodlust's on her too, he thought. *Good.*

Alfray, custodian of the Wolverines' banner, joined them and drove the flag's spar into the semi-frozen earth. The warband's two dozen common soldiers formed a defensive ring around the officers. Noticing one of the grunts had taken a pernicious-looking head wound, Alfray pulled a field dressing from his hip bag and went to staunch the blood.

Sergeants Haskeer and Jup pushed through the troopers. As usual, the former was sullen, the latter unreadable.

'Enjoy your stroll?' Stryke jibed, his tone sarcastic.

Jup ignored it. 'What now, Captain?' he asked gruffly.

'What *think* you, shortarse? A break to pick flowers?' He glared at his diminutive joint second-in-command. 'We get up there and do our job.'

'How?'

Coilla was staring at the leaden sky, a hand cupped over her eyes.

'Frontal assault,' Stryke replied. 'You have a better plan?' It was a challenge.

'No. But it's open ground, uphill. We'll have casualties.'

'Don't we always?' He spat copiously, narrowly missing his sergeant's feet. 'But if it makes you feel better we'll ask our strategist. Coilla, what's your opinion?'

'Hmmm?' Her attention remained fixed on the heavy clouds.

'*Wake up*, Corporal! I said—'

'See that?' She pointed skyward.

A black dot was descending through the gloom. No details were obvious from this distance, but they all guessed what it was.

'Could be useful,' Stryke said.

Coilla was doubtful. 'Maybe. You know how wilful they can be. Best to take cover.'

'Where?' Haskeer wanted to know, scanning the naked terrain.

The dot grew in size.

'It's moving faster than a cinder from Hades,' Jup observed.

'And diving too tight,' added Haskeer.

By this time the bulky body and massive serrated wings were clearly visible. There was no doubt now. Huge and ungainly, the beast swooped over the battle still raging on the plain.

Combatants froze and stared upwards. Some scattered from its shadow. It carried on heedless in an ever-sharper descent, aimed squarely at the rise where Stryke's Wolverines were gathered.

He squinted at it. 'Can anybody make out the handler?'

They shook their heads.

The living projectile came at them unerringly. Its vast, slavering jaws gaped, revealing rows of yellow teeth the size of war helms. Slitty green eyes flashed. A rider sat stiffly on its back, tiny compared to his charge.

Stryke estimated it to be no more than three flaps of its powerful wings away.

'Too low,' Coilla whispered.

Haskeer bellowed, '*Kiss the ground!*'

The warband flattened.

Rolling on to his back, Stryke had a fleeting view of grey leathery skin and enormous clawed feet passing overhead. He almost believed he could stretch and touch the thing.

Then the dragon belched a mighty gout of dazzling orange flame.

For a fraction of a second Stryke was blinded by the intensity of light. Blinking through the haze, he expected to see the dragon smash into the ground. Instead he caught sight of it soaring aloft at what seemed an impossibly acute angle.

Further up the hillside, the scene was transformed. The defenders and some attackers, ignited by the blazing suspiration, had been turned into shrieking fireballs or were already dead in smouldering heaps. Here and there, the earth itself burned and bubbled.

A smell of roasting flesh filled the air. It made the juices in Stryke's mouth flow.

'Somebody should remind the dragonmasters whose side they're on,' Haskeer grumbled.

'But this one eased our burden.' Stryke nodded at the gates.

They were well alight. Scrambling to his feet, he yelled, '*To me!*'

The Wolverines sent up a booming war cry and thundered after him. They met little resistance, easily cutting down the few enemy still left standing.

When Stryke reached the smoking gates he found them damaged enough to offer no real obstacle, and one was hanging crookedly, fit to fall.

Nearby, a pole held a charred sign bearing the crudely painted word *Homefield*.

Haskeer ran to Stryke's side. He noticed the sign and swiped contemptuously at it with his sword, severing it from the upright. It fell and broke in two.

'Even our language has been colonised,' he growled.

Jup, Coilla and the remainder of the band caught up with them. Stryke and several troopers booted the weakened gate, downing it.

They poured through the opening and found themselves in a spacious compound. To their right, a corral held livestock. On the left stood a row of mature fruit trees. Ahead and set well back was a sizeable wooden farmhouse.

Lined up in front of it were at least twice as many defenders as Wolverines.

The warband charged and set about the creatures. In the intense hand-to-hand combat that followed, the Wolverines' discipline proved superior. With nowhere to run, desperation fuelled the enemy and they fought savagely, but in moments their numbers were drastically depleted. Wolverine casualties were much lighter, a handful sustaining minor wounds. Not enough to slow their advance or impede the zeal with which they plundered their foes' milky flesh.

At length, the few remaining defenders were driven back to bunch in front of the entrance. Stryke led the onslaught against them, shoulder to shoulder with Coilla, Haskeer and Jup.

Yanking his blade free of the final protector's innards, Stryke spun and gazed around the compound. He saw what he needed at the corral's fence. 'Haskeer! Get one of those beams for a ram!'

The sergeant hurried away, barking orders. Seven or eight troopers peeled off to run after him, tugging hatchets from their belts.

Stryke beckoned a footsoldier. The private took two steps and collapsed, a slender shaft projecting from his throat.

'*Archers!*' Jup yelled, waving his blade at the building's upper storey.

The band dispersed as a hail of arrows peppered them from an open window above. One Wolverine went down, felled by a shot to the head. Another was hit in the shoulder and pulled to cover by his comrades.

Coilla and Stryke, nearest the house, ran forward to take shelter under the building's overhang, pressing themselves to the wall on either side of the door.

'How many bowmen have *we*?' she asked.

'We just lost one, so three.'

He looked across the farmyard. Haskeer's crew seemed to be taking the brunt of the archers' fire. As arrows whistled around them, troopers gamely hacked at the uprights supporting one of the livestock pen's immense timbers.

Jup and most of the others sprawled on the ground nearby. Braving the volleys, Corporal Alfray knelt as he improvised a binding for the trooper's pierced shoulder. Stryke was about to call over when he saw the three archers were stringing their short bows.

Lying full-length was a less then ideal firing position. They had to turn the bows sideways and aim upwards while lifting their chests. Yet they quickly began unleashing shafts in a steady stream.

From their uncertain sanctuary Stryke and Coilla were

powerless to do anything except watch as arrows winged up to the floor above and others came down in exchange. After a minute or two a ragged cheer broke out from the warband, obviously in response to a hit. But the two-way flow of bolts continued, confirming that at least one more archer was in the building.

'Why not tip the shafts with fire?' Coilla suggested.

'Don't want the place to burn till we get what we're after.'

A weighty crash came from the corral. Haskeer's unit had freed the beam. Troopers set to lifting it, still wary of enemy fire, though it was now less frequent.

Another triumphant roar from the pinned-down grunts was followed by a commotion upstairs. An archer fell, smacking to the ground in front of Stryke and Coilla. The arrow jutting from its chest was snapped in half by the impact.

At the livestock, Jup was on his feet, signalling that the upper storey was clear.

Haskeer's crew ran over with the beam, muscles taut and faces strained with the effort of shifting its mass. All hands to the improvised ram, the warband began pounding the reinforced door, splintering shards of wood. After a dozen blows it gave with a loud report and exploded inwards.

A trio of defenders were waiting for them. One leapt forward, killing the lead rammer with a single stroke. Stryke felled the creature, clambered over the discarded timber and laid into the next. A brief, frenzied trading of blows pitched it lifeless to the floor. But the distraction left Stryke open to the third defender. It closed in, its blade pulling up and back, ready to deliver a decapitating swipe.

A throwing knife thudded hard into his chest. It gave a throaty rasp, dropped the sword and fell headlong.

Stryke's grunt was all Coilla could expect in the way of thanks.

She retrieved the knife from her victim and drew another to

fill her empty hand, preferring a blade in both fists when close quarter fighting seemed likely. The Wolverines flowed into the house behind her.

Before them was an open central staircase.

'Haskeer! Take half the company and clear this floor,' Stryke ordered. 'The rest with me!'

Haskeer's troopers spread right and left. Stryke led his party up the stairs.

They were near the top when a pair of creatures appeared. Stryke and the band cut them to pieces in combined fury. Coilla got to the upper level first and ran into another defender. It opened her arm with a saw-toothed blade. Hardly slowing, she dashed the weapon from its hand and sliced its chest. Howling, it blundered through the rail and plunged to oblivion.

Stryke glanced at Coilla's streaming wound. She made no complaint so he turned his attention to this floor's layout. They were on a long landing with a number of doors. Most were open, revealing apparently empty rooms. He sent troopers to search them. They soon reappeared, shaking their heads.

At the furthest end of the landing was the only closed door. They approached stealthily and positioned themselves outside.

Sounds of combat from the ground floor were already dying down. Shortly, the only noise was the distant, muffled hubbub of the battle on the plain, and the stifled panting of the Wolverines catching their breath as they clustered on the landing.

Stryke glanced from Coilla to Jup, then nodded for the three burliest footsoldiers to act. They shouldered the door once, twice and again. It sprang open and they threw themselves in, weapons raised, Stryke and the other officers close behind.

A creature hefting a double-headed axe confronted them. It went down under manifold blows before doing any harm.

The room was large. At its far end stood two more figures,

shielding something. One was of the defending creatures' race. The other was of Jup's kind, his short, squat build further emphasised by his companion's lanky stature.

He came forward, armed with sword and dagger. The Wolverines moved to engage him.

'*No!*' Jup yelled. '*Mine!*'

Stryke understood. 'Leave them!' he barked.

His troopers lowered their weapons.

The stocky adversaries squared up. For the span of half a dozen heartbeats they stood silently, regarding each other with expressions of vehement loathing.

Then the air rang to the peal of their colliding blades.

Jup set to with a will, batting aside every stroke his opponent delivered, avoiding both weapons with a fluidity born of long experience. In seconds the dagger was sent flying and embedded itself in a floor plank. Soon after, the sword was dashed away.

The Wolverine sergeant finished his opponent with a thrust to the lungs. His foe sank to his knees, toppled forward, twitched convulsively and died.

No longer spellbound by the fight, the last defender brought up its sword and readied itself for a final stand. As it did so, they saw it had been shielding a female of its race. Crouching, strands of mousy hair plastered to its forehead, the female cradled one of their young. The infant, its plump flesh a dawn-tinted colour, was little more than a hatchling.

A shaft jutted from the female's upper chest. Arrows and a longbow were scattered on the floor. She had been one of the defending archers.

Stryke waved a hand at the Wolverines, motioning them to stay, and walked the length of the room. He saw nothing to fear and didn't hurry. Skirting the spreading pool of blood seeping from Jup's dead opponent, he reached the last defender and locked eyes with it.

For a moment it looked as though the creature might speak.

Instead it suddenly lunged, flailing its sword like a mad thing, and with as little accuracy.

Untroubled, Stryke deflected the blade and finished the matter by slashing the creature's throat, near severing its head.

The blood-soaked female let out a high-pitched wail, part squeak, part keening moan. Stryke had heard something like it once or twice before. He stared at her and saw a trace of defiance in her eyes. But hatred, fear and agony were strongest in her features. All the colour had drained from her face and her breath was laboured. She hugged the young one close in a last feeble attempt to protect it. Then the life force seeped away. She slowly pitched to one side and sprawled lifeless across the floor. The hatchling spilled from her arms and began to bleat.

Having no further interest in the matter, Stryke stepped over the corpse.

He was facing a Uni altar. In common with others he'd seen it was quite plain; a high table covered by a white cloth, gold-embroidered at the edges, with a lead candleholder at each end. Standing in the centre and to the rear was a piece of ironwork he knew to be the symbol of their cult. It consisted of two rods of black metal mounted on a base, fused together at an angle to form a simple X.

But it was the object at the front of the table that interested him. A cylinder, perhaps as long as his forearm and the size of his fist in circumference, it was copper-coloured and inscribed with fading runic symbols. One end had a lid, neatly sealed with red wax.

Coilla and Jup came to him. She was dabbing at the wound on her arm with a handful of wadding. Jup wiped red stains from his blade with a soiled rag. They stared at the cylinder.

Coilla said, 'Is that it, Stryke?'

'Yes. It fits her description.'

'Hardly looks worth the cost of so many lives,' Jup remarked.

Stryke reached for the cylinder and examined it briefly before slipping it into his belt. 'I'm just a humble captain. Naturally our mistress didn't explain the details to one so lowly.' His tone was cynical.

Coilla frowned. 'I don't understand why that last creature should throw its life away protecting a female and her offspring.'

'What sense is there in anything humans do?' Stryke replied. 'They lack the balanced approach we orcs enjoy.'

The cries of the baby rose to a more incessant pitch.

Stryke turned to look at it. His green, viperish tongue flicked over mottled lips. 'Are the rest of you as hungry as I am?' he wondered.

His jest broke the tension. They laughed.

'It'd be exactly what they'd expect of us,' Coilla said, reaching down and hoisting the infant by the scruff of its neck. Holding it aloft in one hand, level with her face, she stared at its streaming blue eyes and dimpled, plump cheeks. 'My gods, but these things are *ugly*.'

'You can say that again,' Stryke agreed.

2

Stryke led his fellow orcs and Jup from the room. Coilla carried the baby, a look of distaste on her face.

Haskeer was waiting at the foot of the stairs. 'Find it?' he said.

Nodding, Stryke slapped the cylinder in his belt. 'Torch the place.' He headed for the door.

Haskeer poked a finger at a couple of troopers. 'You and you. Get on with it. The rest of you, *out!*'

Coilla blocked the path of a startled-looking grunt and dumped the baby in his arms. 'Ride down to the plain and leave this where the humans will find it. And try to be . . . *gentle* with the thing.' She hurried off, relieved. The trooper left, clutching the bundle as though it contained eggs, a bemused expression on his face.

There was a general exodus. The appointed arsonists found lanterns and began sloshing oil around. When they'd done, Haskeer dismissed them, then slipped a hand inside his boot for a flint. He ripped a length of shirt off the corpse of a defender and dipped it in oil. Igniting the sodden cloth with a spark, he threw it and ran.

A *whoomp* of yellow flame erupted. Sheets of fire spread over the floor.

Not bothering to look back, he jogged across the compound to catch up with the others.

They were with Alfray. As usual, the corporal was doubling as the warband's surgeon, and as Haskeer arrived he was tying the last stay on a trooper's makeshift splint.

Stryke wanted a casualty report.

Alfray pointed at the bodies of two dead comrades laid out on the ground nearby. 'Slettal and Wrelbyd. Apart from them, three wounded. Though none so bad they won't heal. About a dozen caught the usual minor stuff.'

'So five out of action, leaving us twenty-five strong, counting officers.'

'What's an acceptable loss on a mission like this?' Coilla asked.

'Twenty-nine.'

Even the trooper with the splint joined in the laughter. Although they knew that when it came down to it, their captain wasn't joking.

Only Coilla remained straight-faced, her nostrils flaring slightly, undecided whether they were making her the butt again because she was the newest recruit.

She has a lot to learn, Stryke reflected. *She'd best do it soon.*

'Things are quieter below,' Alfray reported, referring to the battle on the plain. 'It went our way.'

'As expected,' Stryke replied. He seemed uninterested.

Alfray noticed Coilla's wound. 'Want me to look at that?'

'It's nothing. Later.' To Stryke, she added stiffly, 'Shouldn't we be moving?'

'Uhm. Alfray, find a wagon for the wounded. Leave the dead to the scavenging parties.' He turned to the nine or ten troopers hanging around listening. 'Get ready for a forced march back to Cairnbarrow.'

They pulled long faces.

'It'll be nightfall soon,' Jup remarked.

'What of it? We can still walk, can't we? Unless you're all frightened of the dark!'

'Poor bloody infantry,' a private muttered as he passed.

Stryke delivered a savage kick to his backside. '*And don't forget it, you miserable little bastard!*'

The soldier yelped and limped hurriedly away.

This time, Coilla laughed with the others.

Over at the livestock pen a chorus of sound arose, a combination of roars and twittering screeches. Stryke set off in that direction. Haskeer and Jup trailed him. Coilla stayed with Alfray.

Two soldiers were leaning on the corral's fence, watching the milling animals.

'What's going on?' Stryke demanded.

'They're spooked,' one of the troopers told him. 'Shouldn't be cooped up like this. Ain't natural.'

Stryke went to the rail to see for himself.

The nearest beast was no more than a sword's length away. Twice the height of an orc, it stood rampant, weight borne by powerful back legs, taloned feet half buried in the earth. The chest of its feline body swelled, the short, dusty yellow fur bristling. Its eagle-like head moved in a jerky, convulsive fashion and the curved beak clattered nervously. The enormous eyes, jet-black orbs against startlingly white surrounds, were never still. Its ears were pricked and quiveringly alert.

It was obviously agitated, yet its erect pose still maintained a curious nobility.

The herd beyond, numbering upwards of a hundred, was mostly on all fours, backs arched. But here and there pairs stood upright, boxing at each other with spindly arms, wickedly sharp claws extended. Their long curly tails swished rhythmically.

A gust of wind brought with it the fetid odour of the gryphons' dung.

'Gant's right,' Haskeer remarked, indicating the trooper who had spoken, 'their pen should be all of Maras-Dantia.'

'Very poetic, Sergeant.'

As intended, Stryke's derision cut Haskeer's pride. He looked as near embarrassed as an orc was capable of. 'I just meant it was typical of humans to pen free-roaming beasts,' he gushed defensively. 'And we all know they'd do the same to us if we let 'em.'

'All I know,' Jup interjected, 'is that yonder gryphons smell bad and taste good.'

'Who asked *you*, you little tick's todger?' Haskeer flared.

Jup bridled and was about to retaliate.

'Shut up, both of you!' Stryke snapped. He addressed the troopers. 'Slaughter a brace for rations and let the rest go before we leave.'

He moved on. Jup and Haskeer followed, exchanging murderous glances.

Behind them, the fire in the house was taking hold. Flames were visible at the upper windows and smoke billowed from the front door.

They reached the compound's ruined gates. On seeing their commander, the guards stationed there straightened themselves in a pretence of vigilance. Stryke didn't ball them out. He was more interested in the scene on the plain. The fighting had stopped, the defenders either being dead or having run away.

'It's a bonus to win the battle,' Haskeer observed, 'seeing as it was only a diversion.'

'They were outnumbered. We deserved to win. But no loose talk of diversions, not outside the band. Wouldn't do to let the arrow fodder know the fight was set up to cover our task.' Automatically his hand went to the cylinder.

Down below, the scavengers were moving among the dead, stripping them of weapons, boots and anything else useful. Other parties had been detailed to finish off the enemy wounded, and those of their own side too far gone to help. Funeral pyres were already burning.

In the gathering twilight it was growing much colder. A stinging breeze whipped at Stryke's face. He looked out beyond the battlefield to the farther plains, and the more remote, undulating tree-topped hills. Softened by the lengthening shadows, it was a scene that would have been familiar to his forebears. Save for the distant horizon, where the faint outline of advancing glaciers showed as a thin strip of luminous white.

As he had a thousand times before, Stryke silently cursed the humans for eating Maras-Dantia's magic.

Then he cast off the thought and returned to practicalities. There was something he'd been meaning to ask Jup. 'How did you feel about killing that fellow dwarf back in the house?'

'Feel?' The stocky sergeant looked puzzled. 'No different to killing anyone else. Nor was he the first. Anyway, he wasn't a "fellow dwarf". He wasn't even from a tribe I knew.'

Haskeer, who hadn't seen the incident, was intrigued. 'You killed one of your own kind? The need to prove yourself must be strong indeed.'

'He took the humans' part and that made him an enemy. I've no need to prove anything!'

'Really? With so many of your clans siding with the humans, and you the only dwarf in the Wolverines? I think you've much to prove.'

The veins in Jup's neck were standing out like taut cords. 'What's your meaning?'

'I just wonder why we need *your* sort in our ranks.'

I should stop this, Stryke thought, *but it's been building too long. Maybe it's time they beat it out of each other.*

'I earned my sergeant's stripes in this band!' Jup pointed at the crescent-shaped tattoos on his rage-red cheeks. 'I was good enough for that!'

'*Were* you?' Haskeer taunted.

Coilla, Alfray and several troopers arrived, drawn by the fuss. More than one of the soldiers wore a gleeful expression at the prospect of a fight between officers. Or in anticipation of Jup losing it.

Insults were now being openly traded, most of them concerning the sergeants' parentage. To rebut a particular point, Haskeer grasped a handful of Jup's beard and gave it a forceful tug.

'Say that again, you snivelling little fluffball!'

Jup pulled free. 'At least I *can* raise hair! You orcs have heads like a human's arse!'

Words were about to give way to action. They squared up, fists bunched.

A trooper elbowed through the scrum. 'Captain! *Captain!*'

The interruption wasn't appreciated by the onlookers. There were disappointed groans.

Stryke sighed. 'What *is* it?'

'We've found something you should see, sir.'

'Can't it wait?'

'Don't think so, Captain. Looks important.'

'All right. Leave it, you two.' Haskeer and Jup didn't move. 'That's *enough*,' he growled menacingly. They lowered their fists and backed off, reluctant and still radiating hatred.

Stryke ordered the guards to admit no one and told the others to get back to work. 'This better be good, Trooper.'

He guided Stryke back into the compound. Coilla, Jup, Alfray and Haskeer, their curiosity whetted, tagged along behind.

The house was blazing furiously, with flames playing on the roof. They could feel the heat being thrown out as far away as the orchard, where the trooper took a sharp left. The higher branches of the trees were burning, each gust of wind liberating showers of drifting sparks.

Once through the orchard they came to a modest wooden barn, its double doors wide open. Inside were two more grunts, holding burning brands. One was inspecting the contents of a hessian sack. The second was on his knees and staring down through a lifted trapdoor.

Stryke crouched to look at the bag, the others gathering around him. It was filled with tiny translucent crystals. They had a faintly purple, pinkish hue.

'Pellucid,' Coilla said in a hushed tone.

Alfray licked his finger and dabbed the crystals. He took a taste. 'Prime quality.'

'And look here, sir.' The trooper pointed at the trapdoor.

Stryke snatched the torch from the kneeling soldier. Its flickering glow showed a small cellar, just deep enough for an orc to stand without bending. Two more sacks lay on its earthen floor.

Jup gave a low, appreciative whistle. 'That's more than I've seen in all my days.'

Haskeer, his dispute with the dwarf forgotten for the moment, nodded in agreement. 'Think of its value!'

'What say we sample it?' Jup suggested hopefully.

Haskeer added his own petition. 'It wouldn't hurt, Captain. Don't we deserve that much after pulling off this mission?'

'I don't know . . .'

Coilla looked pensive but held her tongue.

Alfray eyed the cylinder in Stryke's belt and injected a note of caution. 'It wouldn't be wise to keep the Queen waiting *too* long.'

Stryke didn't seem to hear. He scooped a palmful of the fine crystals and let them trickle slowly through his fingers. 'This cache is worth a small fortune in coin and influence. Think how it would swell our mistress's coffers.'

'*Exactly*,' Jup eagerly concurred. 'Look at it from her point of view. Our mission successfully accomplished, victory in the battle and a queen's ransom of crystal lightning to boot. She'll probably promote you!'

'Dwell on this, Captain,' Haskeer said. 'Once delivered into the Queen's hands, how much of it are *we* ever likely to see? There's enough human in her to make the answer to that question no mystery to me.'

That did it.

Stryke dusted the last crystals from his hands. 'What she doesn't know about won't hurt her,' he decided, 'and starting out an hour or two later won't make *that* much difference. And when she sees what we've brought, even Jennesta's going to be satisfied.'

3

Some endure the frustration of their will with grace and forbearance. Others see obstacles to their gratification as intolerable burdens. The former embody admirable stoicism. The latter are dangerous.

Queen Jennesta belonged firmly in the second category. And she was growing impatient.

The warband she had entrusted with the sacred mission, the Wolverines, had yet to return. She knew the battle was over, and that it went in her favour, but they had not brought their monarch what she craved.

When they came she would have them skinned alive. If they had failed in their task she would inflict a much worse fate.

An entertainment had been arranged for her while she waited. It was necessary and practical as well as promising a certain pleasure. As usual, it would take place here in her *sanctum sanctorum*, the innermost of her private quarters.

The chamber, deep below her palace at Cairnbarrow, was constructed of stone. A dozen pillars supported the distant vaulted ceiling. Just enough light was provided by a scattering of candelabra and guttering brands, for Jennesta favoured shadows.

Wall hangings depicted complex cabalistic symbols. The floor's time-worn granite blocks were covered by woven rugs bearing equally arcane designs. A high-backed wooden chair, ornately carved but not quite a throne, stood next to an iron brazier of glowing coals.

Two features dominated the apartment. One was a solid chunk of black marble that served as an altar. The other was set in front and below it, of the same material but white, and shaped like a long, low table or couch.

A silver chalice stood on the altar. By it lay a curved dagger, its hilt inlaid with gold, runic devices etched into the blade. Alongside was a small hammer with a weighty, rounded head. It was decorated and inscribed in a similar way.

The white slab had a pair of shackles at each end. She ran her fingertips, slowly and lightly, along its surface. The smooth coolness of the marble felt sensuous to her touch.

A rap at the studded oak door broke her reverie

'Come.'

Two Imperial Guards herded in a human prisoner at spear point. Chained hand and foot, the man wore only a loincloth. Around thirty seasons old, he was typical of his race in standing head and shoulders taller than the orcs prodding him forward. Bruises discoloured his face. Dried blood encrusted his blond hair and beard. He walked stiffly, partly due to the manacles but mostly because of a flogging he had been given after his capture during the battle. Vivid red weals criss-crossed his back.

'Ah, my guest has arrived. Greetings.' The Queen's syrupy tone held pure mockery.

He said nothing.

As she languorously approached, one of the guards jerked the trailing chain at the captive's wrists. The man winced. Jennesta studied his robust, muscular frame, and decided he was suitable for her purpose.

In turn, he inspected her, and it was obvious from his expression that what he saw confounded him.

There was something wrong about the shape of her face. It was a little too flat, a mite wider than it should have been across the temples, and it tapered to a chin more pointed than seemed reasonable. Ebony hair tumbled to her waist, its sheen so pronounced it looked wet. Her dark fathomless eyes had an obliqueness that extraordinarily long lashes only served to stress. The nose was faintly aquiline and the mouth appeared overly broad.

None of this was exactly displeasing. It was rather as if her features had deviated from Nature's norm and pursued their own unique evolution. The result was startling.

Her skin, too, was not quite right. The impression, in the flickering candleglow, was of an emerald hue one moment and a silvery lustre the next, as though she were covered in minute fish scales. She wore a long crimson gown that left her shoulders exposed and clung tightly to the outlines of her voluptuous body. Her feet were bare.

Without doubt she was comely. But her beauty had a distinctly alarming quality. Its effect on her prisoner was to both quicken his blood and excite vague feelings of disgust. In a world teeming with racial diversity, she was totally outside his experience.

'You do not show proper deference,' she said. Her remarkable eyes were mesmeric. They made him feel that nothing could be kept concealed.

The captive dragged himself out of the depths of that devouring gaze. Despite his pain, he smiled, albeit cynically. He glanced down at the chains binding him, and for the first time spoke. 'Even if I were so inclined, I could not.'

Jennesta smiled too. It was genuinely disquieting. 'My guards will be happy to assist,' she replied brightly.

The soldiers forced him roughly to his knees.

'That's better.' Her voice dripped synthetic sweetness.

Gasping from the added discomfort, he noticed her hands. The length of the slender fingers, extended by keen nails half as long again, bordered abnormal. She moved to his side, reaching to touch the welts covering his back. It was done softly, but he still flinched. She traced the angry red lines with the tips of her nails, releasing trickles of fresh blood. He groaned. She made no attempt to hide her relish.

'Damn you, you heathen bitch,' he hissed weakly.

She laughed. 'A typical Uni. Any rejecting your ways must be a heathen. Yet you're the upstarts, with your fantasies of a lone deity.'

'While you follow the old, dead gods worshipped by the likes of these,' he countered, glaring at the orc guards.

'How little you know. The Mani faith reveres gods even more ancient. *Living* gods, unlike the fiction you cleave to.'

He coughed, misery racking his frame. 'You call yourself a Mani?'

'What of it?'

'The Manis are wrong, but at least they're human.'

'Whereas I'm not, and therefore cannot embrace the cause? Your ignorance would fill this place's moat, farmer. The Manifold path is for all. Even so, I am human in part.'

He raised his eyebrows.

'You've never seen a hybrid before?' She didn't wait for an answer. 'Obviously not. I'm of mixed nyadd and human parentage, and carry the best of both.'

'The best? Such a union is . . . *an abomination*!'

The Queen found that even more amusing, throwing back her head to laugh again. 'Enough of this. You're not here to engage in a debate.' She nodded at the soldiers. 'Make him ready.'

He was yanked upright, then goaded to the marble slab, where they lifted him bodily by his arms and legs. The agony of being dumped unceremoniously on its surface made him cry out. He lay panting, his eyes watery. They removed the chains and fastened his wrists and ankles with the shackles.

Jennesta curtly dismissed the guards. They bowed and lumbered out.

She went to the brazier and sprinkled powdered incense on the coals. Heady perfume filled the air. Crossing to the altar, she took up the ceremonial dagger and the chalice.

With an effort, the man turned his head her way. 'At least allow me the mercy of a quick death,' he pleaded.

Now she loomed over him, the knife in her hand. He drew an audible breath and started to recite some prayer or incantation, his panic making the words an incomprehensible babble.

'You're spouting gibberish,' she chided. 'Still your tongue.' Blade in hand, she stooped.

And cut through the loincloth.

She sliced away the material and tossed it aside. Placing the knife on the edge of the slab, she contemplated his nudity.

Slack-jawed, he stammered, 'What—?' His face reddened with embarrassment. He gulped and squirmed.

'You Unis have a very unnatural attitude to your bodies,' she told him, matter-of-factly. 'You feel shame where none should exist.'

She lifted his head with one hand and put the chalice to his lips with the other. 'Drink,' she commanded, sharply tilting the vessel.

Enough of the potion poured down his throat before he gagged and clamped his teeth on the rim. She removed the cup, leaving him coughing and spluttering. Some of the urine-coloured liquid dribbled from the sides of his mouth.

It was quick-acting but short-lived, so she wasted no time. Untying the straps of her gown, she let it fall to the floor.

He stared at her, wide-eyed with disbelief. His gaze took in her generous, jutting breasts. It moved down past her taut midriff to the pleasing camber of her hips, the long, curvaceous sweep of her legs and the luxuriant downy mound at her crotch.

Jennesta had a physical perfection which combined the sumptuous charms of a human woman with the alien heritage of her crossbred origins. He had never seen the like.

For her part, she recognised in him a struggle between the prudery of his Uni upbringing and the innate hunger of male lust. The aphrodisiac would help tilt the balance in the right direction, and deaden the pain of his ill-treatment. If need be she could add the persuasive powers of her sorcery. But she knew the best inducement required no magic.

She slid on to the side of the slab and brought her face close to his. The strange, sweet muskiness of her breath made the hairs on the back of his neck prickle. She blew gently in his ear, whispered shockingly explicit endearments. He blushed again, though this time perhaps not entirely because of abashment.

At last he found his voice. 'Why do you torment me this way?'

'You torment yourself,' she responded huskily, 'by denying the joys of the flesh.'

'Whore!'

Giggling, she leaned nearer, the tips of her swaying breasts tickling his chest. She made as if to kiss him, but drew back at the last. Wetting her fingers, she slowly trailed them around his nipples until they became erect. His breathing grew heavier. The potion was beginning to work.

Swallowing loudly, he summoned enough resolution to utter, 'The thought of congress with you is repulsive to me.'

'Really?' She eased on to him, straddling his body, her pubic hair pressed against his abdomen. He strained at the shackles, but feebly.

Jennesta was enjoying his humiliation, the destruction of his resolve. It heightened her own excitement. She parted her lips and disgorged a tongue that seemed overlong for the cavity of her mouth. It proved coarse-textured when she started licking his throat and shoulders.

Despite himself, he was becoming aroused. She squeezed her legs more firmly against the sides of his sweat-filmed body and caressed him with renewed ardour. A succession of emotions passed rapidly across his face: expectancy, repellence, fascination, eagerness. Fear.

He half cried, half sobbed, 'No!'

'But you *want* this,' she soothed. 'Why else make yourself ready for me?' She lifted herself slightly. Reaching down, she took hold of his manhood and guided it.

Gradually she moved against him, her lithe form rising and falling in a deliberate, unhurried rhythm. His head rolled from side to side, eyes glazed, mouth gaping. Her tempo increased. He writhed and began moaning. The motion grew faster. He started to respond, tentatively at first, then thrusting deeper and harder. Jennesta tossed back her hair. The cloud of raven locks caught pinpoints of light that wreathed her in a nimbus of fire.

Aware he was on the verge of gushing his seed, she rode him mercilessly, building to a frenzy of wanton rapture. He twisted, flailed, shuddered his way to culmination.

Suddenly she had the dagger in both hands, lifting it high.

Orgasm and terror came simultaneously.

The blade plunged into his chest, again, again and again. He shrieked hideously, tearing the skin from his wrists as he fought the shackles. Unheeding, she stabbed and hacked, cleaving at flesh.

His screams gave way to a moist gurgle. Then his head fell back with a meaty thump and he was still.

She cast away the knife and scrabbled with her hands, delving into the gory hollow. Once the ribs were exposed she took up the hammer and pounded at them. They cracked, white shards flying. This obstruction removed, she dropped the hammer and clawed through viscera, arms blood-drenched, to grasp his still faintly beating heart. With an effort she ripped it free.

She lifted the dripping organ to her widening mouth and sank her teeth into its warm tenderness.

Great as her sexual gratification had been, it was as nothing compared to the fulfilment she now experienced. With each bite her victim's life force reinvigorated her own. She felt the flow replenishing her physically and feeding the spring from which she drew her vital magical energies.

Sitting cross-legged on the steaming corpse's chest, her face, breasts and hands smeared with blood, she happily feasted.

At length she was replete. For the time being.

As she sucked the last of the juices from her fingers, a young black and white cat slunk from a dark corner of the chamber. It mewed.

'Here, Sapphire,' Jennesta crooned, patting her thigh.

The she-cat leapt effortlessly and joined her mistress to be petted. Then she sniffed at the mutilated body and began lapping at its open wound.

Smiling indulgently, the Queen got down from the slab and padded to a velvet bellcord.

The orc guards wasted no time in obeying her summons. If they had any feelings about the scene that greeted them, or her appearance, they gave no hint.

'Remove the carcass,' she ordered.

The cat darted for the shadows on their approach. They set to work on the shackles.

'What news of the Wolverines?' Jennesta asked.

'None, my lady,' one of the guards replied, avoiding her gaze.

It wasn't what she wanted to hear. The benefits of the refreshment were already fading. Regal displeasure returned.

She made a silent vow that the warband's deaths would surpass their worst nightmares.

Two Wolverine footsoldiers lay stretched out with their backs against a tree, enraptured by a swarm of tiny fairies fluttering and gambolling above their heads. Soft multicoloured light shimmered on the fairies' wings and their gentle singing tinkled melodiously in the late-evening air.

One of the orcs abruptly shot out a hand and snatched a fistful of the creatures. They squeaked pitifully. He stuffed their wriggling bodies into his mouth and crunched noisily.

'Irritating little bastards,' his companion muttered.

The first trooper nodded sagely. 'Yeah. But good to eat.'

'And stupid,' the second soldier added as the swarm formed again overhead.

He watched them for a while then decided to grab a handful for himself.

They sat chewing, staring dumbly at the smoking embers of the farmhouse on the other side of the compound. The fairies finally got the message and flittered away.

A moment passed and the first orc said, 'Did that really just happen?'

'What?'

'Those fairies.'

'Fairies? Irritating little bastards.'

'Yeah. But good to—' A light kick from a boot against his shin interrupted the discourse.

They hadn't noticed the approach of another trooper standing beside them. He stooped, grunted, 'Here,' and handed over a clay pipe. Swaying slightly, he stumbled off again.

The first soldier raised the pipe and inhaled deeply.

His comrade smacked his lips and pulled a face. He dug a grubby fingernail between his front teeth and picked out something that looked like a minute shiny wing. Shrugging, he flicked it into the grass. The other orc passed him the cob of pellucid.

Nearer the remains of the house, Stryke, Coilla, Jup and Alfray sat around a small campfire sharing their own pipe. Haskeer was using a stick to stir the contents of a black cooking pot hanging over the crackling flames.

'I'll say it one last time,' Stryke told them, mildly exasperated. He pointed to the cylinder in his lap. 'This thing was taken from a heavily armed caravan by Unis who killed the guards. That's the story.' His voice was growing slurred. 'Jennesta wants it back.'

'But why?' Jup wondered, drawing from the pipe. 'After all, it's only a cessage marrier . . . I mean, it's only a message carrier.' Blinking, he handed the pipe to Coilla.

'We know *that*,' Stryke replied. He waved a dismissive, lazy hand. 'Must be an important message. Not our concern.'

Dishing out steaming milky-white liquid from the pot and into tin cups, Haskeer commented, 'I wager this pellucid was part of the caravan's cargo too.'

Alfray, displaying characteristic correctness even in his present state, again tried reminding Stryke of his responsibilities. 'We mustn't linger here too long, Captain. If the Queen—'

'Can't you chirrup a different song?' Stryke interrupted testily. 'Mark me; our mistress will welcome us with open arms. You worry overmuch, sawbones.'

Alfray lapsed into moody silence. Haskeer offered him a cup of the infused drug. He shook his head. Stryke accepted the brew and downed an ample draft.

Coilla had been vacant-eyed and half drowsing under the pellucid's influence. Now she spoke. 'Alfray has a point. Incurring Jennesta's wrath is never a good scheme.'

'Must you nag me too?' retorted Stryke, raising the cup once more. 'We'll be on our way soon, never fear. Or would you deny them a little leisure?' He looked in the direction of the orchard, where most of the Wolverines were taking their ease.

The band's troopers sprawled before a larger fire. There was rude laughter, rough horseplay and raucous singing. A pair engaged in arm-wrestling. Several were slumped in ungainly postures.

Stryke turned back to Coilla. But the scene had changed completely.

She was curled on the ground with her eyes closed. All the others were also prone, one or two of them snoring. The fire was long dead. He returned his gaze to the main band. They too were sleeping, their fire also reduced to ashes.

It was the depth of night. A full panoply of stars dusted the sky.

What had seemed to him no more than an instant of time had proved an illusion.

He should rouse everyone, organise them, issue orders for the march to Cairnbarrow. And he would. Certainly he would. But he needed to rest his leaden limbs and clear the muzziness from his brain. Only a minute or two was all it would take. Just a minute.

His nodding head drooped, chin meeting neck.

A warm stupor crept into every fibre of his being. It was so hard to keep his eyes open.

He surrendered to the dark.

4

He opened his eyes.

The sun blazed directly overhead. He lifted a hand to shield himself from the light and, blinking, slowly rose to a standing position. The carpet of lush sward felt springy underfoot.

Before him stood a distant range of softly rolling hills. Above them, pure-white clouds drifted serenely across a sky of flawless blue. The landscape was verdant, uncorrupted.

Off to his right the view was dominated by the brim of an immense forest. On his left a shallow stream flowed down an incline before curving round a bend and out of sight.

It occurred to Stryke to wonder, in an abstract sort of way, what had happened to the night. And he had no idea where the other Wolverines might be. But these questions did no more than mildly stroke some small corner of his mind.

Then it seemed to him that he could hear other sounds beyond the tumbling water. Sounds resembling voices, and laughter, and the faint, rhythmic pounding of a drum. Their source was either in his head or at the brook's destination.

He followed the stream, walking in it, his boots crunching on the shingle washed smooth by its endless polishing. His sloshing descent inspired rustling in the undergrowth on either side as tiny furtive creatures darted from his path.

A pleasantly warm breeze caressed his face. The air was fresh and clean. It made him feel light-headed.

He reached the point where the rivulet turned. The voices were louder, more distinct, as he rounded the crook.

Before him was the mouth of a small valley. The stream ran on, snaking through a cluster of circular timber huts, roofed with straw. Set to one side was a long-house, decorated with embellished shields of a clan Stryke didn't recognise. War trophies hung there, too; broadswords, spears, the bleached skulls of sabrewolves. The air was perfumed with the fragrance of smoky kindling and roasting game.

There were tethered horses, roaming livestock, strutting fowl.

And orcs.

Males, females, hatchlings. They carried out chores, tended fires, hewed wood, or simply lounged, watching, talking, bragging. In the clearing outside the long-house a group of young tyros sparred with swords and staffs, the beating of a hide tambour harmonising their mock combat.

No one paid him any particular attention as he entered the settlement. All the orcs he saw bore weapons, as was only fitting for their kind, but despite this clan being unknown to him, Stryke didn't feel threatened. Just curious.

Someone came towards him. She strode with easy confidence, and made no move for the sword hanging in its scabbard at her belt. He judged her a head shorter than himself, though her flaming crimson headdress, shot through with streaks of gold, made up the height. Her back was straight, her build attractively muscular.

She showed no surprise at his presence. Indeed her expression was almost passive, or at least as passive as a face so strong and active could be. As she neared him, she smiled, openly and with warmth. He was aware of a faint stirring in his loins.

'Well met,' she said.

Reflecting on her comeliness, he did not immediately respond. When he replied, it was hesitantly. 'Well . . . met.'

'I don't know you.'

'Nor I you.'

She asked, 'What is your clan?'

He told her.

'It means nothing to me. But there are so many.'

Stryke glanced at the unfamiliar shields on the long-house. 'Your clan isn't known to me either.' He paused, captivated by her fetching eyes, before adding, 'Aren't you wary of greeting a stranger?'

She looked puzzled. 'Should I be? Is there a dispute between our clans?'

'Not that I know of.'

She flashed her appealing, sharpened yellow teeth again. 'Then there's no need for caution. Unless you come with evil intent.'

'No, I come in peace. But would you be as welcoming if I were a troll? Or a goblin? Or a dwarf of unknown allegiance?'

Her mystified look returned. 'Troll? Goblin? Dwarf? What are they*?'*

'You do not know of dwarves?'

She shook her head.

'Or gremlins, trolls, elves? Any *of the elder races?'*

'Elder races? No.'

'Or . . . humans?'

'I don't know what they are, but I'm sure there aren't any.'

'You mean there aren't any in these parts?'

'I mean that your words are lost on me. You're odd.' It was said without malice.

'And you speak in riddles,' he told her. 'Where are we in Maras-Dantia that you do not know of the other elder races, or of humans?'

'You must have journeyed a long way, stranger, if your land has a name I've never heard of.'

He was taken aback. 'Are you telling me you don't even know what the world is called?'

'No. I'm telling you it isn't called Maras-Dantia. At least, not

here. And I've never known another orc who spoke of us sharing it with these . . . elder races *and . . .* humans.*'*

'Orcs decide their own fate here? They make war as they choose? There are no humans or—'

She laughed. 'When was it otherwise?'

Stryke furrowed his craggy brow. 'Since before my father's father was hatched,' he muttered. 'Or so I thought.'

'Perhaps you've marched too long in the heat,' she offered gently.

He gazed up at the sun, and a realisation came to him. 'The heat . . . No chill wind blows.'

'Why should it? This isn't the cold season.'

'And the ice,' Stryke continued, ignoring her answer. 'I haven't seen the advancing ice.'

'Where?'

'From the north, of course.'

Unexpectedly, she reached out and grasped his hand. 'Come.'

Even in his confusion he was aware that her touch was agreeably cool and clammy. He allowed her to lead him.

They followed the downward path of the stream until they left the village behind. Eventually they came to a place where the land fell away, and Stryke and the female stood on the edge of a granite cliff. Here the stream became a pool, slipping from its far lip as a waterfall, a foamy cascade that plunged to rocks far below in a greater valley.

The silver thread of a river emerged from somewhere at the foot of the cliff, slicing across olive plains that stretched endlessly in all directions. Only the tremendous forest to their right curbed the ocean of grassland. Vast herds of grazing beasts, too numerous to count, ranged further than Stryke could see. An orc might spend a lifetime hunting here and never want for prey.

The female pointed, dead ahead. 'North,' she said.

There were no encroaching glaciers, no looming slate sky. All he saw in that direction was more of the same; luxuriant foliage, an infinity of green, a thriving abundance of life.

Stryke experienced a strange emotion. He could not explain why, but he had a nagging sensation that all this was somehow familiar, as though he had seen these wondrous sights and breathed deep of this unsullied air before.

'Is this . . . Vartania?' He all but whispered the sacred word.

'Paradise?' She smiled enigmatically. 'Perhaps. If you choose to make it so.'

The alchemy of sunlight and airborne spray birthed an arcing rainbow. They silently marvelled at its multicoloured splendour.

And the soothing rush of water was balm to Stryke's troubled spirit.

He opened his eyes.

A Wolverine grunt was pissing into the ashes of the fire.

Stryke snapped fully awake. *'What the* fuck *do you think you're doing, Private?'* he bellowed.

The grunt scooted off like a scalded whelp, head down, fumbling at his breeches.

Still muzzy from the dream, or vision, or whatever it was, it took a moment for Stryke to realise that the sun had risen. It was past dawn.

'Gods!' he cursed, scrambling to his feet.

He checked his belt for the cylinder, then quickly took in the scene. Two or three of the Wolverines were unsteadily exploring wakefulness, but the rest, including the lookouts he'd posted, lounged all over the compound.

Sprinting to the nearest huddle of sleeping figures, he laid about them with his boot. 'Up, you *bastards*!' he roared. 'Up! *Move yourselves!*'

Some rolled from the kicks. Several came alive with blades in their hands, ready for a fight, then cowered on recognising their tormentor. Haskeer was among them, but less inclined to quail at his commander's rage. He scowled, returning his knife to its sheath with deliberate, insolent slowness.

'What ails you, Stryke?' he rumbled sullenly.

'What ails me? The *new day* ails me, scumpouch!' He jabbed a thumb skyward. 'The sun climbs and we're still here!'

'And whose fault is that?'

Stryke's eyes narrowed dangerously. He moved closer to Haskeer, near enough to feel the sergeant's fetid breath against his face. *'What?'* he hissed.

'You blame us. Yet you're in charge.'

'You'd like to try changing that?'

The other Wolverines were gathering around them. At a distance.

Haskeer held Stryke's gaze. His hand edged to his scabbard.

'Stryke!'

Coilla was elbowing the grunts aside, Alfray and Jup in tow.

'We don't have time for this,' she said sternly.

Captain and sergeant paid her no heed.

'The Queen, Stryke,' Alfray put in. 'We have to get back to Cairnbarrow. Jennesta—'

Mention of her name broke the spell. 'I *know*, Alfray,' Stryke barked. He gave Haskeer a last, contemptuous look and turned away from him.

Sullenly, Haskeer backed off, directing a venomous glare at Jup by way of compensation.

Stryke addressed the warband. 'We'll not march this day, we'll ride. Darig, Liffin, Reafdaw, Kestix; round up horses for all. Seafe, and you, Noskaa; find a couple of mules. Finje, Bhose; gather provisions. Just enough to travel light, mind. Gant, take who you need and release those gryphons. The rest of you, collect up our gear. *Now!*'

The grunts dispersed to carry out their orders.

Scanning his officers, Stryke saw that Alfray, Jup, Haskeer and Coilla looked as bleary-eyed as he probably did himself. 'You'll see they waste no time with those horses and mules, Haskeer,' he said. 'You too, Jup. And I want no trouble from either of you.' He curtly jerked his head to dismiss them.

They ran off, keeping well apart.

'What do you want us to do?' Alfray asked.

'Pick one or two grunts to help divide the pellucid equally among the band. It'll be easier to transport that way. But make it clear they're carrying it, not being given it. And if any of 'em has other ideas, they'll get more than their arses tanned.'

Alfray nodded and left.

Coilla lingered. 'You look . . . strange,' she said. 'Is everything all right?'

'No, Corporal, it isn't.' Stryke's words dripped venom. 'If you hadn't noticed, we should have reported to Jennesta hours since. And that might mean getting our throats cut. *Now do as you're told!*'

She fled.

Wisps of the vision still clung to his mind as he damned the rising sun.

They left behind the ruins of the human settlement, and the trampled, deserted battlefield beneath it, and headed north-east.

An upgrade in their trail took them above the rolling plains. The liberated gryphons were spreading across the grasslands.

Riding beside Stryke at the head of the column, Coilla indicated the view and said, 'Don't you envy them?'

'What, beasts?'

'They're freer than us.'

The remark surprised him. It was the first time she'd made any comment, even indirectly, that referred to the situation their race had been reduced to. But he resisted the temptation to agree with her. These days an orc did well not to speak too freely. Opinions had a way of reaching unintended ears.

He kept his response to a noncommittal snort.

Coilla regarded him with an expression of curiosity, and dropped the subject. They rode on in grim silence, maintaining as rapid a pace as they could over the uneven terrain.

At mid-morning they came to a winding track that led through a narrow ravine. It was deep, with tall grassy walls rising at gentle gradients, making the pass wedge-shaped. The constricted path meant the band could ride no more than two abreast. Most took it single-file. Stony and cramped, the trail slowed them to a trot.

Frustrated at the delay, Stryke cursed. 'We *have* to move faster than this!'

'Using the pass gains us half a day,' Coilla reminded him, 'and we'll make up for more on the other side.'

'Every passing minute is going to sour Jennesta's mood.'

'We've got what she wanted, and a cargo of pellucid as bonus. Doesn't that stand for something?'

'With *our* mistress? I think you know the answer to that, Coilla.'

'We can say we ran into strong opposition, or had trouble finding the cylinder.'

'No matter the story we tell; we aren't there. That's enough.' He glanced over his shoulder. The others were far enough behind to be out of earshot. 'I wouldn't admit this to everybody,' he confided in a hushed tone, 'but Haskeer was right, blast his eyes. I let this happen.'

'Don't be too hard on yourself. We all—'

'*Wait!* Ahead!'

Something was coming towards them from the opposite end of the ravine.

Stryke held up a hand, halting the column. He squinted, trying to identify the low, broad shape moving their way. It was obviously a beast of burden of some sort, and it had a rider. As he watched, several more came into view beyond it.

Down the line, Jup passed the reins to a grunt and

dismounted. He jogged to Stryke. 'What is it, Captain?' he said.

'I'm not sure . . .' Then he recognised the animals. '*Damnation!* Kirgizil vipers!'

Though commonly referred to as such, kirgizils weren't vipers at all. They were desert lizards, much shorter than horses but of roughly the same mass, with wide backs and stumpy, muscular legs. Albino-white and pink-eyed, they had forked tongues the length of an orc's arm. Their dagger-sharp fangs held a lethal venom, their barbed tails were powerful enough to shatter a biped's spine. They were stalking creatures, capable of remarkable bursts of speed.

Only one race used them as war chargers.

The lizards were near enough now to leave no doubt. Sitting astride each was a kobold. Smaller than orcs, smaller than most dwarves, they were thin to the point of emaciation, totally hairless and grey-skinned. But appearances were deceptive. Despite the gangly arms and legs, and elongated, almost delicate faces, they were obstinate, ravening fighters.

Pointed ears swept back from heads disproportionately large in relation to their bodies. The mouth was a lipless slash, filled with tiny, sharp teeth. The nose resembled a feral cat's. The eyes were golden-orbed, glinting with spite and avarice.

Quilled leather collars wrapped their unusually extended necks. Their reed-slim wrists prickled with razor-spike bracelets. They brandished spears and wicked-looking miniature scimitars.

In the business of thievery and scavenging, kobolds had few equals in all Maras-Dantia. They had even fewer when it came to meanness of temperament.

'Ambush!' Jup yelled.

Other voices were raised along the column. Orcs pointed upward. More kirgizil-mounted raiders were sweeping down at them from both sides of the gully. Standing in his saddle, Stryke saw kobolds pouring in to block their exit.

'Classic trap,' he snarled.

Coilla tugged free a pair of throwing knives. 'And we walked right into it.'

Alfray unfurled the war banner. Horses reared, scattering loose shingle. The orcs drew their weapons and turned to face the enemy on every side.

Half befuddled from the pellucid, looted wine and rougher alcohol of the night before, the Wolverines were outnumbered with barely room to manoeuvre.

Blades flashing in the sun, the kobolds thundered in for the attack.

Stryke roared a battle cry and the warband took it up.

Then the first wave was on them.

5

Stryke didn't wait to be attacked.

Digging his heels into the flanks of his horse, he spurred it toward the leading raider, pulling to the left, as though to pass the kobold's charging lizard. The horse shield. Stryke kept it firmly on course, reins wrapped tightly around one hand. With the other he brought his sword up and back.

Caught out by the swiftness of the move, the rider tried to duck. Too late.

Stryke's blade cleaved the air. The kobold's head leapt from its shoulders, flew to the side and hit the trail bouncing. Sitting upright, a fountain of blood gushing from its stump, the corpse was carried past by the uncontrolled kirgizil. It ran on into the melée at Stryke's rear.

He laid into his next opponent.

Coilla lobbed a knife at the raider nearest to her. It buried itself in the kobold's cheek. The creature plunged screaming from its mount.

She singled out another target and threw again, underarm this time, as hard as she could. Her mark instinctively pulled back sharply on its reins, bringing up the viper's head. Her missile struck it squarely in the eye. Roaring with pain, the animal's body pitched to one side, crushing its rider. Both writhed in thrashing agony.

Coilla steadied her horse and reached for more knives.

On foot when the attackers swept in, Jup had armed himself with an axe and was swinging it two-handed. A kobold, unsaddled by a glancing blow from a Wolverine sword, lurched into range. Jup split its skull. Then a mounted attacker side-swiped the dwarf. He spun and chopped deep into the rider's twig-thin leg, completely severing it.

All around, orcs were engaged in bloody exchanges. About a third of them had been de-horsed. Several of the archers had managed to notch their bows and wing bolts at the raiders. But the fight was already too close-quartered to make this feasible for much longer.

Haskeer found himself boxed in. One opponent hacked at him from the trail side. The other delivered slashing downward blows from the gully's slope, its dextrous kirgizil gripping the treacherous incline with ease. Fearful of the lizards, Haskeer's panicking horse bucked and whinnied. He lashed out to the right, to the left and back again.

An orc arrow smacked into the chest of the kobold on the slope, knocking it clean off the viper's back. Haskeer turned full attention to the opponent on his other side. Their blades clashed, returned, clashed once more.

A pass sliced across Haskeer's chin. It wasn't a serious wound, though the steel was keen, but it caught him off balance and he fell from the horse. His sword was lost. As he rolled from pounding hooves and swishing reptilian tails, a spear was hurled at him. It narrowly missed. He struggled to his feet and wrenched it from the ground.

The kobold that had unseated him came in for the kill. Haskeer had no time to straighten the spear. He brought it up to fend off the creature's arcing sword. It sliced the shaft in two, showering slivers of wood. Discarding the shorter end,

Haskeer swung the remainder like an elongated club, swiping the kobold full in the face. The impact sent it crashing to the ground.

Haskeer rushed in and began viciously booting the creature's head. For good measure he jumped on its chest, pounding up and down with all his might, knees bent, fists clenched. The kobold's ribcage snapped and crunched. Blood disgorged from its mouth and nose.

Alfray fought for possession of the Wolverines' banner. A kobold, standing in its stirrups, had hold of the pole. Grimly, Alfray maintained an iron grasp, his knuckles whitening as the rod went back and forth in a bizarre tug-of-war. For such an insubstantial-looking creature, the kobold was tenacious. Avaricious eyes narrowed, spiky teeth bared, it hissed horribly.

It was close to gaining its prize when Alfray delivered an orc's kiss.

Throwing himself forward, he head-butted the kobold solidly in its bony forehead. The creature flew backwards, letting go of the pole as though it were a hot poker. Alfray quickly levelled the shaft and rammed the sharpened end into his assailant's abdomen.

He turned, ready to inflict the same fate on any enemy near enough. What he saw was a Wolverine grunt trading blows with a raider and getting the worst of it. Exploiting an opening, the kobold lunged in, its scimitar swiftly carving a scathing X on the orc's chest. The trooper went down.

Urging on his horse, Alfray galloped full pelt at the kobold, holding the banner pole like a lance. It penetrated the creature's midriff and exited its back with an explosion of gore.

Working his way up the trail, Stryke was heading for his fourth or fifth opponent. He wasn't sure which. He rarely kept count. Two or three kills earlier he'd abandoned the reins, preferring his hands free for combat. Now he held on to and guided the horse solely by applying pressure with his thighs. It was an old orc trick he was adept at.

The kobold he was fast approaching held a large, ornate shield; the first he had seen any of them carrying. That probably made this particular individual a chieftain. Of more concern to Stryke was how the shield might hinder him in killing its owner. He decided to adopt a different strategy.

Just before drawing level with the striding reptile, he grabbed a handful of his horse's mane and jerked it, slowing their pace. Now parallel with the kirgizil, he stretched down and snatched the harness encasing its huffing snout. Careful to avoid the animal's snaking tongue, he heaved the yoke upwards, muscles straining. Half strangulated, the kirgizil lashed and struggled, its taloned feet pawing the ground. It twisted its head, snorting for breath.

Stryke pummelled his heels into his horse's sides, driving it on. The steed was labouring to move, bearing as it was both Stryke's weight and the mass of the viper. Unable to control its mount, the kobold rider leaned from the saddle, impotently swiping at Stryke with its blade.

Finally, its neck bent to an untenable angle, the kirgizil tilted to one side. The kobold let out a dismayed yelp and slid from its back, parting company with the shield. Stryke let go of the lizard's harness. Ignoring the beast as it fought to right itself, he wheeled round the horse to face the fallen kobold. A sharp tug on the mane made the steed rear.

The kobold was on its knees when the hooves came down and stove in its skull.

Stryke looked back. He caught a glimpse of Coilla. She'd lost her mount and was in the thick of the ferocious scrum. Several bandits, parted from their chargers, were moving in on her.

She couldn't hold them off with knife-throws any longer; it was down to close combat. Using her knives as daggers, she stabbed and slashed, spinning and dodging to avoid thrusts from spears and swords.

A leering kobold took a swipe from the edge of her blade across its throat and spiralled away. Another jumped in to take its place. As it raised its sword she darted under it, dealing two rapid stabs to the heart. It collapsed. A third raider appeared in front of her, holding a spear. It was too far away to engage with her daggers, too close for a throw. She stepped back, transfixed by the menacing, barbed spearhead.

From behind, a hatchet came down heavily on the creature's shoulder. With an eruption of blood and sinew, it severed the kobold's spear arm from its trunk. Wailing terribly, the raider fell.

Hefting his gore-spattered axe, Jup ran forward to join her.

'We can't take much more of this!' he yelled.

'Keep killing!'

They fought back to back.

Alfray kicked out at a kobold on foot, while simultaneously crossing swords with another, alongside on its kirgizil. The lizard was snapping at Alfray's spooked horse, and it was all he could do to keep it in check. Nearby, two orc grunts were cutting a lone raider to ribbons.

Haskeer's newly retrieved sword was dashed away by a passing kobold rider. Another raider immediately loomed up, sneering evilly at the Wolverine's empty hands. Its scimitar flashed. Haskeer ducked. The blade whistled overhead. Diving at his opponent, Haskeer drove his massive fist into its face. With his free hand he caught the wrist of the bandit's sword arm and squeezed until the bones popped. The kobold shrieked. Haskeer resumed pounding at its face until it let go of the sword. Scooping it up, he ran the creature through.

Far gone in bloodlust, he turned to an adjacent mounted enemy. The kobold had its back to him, preoccupied with a fight on its other side. Haskeer dragged it from the viper and set to battering it. Its slender arms and legs snapped like dry kindling under the onslaught.

A bellowing grunt tumbled past, swatted by a kirgizil's tail. He collided with a brawling mass of combatants. Orcs and kobolds went down in a tangle of thrashing limbs.

The last ambusher blocking Stryke's path proved skilful as well as obstinate. Instead of hacking and slashing, Stryke was embroiled in something like a fencing match.

As his foe's mount was lower than Stryke's, the Wolverine commander had to lean over to clash blades. That disadvantage, along with the kobold's adeptness at swordplay, made it difficult penetrating the creature's guard. Every blow was parried, each stroke countered.

After a full minute of stalemate, the kobold's blade was the one to break through. It gashed Stryke's upper arm, spraying blood.

Enraged, he renewed his attack with fresh energy. He showered blows on the raider, seeking to overcome its skill with sheer force. The ceaseless buffeting lacked finesse, and the strokes were scarcely aimed, but soon paid dividends. In the face of the lashing storm, the kobold's defences weakened, its reactions slowed.

Stryke's blade sliced through one of the creature's upswept ears. It shrieked. The next pass laid open its shoulder, bringing forth an anguished howl.

Then Stryke landed a vicious blow to the side of the bandit's head and ended it.

Panting, his limbs afire from exertion, he slumped in his saddle. There were no more kobolds on the trail ahead.

Something jolted his horse from behind. The steed bolted. Before he could turn, he felt an impact against his back. A clawed hand snaked around his body and dug painfully into his chest. Hot breath prickled the nape of his neck. The other hand appeared, clutching a curved dagger, and made for his throat. He grabbed the wrist and checked its upward transit.

The horse was running, unrestrained. From the corner of his eye, Stryke saw a riderless kirgizil passing them; the mount his attacker must have leapt from.

Stryke twisted the wrist he held, intent on breaking it. At the same time he repeatedly jabbed the elbow of his other arm into the kobold's solar plexus. He heard a guttural moan. The dagger slipped from its hand and fell away.

Another mounted bandit appeared at his side. It was waving a scimitar.

He kicked out, his boot thudding against the creature's wiry shoulder. The momentary loss of concentration loosened his grip on the kobold at his back. Its hands quickly withdrew. Stryke jabbed his elbow again, sinking it deep in flesh. Once more he aimed a kick at the mounted raider. This time he missed.

His horse thundered on. The kobold on the viper kept pace, and drew ahead a little.

Now the tiny, loathsome hands were eagerly scrabbling at Stryke's belt. He managed to half turn and lash out at the unwanted passenger. His knuckles struck its face, but ineffectually.

Avidly, the hands encircled his waist again, probing, searching. And he realised what the bandit was after.

The cylinder.

No sooner had the thought occurred than the kobold reached its goal. With a triumphant hiss, it seized the artefact and pulled it free.

As he felt the prize being tugged away, it seemed to Stryke that time slowed, became pliable, stretching the following instant to an eternity.

Laggard-paced, as though seen with a dreamer's eye, several things happened at once.

He caught the horse's flailing reins and yanked on them with all his might. The steed's head whiplashed back. A great shudder ran through its body.

The mounted kobold slowly rose in its saddle, arm outstretched, taloned hand open.

An object sailed leisurely over Stryke's right shoulder. It turned end over end, burnished surface briefly flashing reflected sunlight as it descended.

Time's frantic tempo returned.

The rider snatched the cylinder from the air.

Stryke's horse went down.

He hit the ground first, rolling the width of the trail. The kobold sitting behind fetched up a dozen paces away. Vision swimming, breath knocked out of him, Stryke watched as his horse struggled to its feet and galloped off. It headed for the far end of the gully, the same direction as the raider bearing the cylinder.

A groan came from the kobold that had fallen with him. Possessed of a berserk frenzy, Stryke stumbled over to the creature and vented his anger. Kneeling on its chest, he reduced its face to a bloody pulp with the hammering of his fists.

The air was rent by a keening, high-pitched blast of sound.

He looked up. Well clear by now, the escaping bandit held a slender, copper-coloured horn to its lips.

As the intonation reached the raiders engaging Coilla and Jup, they backed off and began to run.

Jup took a last, wide swing at his fleeing opponent and shouted, 'Look!'

All the kobolds were withdrawing. Most retreated on foot; some dashed to mount loose kirgizils. They ran and rode in the direction of the gully's entrance, or up its steep sides. A handful of orcs harried the escaping creatures, but most were licking their wounds.

Coilla saw Stryke loping towards them. 'Come on!' she said.

They rushed to meet him.

'The cylinder!' he raged, half demented.

No further explanation was necessary. It was obvious what had happened.

Jup carried on along the trail, legs pumping, a hand shading his eyes as he peered into the distance. He made out the kirgizil and its rider, climbing the wall of the gully at its far end. As he watched, they reached the top. They were outlined against the sky for a second before disappearing.

He trotted back to Stryke and Coilla.

'Gone,' he reported baldly.

Stryke's face was black with fury. Without a word to either of them, he turned and headed for the rest of the band. Corporal and sergeant exchanged barren glances and followed.

Where the fighting had been most intense the ground was littered with kobold dead and wounded, downed horses and kirgizils. At least half a dozen orcs had more than superficial injuries, but were still on their feet. One was stretched on the ground and being tended by comrades.

Sighting their commander, the Wolverines moved to him.

Stryke marched to Alfray, eyes blazing. 'Casualties?' he barked.

'Give me a chance, I'm still checking.'

'Well *roughly*, then.' The tone was menacing. 'You're supposed to double as our combat physician; *report*.'

Alfray glowered. But he wasn't about to challenge the Captain in his present mood. 'Looks like no loss of life. Though Meklun yonder's in a bad way.' He nodded at the downed trooper. 'Others took deep wounds, but can stand.'

Haskeer, wiping blood from his chin, said, 'Lucky as devils, us.'

Stryke glared at him. *'Lucky?* Those bastards took the cylinder!'

Palpable shock ran through the band.

'Thieving little *fuckers*,' Haskeer responded indignantly. 'Let's get after 'em!'

The Wolverines chorused approval.

'Think!' Stryke bellowed. 'By the time we've cleared this shambles, rounded up the horses, tended our wounded—'

'Why not send a small party after them now, and the rest can follow?' Coilla suggested.

'They'd be well outnumbered, and those kirgizils can go where we can't. The trail's cold already!'

'But what good is it if we wait until we sort ourselves?' Alfray put in. 'Who knows where they've gone?'

'There's plenty of their wounded lying about,' Haskeer reminded them. 'I say we make 'em tell us.' He slipped out a knife and flicked his finger against its edge to underline the point.

'Can *you* speak their infernal language?' Stryke demanded. 'Can *any* of you?' They shook their heads. 'No, I thought not. So torture's hardly the answer, is it?'

'We should never have entered this valley without scouting it first,' Haskeer grumbled lowly.

'I'm just in the mood for your griping,' Stryke told him, his expression like flint. 'If you've got something to say about how I'm leading this band, let's hear it now.'

Haskeer held up his hands in a placating gesture. 'No, chief.' He turned on an empty grin. 'Just . . . thinking aloud.'

'Thinking's not your strong point, Sergeant. Leave it to me. And that goes for *all* of you!'

A tense silence descended. Alfray broke it. 'What do you want us to do, Captain?' he asked.

'Find as many horses as we can, for a start. If Meklun can't ride, make a litter for him.' He bobbed his head at the carnage. 'Don't leave any kobolds alive. Cut their throats. Get on with it.'

The Wolverines melted away.

Coilla remained, looking at him.

'Don't say it,' he told her. 'I know. If we don't get that damn thing back for Jennesta, we're as good as dead.'

6

Jennesta stood on the highest balcony of her palace's tallest tower.

The eastern ocean was to her back. She looked north-west, where curling yellow mist rose over Taklakameer, the inland sea. Beyond that, she could just make out the city spires of Urrarbython, on the margin of the Hojanger wastelands. In turn, Hojanger eventually gave way to the ice field dominating the horizon, bathed by a crimson sun.

To Jennesta it resembled a frozen tidal wave of blood.

An icy breeze swept in, acute as a blade, stirring the heavy cerise drapes on the balcony's entrance. She wrapped the cloak of milky-hued sabrewolf pelts tighter around herself. Autumnal conditions belied the season, and each passing year was worse.

The advancing glaciers and frigid winds were harbingers of the encroaching humans; ever expanding their hold, tearing the heart from the land, interfering with the balance.

Eating Maras-Dantia's magic.

She heard that in the south, where they were most densely concentrated and sorcery worked poorly if at all, humans had even abandoned the hallowed name and taken to calling the world Centrasia. At least the Unis had, and they were still more numerous than the Manis.

Not for the first time, she fell to wondering what her mother, Vermegram, would have made of the schism. There was no doubt she would favour the Followers of the Manifold Path. After all, they adhered to pantheistic tenets remarkably similar to those of the elder races. Which was why Jennesta herself supported their cause, and would continue to do so for as long as it suited her. But whether her mother, a nyadd, would have approved of Jennesta actually siding with incomers was a moot point. Notwithstanding Vermegram's human consort.

And what of him? Would Jennesta's father have approved of Unity and its nonsensical monotheistic creed?

Whenever she dwelt on these matters she always came up against the ambiguity of her hybrid origins. Inevitably, that led to thoughts of Adpar and Sanara, and anger rose.

She brought her mind back to the artefact. It was the key to her ambitions, to victory, and it was slipping out of her grasp.

Turning, she entered the chamber.

An attendant stepped forward and took her cloak. Slimly built, almost petite, the servant was pallid-skinned and dainty of face. The sandy hair, powder-blue eyes with long golden lashes, button nose and sensuous lips were typically androgynous.

The servant was new, and Jennesta was still uncertain whether the creature was predominantly male or female. But everyone had that problem with elves.

'General Kysthan is here, Your Majesty,' he or she announced in a piping, sing-song voice. 'He, er, has been waiting for some time.'

'Good. I'll see him now.'

The elf ushered in the visitor, bowed discreetly and left.

Kysthan was probably in late middle-age, as far as she could tell, and in orc terms, distinguished-looking. He had ramrod-backed military bearing. An accumulation of criss-crossed tattoos on both cheeks recorded his rise through the ranks. His expression spoke of unease, and not a little apprehension.

There were no opening formalities.

'I can see from your face that they haven't come back,' she said, regal displeasure barely in check.

'No, Your Majesty.' He failed to meet her eyes. 'Perhaps they ran into greater opposition than expected.'

'Reports from the battle don't indicate that.'

He made no reply.

'What do you propose doing about it?'

'A detachment will be sent with all speed to find out what's happened to them, my lady.'

'Are we dealing with treachery here?'

The General was offended. 'We've never had reason to doubt the loyalty of any of the Wolverines,' he replied gravely. 'Their service records are excellent, and—'

'I know *that*. Do you think I'd send them on so sensitive a mission if it were otherwise? Do you take me for such a fool?'

Kysthan's gaze fell to his feet. 'No, my lady.'

'"*No, my lady*",' she mimicked sarcastically. After a tense pause she added, 'Tell me about their leader, this Stryke.'

He produced several sheets of parchment from inside his jerkin. She noticed that his hands were trembling slightly.

'I had few dealings with him personally, Your Majesty. But I know he's from a good clan. Been in military service since hatching, of course. And he's bright.'

'For an orc.'

'As you say,' Kysthan muttered. He cleared his throat, awkwardly, and consulted the papers. 'It seems that he decided early on to increase his chances of promotion by applying total dedication to every duty given to him. His superior officers report that he always obeyed orders instantly and took beatings without complaint.'

'Intelligent *and* ambitious.'

'Yes, my lady.' The General shuffled his notes, a task soldier's hands were too gauche to achieve with grace. 'In fact, it was during his very first detail that—'

'What was it?'

'Hmm?'

'His first detail. What was it?'

'He was assigned as a menial to the dragonmasters, working in the pens.' Kysthan scrutinised the parchment. 'Shovelling dragon dung.'

A small gesture of her hand indicated he should continue.

'While on that detail he caught the eye of an officer who recommended his promotion from drone to footsoldier. He did well and was made a corporal, then sergeant. He was raised to his present rank shortly after. All within four seasons.'

'Impressive.'

'Yes, ma'am. Of course, up to then he'd served exclusively in the Expeditionary Force of the United Orc Clans—'

'Although in truth it does not represent all orc clans and is frequently far from united.' She smiled at him with all the warmth of a Scilantium pit spider. 'Is that not so, General?'

'It is so, my lady.'

She relished his humiliation.

'As you know,' he went on, 'the Orc Supreme Council of War, short of coin to feed and supply the troops, was forced into certain economies. One of those economies involved several thousand warriors being . . .'

'The word is *sold*, General. To me. You were part of the purchase, as I recall.'

'Yes, Majesty, as was Stryke. We both came into your gracious service at that time.'

'Don't ooze. I despise crawlers.'

He blushed, a light cerulean tint colouring his cheeks.

'How long before the detachment you'll send reports back?' she asked.

'About five days, assuming they don't run into problems.'

'Then they must be careful not to. Very well. I expect this . . . *shit shoveller* to be brought here in five days at most. But be clear, General; what he holds is mine, and I will have it. I want the cylinder above all else. Bringing back the Wolverines for punishment is secondary. *Everything* is secondary to the cylinder. Including the lives of Stryke and his band.'

'Yes, my lady.'

'The lives of those sent after them are also expendable.'

He hesitated before replying, 'I understand, my lady.'

'Be sure you do.' She made a series of swift, mysterious movements with her hands. 'And lest you forget . . .'

The General looked down. His uniform was smouldering. It caught fire. The blaze enveloped his jerkin, and instantly spread to his arms and legs. Intolerable heat scorched his limbs. Smoke billowed.

Nostrils smarting from the odour of singeing, he beat at the flames. His palms stung and blistered. Fire leapt to his shoulders, neck, face. It completely engulfed him. His flesh blackened. Excruciating agony seared his body.

He cried out.

Jennesta's hands moved again, in a perfunctory, almost dismissive motion.

There was no fire. His clothes were not charred. The smell of burning had vanished, and there were no blisters on his hands. He felt no pain.

Dumbly, he stared at her.

'If you or your subordinates fail me,' she stated evenly, 'that's just a taste of what you'll get.'

Embarrassment, shame, and above all fear were stamped on his features. 'Yes, Majesty,' he whispered.

His reaction was gratifying. She enjoyed making a grown orc quake.

'You have your orders,' she told him.

He bowed stiffly and turned to the door.

Once the General had left, Jennesta sighed. Making for a couch, she sank into its plump cushions. She was drained. With the natural energy sources so depleted, even casting a simple glamour took considerable effort. Though it was worth it to keep her underlings in line. But now she would have to replenish her powers. The other way.

She remembered the elf servant.

And decided that might be an agreeable way of doing it.

In the corridor outside, Kysthan's upright demeanour deserted him. His nerve was near doing the same. He slumped against a wall, eyes closed, slowly expelling the breath he'd been holding.

It wouldn't do for him to be seen this way. He fought to pull himself together.

After a moment he straightened his shoulders and ran the back of his hand across his sweat-sheened brow. Then with measured deliberateness he resumed his short journey.

The curving passageway took him to an adjacent anteroom. A young officer snapped to attention when he entered.

'As you were, Captain,' the General told him.

The officer relaxed, marginally.

'You're to leave immediately,' Kysthan said.

'How long do we have, sir?'

'Five days, maximum.'

'That's tight, General.'

'It's as long as she'll allow. And let me make myself plain, Delorran. You're to bring back that artefact. If you can return with the Wolverines too, that's fine. But should they prove . . . uncooperative, she'll settle for their heads. Given your past history with Stryke, I imagine you have no problem with that.'

'None, sir. But . . .'

'But what? You'll outnumber them at least three to one. That seems like good odds to me. Or have I got the wrong orc for the job?'

'*No*, sir,' Delorran quickly responded. 'It's just that the Wolverines' kill tally is one of the highest of any of the warbands in the horde.'

'I know that, Captain. It's why I've assigned the best troopers we have to this mission.'

'I'm not saying it's going to be impossible, sir. Just difficult.'

'Nobody promised you an easy ride.' He stared hard at the officer's earnest face, and added, 'Her Majesty's position is that, as with the Wolverines, the loss rate of the troopers under your command is . . . without limit.'

'Sir?'

'Do I have to spell it out? You will spend as many lives on this mission as may be necessary.'

'I see.' His tone was doubtful, troubled.

'Look at it this way, Delorran. If you return without her prize, she'll have you all put to death anyway. Horribly, knowing her. Weigh that against losing only some of your troop, and your certain promotion. Not to mention evening the score in the grievance you have with Stryke. Of course, if you'd prefer me to find someone else—'

'No, General. That won't be necessary.'

'Anyway, such talk could be pointless. Your quarry may already be dead.'

'The Wolverines? I doubt it, sir. I'd say they weren't that easy to kill.'

'Then why no word from them? If they're not dead it's just as unlikely they've been captured. They might have fallen prey to one of the afflictions the humans spread, of course, but I think them too careful for that. Which only leaves betrayal. And there were no grounds to believe any of them might turn out traitors.'

'I'm not so sure. Not all orcs are happy with our present situation, as you know, sir.'

'Do you have reason to believe Stryke and his band harboured such thoughts?'

'I claim no knowledge of their thoughts, sir.'

'Then keep your fancies to yourself, that kind of talk is dangerous. Think only of the cylinder. It has the highest priority. I'm relying on you, Delorran. If you fail, we both suffer Jennesta's wrath.'

The Captain nodded grimly. 'Stryke's death will prevent that fate. I won't let you down, sir.'

They were ready to move. The only disagreement was where.

'I say we get ourselves back to Cairnbarrow and confess all to Jennesta,' argued Haskeer. A handful of his supporters in the assembled warband murmured approval. 'We have pellucid, and that should stand for *something*. Let's go back and throw ourselves on her mercy.'

'We'd be in for a hard landing, comrade,' Alfray said. 'And the crystal wasn't what she sent us for.'

'Alfray's right,' Stryke agreed. 'The only chance we have is to regain that cylinder.'

'If we are going to look for it, why don't we send one or two of the band to Jennesta to explain what the rest of us are doing?' Alfray suggested.

Stryke shook his head. 'To their deaths? No. All of us and the cylinder, or not at all.'

'But where do we look?' Coilla wanted to know.

'It has to be the kobolds' homeland,' Jup said.

'All the way to Black Rock?' Haskeer scoffed. 'That's long odds, shortshanks.'

'Can you think of a *better* idea?'

Haskeer's resentful silence indicated he couldn't.

'They could have gone anywhere,' Coilla told the dwarf.

'True. But we don't know where anywhere is. Black Rock we know how to get to.'

Stryke smiled thinly. 'Jup's got a point. We might spend our lives combing this countryside for those bastards. Black Rock makes more sense, and if the group that robbed us aren't there now, they might turn up.'

Haskeer spat. *'Might.'*

'You want to head back to Cairnbarrow, Sergeant, go ahead.' Stryke scanned the Wolverines' faces. 'That goes for anybody here. You can tell Jennesta where we've gone before she skins you.'

Nobody took him up on the offer.

'It's settled, then; Black Rock. What do you think, Alfray, a week?'

'About that. Maybe more 'cause of the horses we lost. Five or six of us are going to have to double up. And don't forget Meklun. It was bad luck not finding a wagon at Homefield. Dragging him's going to slow us.'

Heads turned to the wounded trooper, strapped to his makeshift litter. His face was deathly pale.

'We'll look for more horses on the way,' Stryke said, 'maybe a wagon.'

'We could always leave him,' Haskeer put in.

'I'll remember that if you ever catch a bad wound yourself.'

Haskeer frowned and shut up.

'What about splitting into two groups?' proposed Coilla. 'One of the fit, going ahead to Black Rock; the other Meklun, the walking wounded and some able bodies, following on.'

'No. Too easy pickings for more ambushes. I've lost the cylinder, I don't want to lose half the band as well. We stick together. Now let's get out of here.'

Some of the Wolverines' less essential kit had to be discarded, and the pellucid redistributed, to make up for the shortage of horses. There were a few petty squabbles over who had to share mounts, but several well-aimed kicks from the officers restored order. Iron rations and water were shared out. Meklun's litter was harnessed.

It was late afternoon before they set off on a southerly bearing. This time Stryke didn't neglect to send scouts ahead of the main party.

He rode at the head of the column, Coilla beside him.

'What do we do when we get to Black Rock?' she said. 'Would you have us take on the whole kobold nation?'

'The gods alone know, Coilla. I'm making this up as I go along, if you hadn't noticed.' He glanced behind him and added in a conspiratorial tone, 'But don't tell them that.'

'This is all we can do, isn't it, Stryke? Make for Black Rock, I mean.'

'Only thing *I* could think of. Because the way I see it, if we can't get the cylinder back, at least we can have the glory of dying while we try.'

'I see it that way too. Though it seems a pity we have to do it for Jennesta, and a human cause.'

There she goes again, he thought. *What does she expect me to say?*

He was tempted to speak frankly, but didn't have the chance.

'You've no idea what's in the cylinder?' she wondered. 'You were given no hint as to why it's so important?'

'Like I said, Jennesta didn't take me into her confidence,' he replied wryly.

'Yet the kobolds obviously thought it was worth facing a warband to gain it.'

'You know kobolds, the thieving little swine. They'll go for anything they think they can get away with.'

'Your reckoning is that they were just acting on a venture?'

'Yes.'

'So with all sorts of travellers crossing these parts, including merchant caravans, who wouldn't give them half the fight we did, they pick on us, a heavily armed band of a race that lives for combat. All on the off-chance we'd have something worth stealing. Does that seem likely?'

'You're saying they were after the cylinder? But how would they know we had it? Our mission was secret.'

'Perhaps our secret mission wasn't so secret after all, Stryke.'

[illegible] these parts, in the [illegible] [illegible] [illegible] [illegible] [illegible] [illegible] [illegible]

7

[illegible]

7

'. . . and ram what's left up your butt!' Stryke concluded.

His captain's feelings having been made clear, in vivid detail, Haskeer glowered murderously and tugged on his horse's reins. He cantered back to his place in the column.

'Don't bite *my* head off,' Coilla ventured, 'but didn't he have a point about stopping to rest?'

'Yes,' Stryke grunted, 'and we will. If I give the order now, though, it'll look like his doing.' He nodded at a rise further along the trail. 'We'll wait till we get to the other side of that.'

They hadn't stopped since setting out, travelling through the night and the new morning. Now the sun was at its highest point, its meagre warmth finally dispelling the lingering chill.

The bluff surmounted, Stryke called a halt. A couple of troopers were sent ahead to alert the forward scouts. Meklun's litter was disengaged from the horse dragging it, and the makeshift stretcher carefully laid flat. Alfray pronounced him little improved.

As fires were lit and horses watered, Stryke went into a huddle with the other officers.

'We're not making bad headway,' he announced, 'despite the handicaps. But it's time for a decision on our route.' He drew a dagger and knelt. 'The human settlement . . . what was it called?'

'Homefield,' Jup offered.

Stryke made a cross in a patch of hardened mud. 'Homefield was here, in the northern end of the Great Plains, and the nearest hostile human colony to Cairnbarrow.'

'Not any more,' Haskeer remarked with dark glee.

Disregarding him, Stryke slashed a downward line. 'We've been moving south.' He carved another cross at the line's end. 'To here. We need to turn south-east for Black Rock. But we've got a problem.' To the right and down a little from the second cross, he gouged a circle.

'Scratch,' Coilla said.

'Right. The trolls' homeland. It's smack in the path of the most direct route to Black Rock.'

Haskeer shrugged his shoulders. 'So?'

'Given how belligerent trolls can be,' Jup told him, 'we should avoid it.'

'*You* might want to run from a fight; *I* don't.'

'We've no need of one, Haskeer,' Stryke intervened coolly. 'Why make extra trouble for ourselves?'

' 'Cause going round Scratch will cost us time.'

'We'll lose a lot more if we get caught up in a fight there, and a fully armed warband riding through their territory is just the thing to start one. No, we'll skirt the place. Question is, which way?'

Coilla jabbed her finger at the improvised map. 'The next shortest way would be to head due east now, toward Hecklowe and the coast. Then we'd make our way south, through or around Black Rock Forest, to Black Rock itself.'

'I'm not happy about going near Hecklowe either,' Stryke said. 'It's a free port, remember. That means plenty of other elder races. We're bound to tangle with at least one that has a grudge against orcs. And the forest's infested with bandits.'

'Not to mention that turning east from here takes us a bit too close to Cairnbarrow for comfort,' Alfray added.

'The advantage of approaching Black Rock from the forest side is that we'd have the cover of trees,' Jup put in.

'That's scant return for all the risks we'd run.' Stryke employed his knife again, extending the line down beyond the elliptical shape he'd drawn. 'I think we have to carry on south, past Scratch, *then* turn east.'

Coilla frowned. 'In which case, don't forget this.' She leaned over and used her finger to outline a small cross below Scratch. 'Weaver's Lea. A Uni settlement, like Homefield, but much bigger. Word is that the humans there are more fanatical than most.'

'Is that possible?' Jup asked drily of no one in particular.

'We'd have to pass between the two,' Stryke granted. 'But it's all flat plains in those parts, so at least we could see trouble coming.'

Alfray studied the markings. 'It's the longest route, Stryke.'

'I know, but it's also the safest. Or the least dangerous, anyway.'

'Whatever damned route we take,' Haskeer rumbled, 'nobody's said anything about Black Rock being a short piss away from *there*.' He plunged his own knife into the ground, to the right of Coilla's crude addition.

Jup glared at him. 'That's supposed to mean Quatt, is it?'

'Where your kind comes from, yes. Being so close should make you feel at home.'

'When are you going to stop blaming me for the wrong done by all dwarves?'

'When your race stops doing the humans' dirty work.'

'I answer for myself, not my whole race. Others do what they must.'

Haskeer bridled. 'There's no *must* about helping the incomers!'

'What do you think *we're* doing? Or are you too stupid to notice who Jennesta's allied with?'

As with most spats between the sergeants, this one escalated rapidly.

'Don't lecture *me* on loyalty, rat's prick!'

'Go shove your head up a horse's arse!'

Faces twisted with malice, they both began to rise.

'*Enough!*' Stryke barked. 'If you two want to tear each other apart, that's fine by me. But let's try to get home alive first, shall we?'

They eyed him, weighed the odds for a second, then backed off.

'You've all got your duties,' he reminded them. 'Move yourselves.'

Haskeer couldn't resist a parting shot. 'If we're going anywhere near Quatt,' he snarled, 'better watch your backs.' He shot the dwarf a malicious look. 'The locals are treacherous in those parts.'

He and his fellow officers scattered to their chores. But Stryke motioned for Jup to stay.

'I know it's hard,' he said, 'but you have to hold back when you're provoked.'

'Tell Haskeer that, Captain.'

'You think I haven't? I've made it clear he's heading for a flogging, and not for the first time since I've led this band.'

'I can take the insults about my race. The gods know I'm used to that. But he never lets up.'

'He's bitter for his own reasons, Jup. You're just a handy scapegoat.'

'It's when he questions my allegiance that my blood really boils.'

'Well, you have to admit your race is notorious for selling its loyalty to the highest bidder.'

'Some have, not all. *My* loyalty isn't for sale.'

Stryke nodded.

'And there are those among the dwarves who say similar things about orcs,' Jup added.

'Orcs fight only to further the Mani cause, and indirectly at that. We've little choice in the matter. At least your race has free will enough to decide. We were born into military service and have known no other way.'

'I know that, Stryke. But you *do* have a choice. You could determine your own fate, as I did when I chose which side to back.'

Stryke didn't like the way the conversation was going. It made him uneasy.

He avoided a direct reply by steering Jup to the topic he'd wanted to raise in the first place. 'Maybe we orcs have a choice, maybe we don't. What we haven't got is farsight. Dwarves have, and we could use it now. Has your skill improved?'

'No, Stryke, it hasn't, and I've been trying, believe me.'

'You're sensing nothing?'

'Only vague . . . traces is the nearest word, I suppose. Sorry, Captain; explaining to somebody from a race with no magical abilities isn't easy.'

'But you are getting traces. Of what? Kirgizil tracks? Or—'

'As I said, traces is an inexact word. Language isn't enough to describe the skill. The point is that what I'm picking up doesn't help us. It's weak, muddled.'

'Damn.'

'Perhaps it's because we're still too close to Homefield. I've often noticed that the power seems lower where humans are concentrated.'

'It could come back the further away we get, you mean?'

'It *might*. Truth to tell, farsight was always pretty basic in dwarves anyway, and nobody really knows how we or the other elder races draw the power, except it comes from the earth. If humans are digging and tearing in one place they can sever a line of energy, and it bleeds, starving wherever else it goes. So in some areas magic works, in others it doesn't.'

'Know what I've never understood? If they're eating the magic, why don't they use it against us?'

Jup shrugged. 'Who can say?'

After a couple of hours' fitful sleep, the Wolverines resumed their journey.

Far to their right flowed the Calyparr Inlet, marked by a fringe of trees. To their left, the Great Plains rolled in seemingly endless profusion. But the scene was askew. What had once been fecund now lacked vitality, and it seemed that much of the colour had washed out of the landscape. In many places the grass was turning yellow and dying in patches. Low-growing shrubbery was stunted and brittle. Tree barks were patterned with sickly parasitic growths. A brief fall of light rain was tawny-hued and smelt unwholesome, as though sulphurous.

Dusk saw them arriving at a point roughly parallel with Scratch. If they continued at the same rate, Stryke reckoned, they could turn west at dawn.

Riding alone at the head of the file, he was preoccupied with weightier thoughts than navigation. He pondered the mystery of the dreams that were afflicting him, and his sense of futility in the face of the odds stacked against them was growing. But what would happen if they didn't find the kobold raiding party, and the cylinder, was something he tried not to think about.

Melancholy had as cold a grip on him as the chill night air by the time one of the advance scouts appeared. The grunt was approaching at speed, his mount's nostrils huffing steamy clouds.

Reaching the column, he reined in sharply and wheeled the sweating horse about.

Stryke put out a hand to catch the trooper's reins, steadying his ride. 'What is it, Orbon?'

'Encampment ahead, sir.'

'Do they have horses?'

'Yes.'

'Good. Let's see if we can parley for some.'

'But Captain, it's an orc camp, and it looks deserted.'

'Are you sure?'

'Zoda and me have been watching the place, and there's no sign of anything stirring 'cept the horses.'

'All right. Go back to him and wait for us. Don't do anything till we get there.'

'Sir!' The scout goaded his steed and galloped off.

Stryke called forward his officers and explained the situation.

'Is an orc camp something you'd expect to come across in these parts?' Jup asked.

'They're more common in our native northern regions, it's true,' Stryke explained, 'but there are a few nomadic orc clans. I suppose it could be one of those. Or a military unit on a mission, like us.'

'If the scouts are reporting no activity, we should approach with caution,' Coilla suggested.

'That's my feeling,' Stryke agreed. 'It may be an orc encampment, but that doesn't mean it's orcs we'll find there. Until we know better, we treat it as hostile. Let's go.'

Ten minutes later they found Orbon waiting for them by a large copse. Its trees shed brown leaves and the bushes were turning autumnal colours, though summer's mid point was still a phase of the moon away.

Stryke had the band quietly dismount. The healing wounded were left with Meklun and the horses. Orbon in the lead, the rest stealthily entered the grove.

Ten paces in, the ground began to slope, and it was soon clear that the copse sheltered a sizeable trench-shaped indentation. They descended on a pulpy carpet of leaves to a fallen tree where Zoda, stretched full-length, kept watch.

Enough dappled light from the setting sun penetrated the swaying canopy to show what lay below.

Two modest roundhouses, topped with thatch, and a third, smaller still, its roof incomplete. Five or six lean-tos built of angled, lashed saplings covered by irregular-shaped remnants of coarse cloth. Sluggish spring water trickling feebly through churned mud. A pair of tree stumps and a connecting bough forming a roughly constructed hitching rail. Seven or eight cowed, strangely silent horses tethered to it.

As Stryke took it all in, the memory of the dream or vision he'd had came back to him, but in diametric opposition to what he now saw. The orc settlement in his dream had had a feeling of permanence. This was itinerant and ramshackle. The dream was redolent with light and clean air. This was dark and stifling. The dream was life-affirming. This spoke of death.

He heard Coilla whisper, 'Abandoned, you think?'

'Wouldn't be surprised,' Alfray replied in hushed tones, 'bearing in mind it's close to Scratch *and* not that far from a Uni colony.'

'But why leave the horses?'

Stryke roused himself. 'Let's find out. Haskeer, take a third of the band and work your way round to the other side. Jup, Alfray, move another third to the right flank. Coilla and the rest, stay with me. We go in on my signal.'

It took a few minutes for the groups to position themselves. When he was sure all were in place, Stryke stood and made a swift chopping motion with his arm. The Wolverines drew their weapons and began moving down toward the camp in a pincer formation.

They reached level without incident, save the nervous shying of several of the horses.

Around the crude dwellings the ground was strewn with

objects of various kinds. An upended cooking cauldron, broken pottery, a trampled saddlebag, the bones of fowl, a discarded bow. Ashes of long-dead fires were heaped in several places.

Stryke led his detachment to the nearest roundhouse.

He raised a finger to his lips, and pointed with his blade to deploy the group around the shanty. When they were in place, he and Coilla crept to the entrance. It had no door; a piece of tattered sacking served the purpose. Swords up, they positioned themselves.

He nodded. Coilla ripped aside the cloth.

An overpoweringly foul smell hit them like a physical blow. It was mouldy, sweet, sickly and unmistakable.

The odour of decaying flesh.

Covering his mouth with his free hand, Stryke stepped inside. The light was poor, but it only took a few seconds for his eyes to adjust.

The hut was filled with dead orcs. They lay three and four deep on makeshift cots. Others completely covered the floor. A pall of corruption hung heavy in the air. Only the scurrying of carrion disturbed the stillness.

Coilla was at Stryke's side, palm pressed against her mouth. She tugged at his arm and they backed out. They retreated from the entrance and gulped air as the rest of their group craned for a look inside the hut.

Stryke moved to the second of the larger roundhouses, Coilla in tow, arriving as Jup emerged ashen-faced. The stench was just as strong. A glance at the interior revealed an identical scene of huddled corpses.

The dwarf breathed deeply. 'All females and young ones. Dead for some time.'

'The same over there,' Stryke told him.

'No adult males?'

'None I could see.'

'Why not? Where are they?'

'I can't be sure, Jup, but I think this is a dispossessed camp.'

'I'm still learning your ways, remember. What does that mean?'

'When a male orc's killed in military service, and his commander says it's cowardice, the dead warrior's mate and orphans are cast out. Some of the dispossessed band together.'

'The rule's being rigidly applied since we came under Jennesta,' Coilla added.

'They're left to fend for themselves?' Jup asked.

Stryke nodded. 'It's an orc's lot.'

'What did you expect?' Coilla said, reading the dwarf's expression. 'A stipend and a tithed farm?'

Jup ignored the sarcasm. 'Any idea what killed them, Captain?'

'Not yet. Mass suicide's not impossible, though. It's been known. Or maybe they—'

'Stryke!'

Haskeer was standing by the smallest hut, waving him over. Stryke went to him. Coilla, Jup and some of the others followed.

'One of 'em's still alive in there.' Haskeer jerked his thumb at the entrance.

Stryke peered into the gloom. 'Get Alfray. And bring a torch!' He entered.

There was just one prone figure, lying on a bed of filthy straw. Stryke approached, and heard strained breathing. He stooped. In the poor light he could just make out the features of an old orc female. Her eyes were closed and her face glistened under a film of perspiration.

A murmur at Stryke's back heralded Alfray's arrival.

'Is she wounded?'

'Can't tell. Where's that torch?'

'Haskeer's bringing it.'

The aged orc's eyes opened. Her lips trembled, as though she were trying to say something. Alfray bent to listen. There was a final outrush of breath, like a sigh, and the distinctive sound of the death rattle.

Haskeer came in with a burning brand.

'Give it here.' Alfray took the torch and held it over the dead female. *'Gods!'*

He quickly pulled away from her, nearly colliding with Stryke.

'What is it?'

'Look.' Alfray stretched the torch at arm's length, bathing the corpse in light.

Stryke saw.

'Get out,' he said. 'Both of you. *Now!*'

Haskeer and Alfray scrambled to exit, Stryke in their wake.

Outside, the rest of the band had gathered.

'Did you touch her?' Stryke demanded of Haskeer.

'Me? No . . . no, I didn't.'

'Or any of the other dead?'

'No.'

Stryke turned to the Wolverines. 'Did *any* of you touch the corpses?'

They shook their heads.

'What's going on, Stryke?' Coilla asked.

'Red spot.'

Several of the band stepped back on reflex. Exclamations and curses ran through the ranks. Grunts began covering their mouths and noses with kerchiefs.

Jup hissed, '*Bastard* humans.'

'The horses can't get it,' Stryke said. 'We'll take them. I want us out of here fast. And burn everything!'

He snatched the torch from Alfray and hurled it into the hut.

The straw caught immediately. In seconds the interior was an inferno.

The band dispersed to spread the fire.

8

Delorran's boot crunched against something. Looking down, he found he'd trodden on a broken slab of wood displaying part of a neatly painted word.

It read: *Homef*

He kicked it aside and returned his attention to the burnt-out human settlement. His troopers were sifting through the ruins, rummaging in debris, upending charred planks, disturbing clouds of ash dust.

The search had begun before dawn. Now it was early afternoon and they were no nearer finding anything of importance, least of all the cylinder. Nor was there any sign of what had happened to the Wolverines. That much had been obvious from shortly after they arrived, and Delorran had sent out parties to scour the surrounding area for clues. None had yet returned.

He paced the compound. An unseasonable wind was gusting in from the north, picking up bite as it funnelled over the chalky line of far-off glaciers. The Captain puffed into his cupped hands.

One of his sergeants came away from the search and trotted toward him. He shook his head as he approached.

'Nothing?' Delorran said.

'No, sir. Neither the item or any orc bones in the ashes. Only human.'

'And we know none of the scavengers reported collecting Wolverine corpses for their pyres after the battle, except possibly a couple of grunts. Stryke and most of his officers are well enough known to be recognised, so we can take that as true.'

'Then you reckon they're still alive, sir?'

'I never really doubted it. I couldn't see a quality band losing out to the kind of opposition they met here. The real mystery is what's happened to them.'

The sergeant, a stolid veteran, his tattoos of rank fading, was better suited to combat than solving riddles. The best he could do was remind Delorran of another puzzle. 'What about the empty cellar in the barn, Captain? You think that's anything to do with it?'

'I don't know. But a cleaned-out silo, not even a grain, at a time when you'd expect to find corn down there seems odd. I'd wager the humans were using it to store *something*.'

'Loot?'

'Could be. What it comes to is that the Wolverines aren't dead, they're gone; and it looks like they've taken at least one valuable with them.'

Delorran's rivalry with the Wolverines' leader and his belief that he, not Stryke, should have been given command of the band was widely known. As was the long-standing animosity between their respective clans. Aware of the possibility that Delorran might have his own reasons for questioning Stryke's honesty, and the shoals of inter-clan politics, the sergeant made no comment. He kept to a neutral 'Permission to resume duties, sir.'

The Captain waved him away.

Well beyond mid point, the arching sun continued its

inexorable journey across the sky. Half his allotted time used up, Delorran's apprehension was growing. He should be heading back for Cairnbarrow in the next couple of hours to meet the deadline. And quite possibly his death.

A rapid decision had to be made.

There were three options. Finding the cylinder here and returning home in triumph seemed less likely by the minute. That left going back without it and facing Jennesta's wrath, or disobeying orders and continuing to look for the Wolverines.

Cursing the Queen's impatience, he agonised about what to do.

His deliberations were interrupted by the appearance of two of the scouts he'd sent out earlier.

They reined in their lathering horses beside him. One rider was a lowly grunt, the other a corporal. The latter dismounted.

'Pack four reporting, sir!'

Delorran gave him a curt nod.

'I think our group's come up with something, sir. We've found signs of a fight south of here, in a small valley.'

A fragile hope stirred in the Captain's breast. 'Go on.'

'The place is littered with dead kobolds, kirgizils and horses.'

'Kobolds?'

'From the lizard tracks down the valley sides it looks like they ambushed somebody.'

'Doesn't mean it was the Wolverines. Unless you found any of their bodies.'

'No, sir. But we came across discarded rations; standard orc issue. And this.' The corporal dug into his belt pouch and retrieved the find. He dropped it on to Delorran's outstretched palm.

It was a necklace of three snow-leopard fangs, its strand broken.

Delorran stared at it, absently fingering the five identical trophies looped around his own throat. Orcs were the only race that wore these particular emblems of their mettle, and they were a prerequisite of the officer class.

He made his decision.

'You've done well.'

'Thank you, sir.'

'Your group will lead us to this valley. Meanwhile, I want you to find yourself a fresh horse and carry out a special mission.'

'Yes, sir.'

'Congratulations, Corporal. You're going to get home earlier than the rest of us. I need you to carry a message to Cairnbarrow with all speed. For the Queen.'

'Sir.' This time there was a slight hesitancy in the corporal's response.

'You're to deliver the message to General Kysthan personally. No one else. Is that understood?'

'Sir.'

'The General is to tell Jennesta that I have a lead on where the Wolverines have gone and am in hot pursuit. I'm sure I can catch them and return the item the Queen desires. I beg more time, and will send further messages. Repeat that.'

The corporal paled a little as he recited it. He didn't doubt it wasn't what Jennesta would want to hear. But he was disciplined enough, or fearful enough, to obey orders without question.

'Good,' Delorran said. He handed back the necklace. 'Give this to the General and explain how it was found. Best pick a couple of troopers to go with you, and burn hell for leather. Dismissed.'

Gloomy-faced, the corporal remounted and made off, the silent grunt in his wake.

Delorran was giving Jennesta no choice. It was a dangerous ploy, and his only chance of surviving it lay in recovering the artefact. But he couldn't see another way.

He consoled himself with the thought that she had to be amenable to reason, notwithstanding her dreadful reputation.

Jennesta finished eviscerating the sacrifice and laid down her tools.

Her work had left a sizeable opening in the cadaver's chest, and entrails dangled wetly from his excavated abdomen. But her skill was such that only one or two tiny crimson flecks stained her diaphanous white shift.

She went to the altar and used the flame of a black candle to light another bundle of incense sticks. The heady fug already perfuming the chamber grew thicker.

A pair of her orc bodyguards were moving back and forth clutching heavy buckets in both hands. One of them spilled a dribble of the contents, leaving a thin trail on the flagstones.

'Don't waste that!' she snapped irritably. 'Unless you want to replace it yourselves!'

The guards exchanged furtive looks, but exercised more care as they lugged their pails to a large round tub and emptied them into it. The tub was built like a barrel, with seasoned wooden uprights sealed at the joins and embraced by metal hasps. It differed from a barrel in having much lower sides, and in being big enough to comfortably hold a reclining drey horse, should Jennesta choose to use if for such a purpose. Which as far as her orc attendants were concerned was not beyond the bounds of possibility.

She walked over to the vessel and contemplated its interior. The orcs returned, the muscles on their arms standing out as they hauled four more buckets. Jennesta watched as they tipped in the load.

'That'll do,' she said. 'Leave me.'

They bowed, demonstrating a peculiarly orcish form of

inelegance. The echoing thump of the weighty door marked their departure.

Jennesta turned back to the tub of fresh blood.

She knelt and breathed deep of its unique aroma. Then she swished her fingertips through the viscous liquid. It was warm, not far short of body temperature, which made it a better medium. As an agent of the ritual it would intensify the power that had once come naturally but these days had to be nourished.

Her cat sashayed into range, meowing.

Jennesta stroked her between the ears, light fingers softly massaging the animal's furry crown. 'Not now, my love, I have to concentrate.'

Sapphire purred and slunk away.

Jennesta focused on her meditations. Brow furrowed, she began reciting an incantation in the old tongue. The strange concatenation of guttural and singsong phrases rose from a near whisper to something resembling a shriek. Then it fell and climbed again.

The candles and torches scattered around the chamber billowed in an unseen wind. Somehow the very atmosphere seemed to compress, to converge and bear down on the tub's scarlet cargo. The blood rippled and churned. It sloshed about disgustingly. Bubbles appeared and burst, sluggishly, releasing wisps of foul-smelling rust-coloured vapour.

Then the surface settled and rapidly coagulated. A crust formed. It took on a different aspect, a rainbow effect, like oil on water.

Beads of perspiration dotted Jennesta's forehead and lank strands of hair were plastered to it. As she looked on, the clotted gore gently shimmered as though lit by an inner radiance. A wavering image started to form slowly on the lustre.

A face.

The eyes were its most striking feature. Dark, flinty, cruel.

Not unlike Jennesta's own. But overall the face was much less human than hers.

In a voice that might have been coming from the depths of a fathomless ocean, the phantasm spoke.

'What do you want, Jennesta?' There was no element of surprise in the imperious, disdainful tone.

'I thought it was time we talked.'

'Ah, the great champion of the incomers' cause deigns to speak to me.'

'I do *not* champion humans, Adpar. I simply support certain elements for my own benefit. And for the benefit of others.'

That was greeted by a mocking laugh. *'Self-deceiving as ever. You could at least be honest about your motives.'*

'And follow *your* example?' Jennesta retorted. 'Pull your head from the sand and join with me. Then perhaps we'd stand a better chance of preserving the old ways.'

'We live *the old ways here, without stooping to consort with humans, or asking their permission. You'll come to regret allying yourself with them.'*

'Mother might have taken a different view on that.'

'The blessed Vermegram was great in many ways, but her judgement was not perfect in all respects,' the apparition replied frostily. *'But we cover old ground. I don't suppose it was your intention to engage in small talk. Why are you troubling me?'*

'I want to ask you about something I've lost.'

'And what might that be? A hoard of gems, perhaps? A prized grimoire? Your virginity?'

Jennesta clenched her fists and held her building irritation in check. 'The object is an artefact.'

'Very mysterious, Jennesta. Why are you telling me this?'

'The thought occurred that you might have . . . heard word of its whereabouts.'

'You still haven't said what it is.'

'It's an item of no value to anyone but me.'

'That's not very helpful.'

'Look, Adpar, either you know what I'm talking about or you don't.'

'I can see your difficulty. If I know nothing of this artefact, *you don't want to run the risk of giving details lest it whet my interest. If I do know, it must be because I had a hand in taking it from you. Is that what I'm accused of?'*

'I'm not accusing you of anything.'

'That's just as well, because I have no idea what you're talking about.'

Jennesta wasn't sure if this was the truth, or whether Adpar was playing a familiar game. It aggravated her that she still couldn't tell after all these years. 'All right,' she said. 'Leave it be.'

'Of course, if this . . . whatever it is is something you want so badly, perhaps I should take an interest in it . . .'

'You'd be well advised to stay out of my affairs, Adpar. And if I find you had anything to do with what I've lost—'

'You know, you look peaky, dear. Are you suffering from a morbidity?'

'No I am not!'

'I expect it's the drain of energy in your part of the country. There isn't anything like as much of a problem here. I wonder if there could be a connection? Between the thing you've lost and your need to make up for the missing energy, I mean. Could it be a magical totem of some kind? Or—'

'Don't play the innocent, Adpar, it's so bloody infuriating!'

'No more than being suspected of theft!'

'Oh, for the gods' sake go and—'

A little undulation started up the side of the conjured face. From a pinpoint epicentre, tiny waves moved indolently across the surface, distorting the face and lapping against the tub's wall.

'Now look what you've done!' Adpar complained.

'Me? *You,* more like it!'

A miniature sparkling whirlpool curled into existence, turning lethargically. The eddies calmed down and an oval silhouette appeared. Gradually it became more distinct.

Another face appeared on the soupy crimson surface.

It, too, had eyes that were striking, but for the opposite reasons that Jennesta and Adpar's were. Of the three, it had features most resembling a human's.

Jennesta adopted an expression of distaste. *'You,'* she said, making the word sound like a profanity.

'I should have known,' Adpar sighed.

'You're disturbing the ether with your bickering,' the new arrival told them.

'And you're disturbing us with your presence,' Jennesta retorted.

'Why can't we ever communicate without you butting in, Sanara?' Adpar asked.

'You know why; the link is too strong. I can't avoid being drawn in. Our heritage binds us together.'

'One of the gods' crueller tricks,' Jennesta muttered.

Adpar piped up with, *'Why don't you ask Sanara about your precious bauble?'*

'Very funny.'

'What are you talking about?' Sanara wanted to know.

'Jennesta's lost something she's desperate to get back.'

'Leave it, Adpar.'

'But surely, of us all Sanara is in a location where a boost to magic is most needed.'

'Stop trying to stir trouble!' Jennesta snapped. 'And I never said the artefact had to do with magic.'

'I'm not sure I'd want to be involved with something you've lost, Jennesta,' Sanara remarked. *It's likely to be troublesome, or dangerous.'*

'Oh, shut up, you self-righteous prig!'

'That's very unkind,' Adpar said with transparently false sympathy. *'Sanara has some terrible problems at the moment.'*

'Good!'

Relishing Jennesta's exasperation, Adpar burst into derisive laughter. And Sanara looked on the point of mouthing some piece of wholesome advice Jennesta was bound to find nauseating.

'You can both go to hell!' she raged, bringing her fists down hard on the pair of smug faces.

Their images fragmented and dissolved. Her pummelling split the gory crust. The blood was cool now, almost cold, and it splashed as she rained wrathful blows, showering her face and clothing.

Fury vented, Jennesta slumped, panting, by the side of the tub.

She berated herself. When would she learn that contact with Adpar, and inevitably Sanara, never did anything to improve her temper? The day was fast approaching, she decided for the hundredth time, when the link between them all would have to be severed. Permanently.

Sensing a titbit, in the way of cats, Sapphire arrived and rubbed sensuously against her mistress's leg. A scab of congealed blood had stuck to Jennesta's forearm. She peeled it off and dangled it in front of the animal. Sapphire sniffed it, whiskers quivering, then sank her teeth into the scummy treat. She made wet, mushy sounds as she chewed.

Jennesta thought of the cylinder, and of the wretched warband she had been foolish enough to send for it. More than half the time she had granted for the item's return was used up. She would have to make contingency plans in the event of Kysthan's emissary failing to recover her prize. Though even the gods wouldn't be able to help him if he hadn't.

But she would have what was hers. The warband would be

hunted down like dogs and delivered to her justice, whatever it took.

She idly licked the blood from her hands and dreamed of torments to inflict on the Wolverines.

9

'You must feel bad,' Stryke said.

Alfray touched his bare neck and nodded. 'I took my first tooth at thirteen seasons. Haven't been parted from the necklace since. Till now.'

'Lost in the ambush?'

'Had to be. So used to wearing it, I didn't even notice. Coilla pointed it out today.'

'But you won the trophies, Alfray. Nobody can take that away. You'll replace them, given time.'

'Time I haven't got. Not enough to gain another three, anyway. Oldest in the band, Stryke. Besting snow leopards unarmed is a sport for young orcs.'

Alfray fell into a brooding silence. Stryke let him be. He knew what a blow to his pride it was to lose the emblems of courage, the symbols that testified to full orchood.

They rode on at the head of the convoy.

None spoke of it, but what they had seen at the orc encampment, and their perilous situation, hung heavy on the entire band. Alfray's melancholy chimed with the Wolverines' generally gloomy mood.

With horses for all, they made better progress, though

Meklun, unable to ride and still on his litter, continued to slow them. Several hours earlier they had veered south-west, cutting across the Great Plains toward Black Rock. Before the day was out they should have reached a point midway between Scratch and Weaver's Lea.

Stryke's hope was that they'd pass through the corridor without meeting trouble from either disputatious trolls to the north or zealous humans in the south.

The terrain had begun to change. Plains were giving way to hilly country, with shallow valleys and winding trails. Scrub was more prevalent. Pastures shaded into heathlands. They were nearing an area dotted with human settlements. Stryke decided it was safer to treat them all as hostile, whether Uni or Mani.

A commotion down the line broke his train of thought. He looked back. Haskeer and Jup were squabbling loudly.

Stryke sighed. 'Keep our heading,' he told Alfray, and swung his horse out.

In the moment it took to gallop to them, the sergeants had come close to blows. They quietened on seeing him.

'You two my joint seconds or spoilt hatchlings?'

'It's his fault,' Haskeer complained. 'He—'

'*My* fault?' Jup snapped. 'You bastard! I should—'

'Shut it!' Stryke ordered. 'You're supposed to be our chief scout, Jup; earn your keep. Prooq and Gleadeg need relieving. Take Calthmon, and leave your shares of crystal with Alfray.'

Jup shot his antagonist a parting scowl and spurred off.

Stryke turned his attention to Haskeer. 'You're pushing me,' he said. 'Much more and I'll have the skin off your back.'

'Shouldn't have his kind in the band,' Haskeer muttered.

'This isn't a debate, Sergeant. Work with him or make your own way home. Your choice.' He headed back to the column's prow.

Haskeer noticed that the grunts within hearing distance of the dressing-down were staring at him. 'We wouldn't be in this mess if we were properly led,' he grumbled sourly.

The troopers looked away.

When Stryke reached Alfray, Coilla came forward to join them.

'On this bearing we'll be passing nearer Weaver's Lea than Scratch. What's our plan if we meet trouble?' she asked.

'Weaver's Lea's one of the older Uni settlements, and one of the most fanatical,' Stryke said. 'That makes them unpredictable. Just bear that in mind.'

'Uni, Mani, who cares?' Alfray put in. 'They're all *humans*, aren't they?'

'We're supposed to be helping the Manis,' Coilla reminded him.

'Only because we've no choice. What choice did we *ever* have?'

'All we wanted, once,' Stryke told him. 'Anyway, it makes sense to support the Manis. They're less hostile to the elder races. More important, it helps us to have the humans divided. Think how much worse it'd be if they were united.'

'Or if one side won,' Coilla added.

Ahead of the column, and out of its sight, Jup and Calthmon took over as pathfinders. Jup watched as the pair of troopers they had relieved, Prooq and Gleadeg, rode back towards the main party.

Only now was he beginning to calm down from his latest tangle with Haskeer. He goaded his mount, a mite harder than necessary, and concentrated on trail-blazing.

The landscape grew more cluttered. Hillocks and clumps of trees were increasingly common, taller grass made the track less certain.

'Know these parts, Sergeant?' Calthmon asked. He spoke

quietly, as though a raised voice might betray their presence, despite the wilderness in all directions.

'A little. From here on we can expect the terrain to alter quite a bit.'

As though on cue, the track they followed dipped and started to curve. The undergrowth on either side thickened. They began to round a blind bend.

'But if the band keeps to its present path,' Jup continued, 'we shouldn't have anything . . .'

A roadblock stretched across the trail.

' . . . to worry about.'

The barricade was made up of a side-on farm wagon and a wall of sturdy tree trunks. It was guarded by humans dressed uniformly in black. They numbered at least a score and were heavily armed.

Jup and Calthmon pulled back on their reins just as the humans spotted them.

'Oh *shit*,' Jup groaned.

A great yell went up from the roadblock. Waving swords, axes and clubs, all but a handful of the humans rushed to mount their horses. Dwarf and orc fought to turn their own steeds.

Then they were racing away, pursued by a howling posse baying for blood.

'One day a member of the United Expeditionary Force, the next bartered into Jennesta's service,' Stryke recalled. 'You know how it was.'

'I do,' Coilla replied, 'and I expect you felt the same way I did.'

'How so?'

'Weren't *you* angry at having no say in the matter?'

Again, he was confounded by her frankness. And by her accurate reading of his feelings. 'Perhaps,' he conceded.

'You're at war with your upbringing, Stryke. You can't bring yourself to admit it was an injustice.'

The way she had of gauging his innermost thoughts was discomforting for Stryke. He answered in a roundabout fashion. 'It was hardest on the likes of Alfray.' A jab of his thumb indicated their field surgeon, down the line, riding next to Meklun's litter. 'Change isn't easy at his age.'

'It's you we were talking about.'

His response was deferred by the sight of Prooq and Gleadeg appearing on the trail ahead. They galloped to him.

'Advance scouts reporting, sir,' Prooq recited crisply. 'Sergeant Jup's taken over.'

'Anything we should look out for?'

'No, sir. The way forward seemed clear.'

'All right. Join the column.'

The troopers left.

'You were saying,' Coilla prompted. 'About the change.'

Are you just naturally single-minded, Stryke thought, *or is there a reason for all these questions?* 'Well, things didn't change that much for me under our new mistress,' he said. 'Not at first. I kept my rank, and I could still fight the real enemy, if only one faction of them.'

'And you were given command of the Wolverines.'

'Eventually. Though not everybody liked it.'

'What did you think about finding yourself serving a part-human ruler?'

'It was . . . unusual,' he responded cautiously.

'You resented it, you mean. Like the rest of us.'

'I wasn't happy,' he admitted. 'As you said yourself, we're in a tough spot. Victory for either Manis or Unis can only strengthen the human side.' He shrugged. 'But it's an orc's lot to obey orders.'

She looked at him long and hard. 'Yes. That's what it's come to.' There was no misreading her bitterness.

He felt an affinity, and wanted to take the conversation further.

A nearby grunt shouted something. Stryke couldn't make it out. The rest of the band started yelling.

Jup and Calthmon were returning, riding all-out.

Stryke raised himself in his stirrups. 'What the—?'

Then he saw the mob of humans chasing them. They were black-garbed, in long frock coats and breeches of coarsely woven cloth, with high leather boots. He reckoned their number matched the Wolverines'. There was no time to charge.

'Close ranks!' he roared. *'To me! Close up!'*

The band surged forward, rallying to their commander. Swiftly the horses were formed into a defensive semi-circle facing the enemy, with Meklun's litter behind them. The company drew their weapons.

Jup and Calthmon's pursuers slowed on seeing the band, allowing the pair to increase their lead. But they still kept coming, spreading out from a bunch to a line.

'Hold fast!' Stryke ordered. 'No quarter and no retreat!'

'As if we would,' Coilla remarked in a gallows-humour tone. She swiped the air with her blade, limbering for a fight.

Cheered on by their comrades, Jup and Calthmon reached the Wolverines, their steeds lathering.

Two heartbeats later the humans came in like a storm tide.

Many of the horses of both groups wheeled round at the last moment, their riders engaging side-on.

Stryke faced a heavily bearded, weather-beaten attacker, eyes flaming with bloodlust. He brandished a hatchet and was swinging it wildly, but the weapon was being used with more energy than precision.

Blocking a pass, Stryke delivered a thrust of his own. His opponent's horse bucked and the sword plunged harmlessly over the human's shoulder. Stryke quickly returned the blade and parried another swing. They exchanged half a dozen ringing blows. The human overreached himself. Stryke chopped down hard on his exposed arm, severing hand from wrist. It fell away, still clutching the axe.

Gushing blood and bellowing, the human took a death stroke to the chest and went down.

Stryke turned to a second assailant as Coilla dispatched her first. She wrenched free her blade just in time to throw up a guard. It stopped a swipe from a dumpy, muscular individual armed with a broadsword. Batting off several more lunges, she sent a whistling slash at the human's head. He ducked and avoided it.

Without pause, Coilla went in again, ramming her sword low. Unexpectedly dextrous, the human twisted in his saddle and the blade pierced only air. He went on the offensive again. Holding him at bay with the sword, Coilla's other hand found her belt and plucked a knife. She flung it underarm and punctured his heart.

Off to the left, Haskeer held his sword two-handed, flapping reins forgotten, as he laid about the enemy. He split skulls, caved chests, hacked deep into limbs. Pink flesh was lacerated, bones cracked, ruby showers soaked all in range. Far gone in berserk frenzy, Haskeer took no account of human or animal, his blade carving horses and riders alike.

In the screaming, trampling chaos, a handful of the attackers flowed around the defensive barrier to strike at the Wolverines' vulnerable rear. Alfray and a couple of grunts turned to deal with the threat. Battle raged about Meklun's litter, crashing hooves and plummeting bodies failing to stir the insensible form.

Almost toppled from his mount by a club's glancing blow, in righting himself Alfray slashed his foe's saddle straps. The human pitched to one side and hit the ground. As he struggled to his feet, a riderless horse flattened him.

Joining the defence of the band's rump, Jup side-swiped one of two raiders who had Alfray boxed in. Dwarf and human crossed swords. Jup laid open the man's arm and followed through by planting cold steel in his ribcage.

A human's sword connected with Stryke's and bounced off. Stryke's response was a grievous blow to the other's neck, hewing flesh to the bone. The next to take the victim's place got equally short shrift. He managed to conjoin with Stryke's blade twice before a raking sword tip ribboned his face and sent him howling.

Fighting with sword and dagger, Coilla held off a pair of aggressors employing a crude pincer movement. One caught the long blade's edge across his throat. A second later the other halted the short blade's flight with his chest.

There being no other opponent to deal with, she turned her attention to Stryke. He was locked in combat with a scrawny, long-limbed antagonist, sandy-haired and blotchy-skinned. She judged it an adolescent of the species, and its artless movements betrayed a life unsullied by warfare. The youth's fear was palpable.

Stryke put an end to it with a swinging blow to the thorax. A smartly administered follow-through to the neck brought clean decapitation. Coilla's face was speckled with red drizzle from the spray.

She wiped the back of a hand across her eyes and spat to clear her mouth. It was a purely reflex action, undertaken with no more distaste than if the liquid had been rainwater. 'They're finished, Stryke,' she stated flatly.

He didn't need her confirmation. Human corpses littered the area. Only two or three remained alive to engage the band, and all were getting the worst of it. Haskeer was beating one over the head repeatedly with what looked like a cudgel. Closer examination showed it to be a human arm, white bone protruding from its sticky end.

A handful of the enemy were fleeing on horseback. About a third of the Wolverine grunts, whooping triumphantly, started after them. Stryke bawled and they abandoned the chase, though returning reluctantly. The human survivors disappeared from view.

Alfray knelt by Meklun's litter. The band began gathering discarded weapons and binding their wounds. Haskeer and Jup made their separate ways to Stryke and Coilla's side.

'Seems the injuries we took weren't too serious,' Jup related.

'No wonder,' Haskeer sneered. 'They fought like pixies.'

'They were farmers, not fighters. Uni zealots, by the look of them, probably out of Weaver's Lea. Hardly a true warrior among 'em.'

'But you didn't know that,' Haskeer growled accusingly.

'What you getting at?' Jup demanded.

'You brought them straight to us. What kind of idiot does something like that? You put the whole band in danger.'

'What did you expect me to do, meathead?'

'You should have led them away from here, taken them somewhere else.'

'Then what? Were Calthmon and me supposed to have lost ourselves out there?' He swept a hand at the wilderness. 'Or let 'em take us to protect *you*?'

Haskeer glared at him. 'That would've been no great loss.'

'Well, fuck you, pisspot! This is a warband, remember? We stick together!'

'They're gonna have to stick *you* together when I'm finished, you little snot!'

'Hey!' Coilla snapped. 'How about you two shutting your mouths long enough for us to get out of here?'

'She's right,' Stryke said. 'We don't know how many more humans might be heading for us. And farmers or not, if there's enough of them, we've got a problem. Where did you run into them, Jup?'

'Roadblock,' he replied sullenly. 'Up the trail.'

'So we have to find another way forward.'

'More time wasted,' Haskeer grumbled.

The shadows were lengthening. Another couple of hours and they'd be travelling in the dark, a prospect Stryke didn't welcome if there were rampaging mobs of humans on the loose. 'I'm doubling the number of scouts riding ahead,' he decided, 'and I want four covering our rear. You're in charge of that, Haskeer. I'll organise the advance scouts myself. Get on and pick your detail.'

Glowering, the sergeant moved away.

'I'm going to check on Meklun,' Stryke told Coilla and Jup. 'You two get the column moving, but keep it slow until the outriders have left.'

He trotted off.

The dwarf gave Coilla a rueful look.

'Spit it out,' she told him.

'This all seemed so simple when it started; now things are getting complicated,' he complained. '*And* more dangerous than I counted on.'

'What's the matter, you want to live forever?'

Jup thought about it.

'Yes,' he said.

10

Jennesta had made the woman's end swift compared to her normal practice. Not through any sense of mercy, but rather a mixture of boredom and the need to attend to more pressing matters.

She climbed down from the altar and unstrapped the bloodied unicorn horn she used as a dildo. With the deft skill of experience she quickly disembowelled the human's corpse; so speedily that the heart was still throbbing as she raised it to her mouth.

The repast was no more than adequate. Her tastes were growing either more refined or more jaded.

Physically and magically refreshed, but hardly better tempered, she sucked the juices from her fingers and brooded about the cylinder. The deadline she'd imposed on the hunting party was nearly up. Whether they'd succeeded or not, the time had come to hedge her bets and increase pressure in the search for the Wolverines.

It felt cold. The chill penetrated even here, in her inner sanctum. A log fire had been laid in the huge hearth but remained unlit. Jennesta stretched a hand. A pulsing bolt of luminescence, straight as a die, stabbed the air silently. The fire ignited with a roar. Basking in its warmth, she remonstrated with herself for needlessly wasting the energy just obtained. But, as ever, her delight at manipulating physicality was the stronger emotion.

Reaching out, she tugged a bell pull. Two orc guards entered. One had a bolt of sacking under his arm.

'You know what to do,' she told them. Her tone was offhand and she didn't bother looking their way.

They set about cleaning up the mess. The sacking was shaken out and placed on the floor. Taking the body by its wrists and ankles, the guards lowered and covered it.

Uninterested, Jennesta pulled the cord again, twice this time.

As they left, the orcs passed another attendant coming in. Momentarily wide-eyed at the sight of their blood-soaked bundle, the elf hastily adopted a bland, impassive expression.

The menial was new, and Jennesta found it as hard to guess its sex as she had its recent predecessor. Although she'd found out in the end, of course. She made a mental note, again, to slow down the rate at which she was getting through the servants. None of them was around long enough to learn the job.

Curtly instructed, the elf assisted the Queen in dressing. Jennesta chose black, as was her custom for excursions outside the castle; skin-tight leather top and riding breeches, the latter tucked into thigh-high, tall-heeled boots of the same material. Over this she donned an ankle-length sable cloak, fashioned from the pelts of forest bears. Her hair was pinned up under a matching fur cap.

She discharged the servant brusquely. The elf retreated, bowing low and ignored.

Jennesta went to a table by the altar and inspected a collection of coiled whips. She selected one of her favourites to complete her ensemble. Slipping a slender hand through its wrist thong, she walked to the door, pausing for a second to check herself in an adjacent mirror.

The orc bodyguards outside snapped to attention as she exited, then made to accompany her. She dismissed them with a careless wave and they resumed their positions. Following the corridor, she came to a staircase, lit by burning torches in iron brackets every ten or twelve steps. As she climbed, she lifted the hem of her cloak, almost daintily, to stop the trim getting dirty.

She reached a door. An orc sentry opened it for her. Jennesta stepped out into a large courtyard surrounded by high walls, the castle towers looming far above. It was dusk and the air was frigid.

A dragon was tethered in the centre of the quadrant, one foreleg ringed by an iron fetter the size of a barrel. An equally colossal chain ran from the shackle and encircled the stump of a mature oak.

The dragon's snout was buried in a small mountain of fodder that blended hay, brimstone, the carcasses of several whole sheep and other, less identifiable titbits. Ample quantities of steaming droppings, containing white slithers of bone and shiny clinker, had already been deposited at the beast's rear end.

Jennesta pressed a delicate lace handkerchief to her nose.

The dragon's handler walked towards her. She was dressed in tan-coloured garb of various shades. Her jerkin and trews were chestnut and soft as chamois, her sturdy knee boots mahogany-hued brushed suede. The only variation was a white and grey feather in her narrow-brimmed hat, and discreet cords of gold about her neck and wrists. Unusually tall even by the standards of her rangy species, she wore a proud, near-haughty expression.

The Dragon Dam's race always intrigued Jennesta. She had never had a brownie. But she harboured a small, grudging respect for them, too. Or at least as much as she was capable of feeling for any other than herself. Perhaps because, like her, brownies were hybrids, the offspring of unions between elves and goblins.

'Glozellan,' Jennesta said.

'Majesty.' The Mistress of Dragons gave a minimal bow of her head.

'You've had your briefing?'

'Yes.'

'And my orders are understood?'

'You wish dragon patrols sent out to search for a warband.' Her voice was high-pitched, reedy.

'The Wolverines, yes. I sent for you in person to emphasise how vital your mission is.'

Should Glozellan have thought it strange that the Queen wanted her own followers hunted down, she didn't betray the fact. 'What would you have us do if we find them, my lady?'

Jennesta didn't like the *if*, but let it pass. 'That's where you and your fellow handlers must take the initiative.' She selected her words with care. 'In the case of sighting the band in a place where they can be captured, our land forces are to be alerted. But if there's the slightest possibility of the Wolverines escaping, they are to be destroyed.'

Glozellan's pencil-thin eyebrows rose. She knew better than to comment more explicitly, let alone protest.

'If you have to kill them you'll send word immediately,' Jennesta continued, 'and guard their remains, with your lives if necessary, until reinforcements arrive.' She was confident that the cylinder was capable of withstanding the heat of a dragon's breath. Fairly confident anyway. There was an element of unavoidable risk.

The dragon chewed noisily on the spine of a sheep.

After mulling over what had been said for a moment, Glozellan replied, 'We'd be looking for a small group. We don't know exactly where they are. It won't be easy, unless we fly low. That leaves us vulnerable.'

Jennesta's composure was strained. 'Why does everyone bring me problems?' she snapped. 'I want solutions! *Do as I say!*'

'Your Majesty.'

'Well, don't just stand there! Get on with it!'

The Dragon Dam nodded, turned and loped to her mount. Having clambered up the rigging to the saddle, she signalled an orc guard waiting by a far wall. He approached bearing a mallet. Several heavy blows to the shackle clasps released the chain. The guard retired to a safe distance.

Glozellan stretched forward, a lean hand on either side of the dragon's neck. It twisted its head, bringing a cavernous ear to her face. She whispered into it. Sinewy wings spread and billowed with a leathery crackling sound. The dragon let out a thunderous roar.

Gigantic muscles in its legs and flanks stood out like smooth scaly boulders. The wings flapped, sluggishly at first then with gathering speed, displacing great gusts of air that lashed the courtyard with the strength of a minor storm.

Jennesta held on to her cap and her cloak swirled as the dragon rose. The feat seemed impossible for such a behemoth, but the miracle was achieved, marrying the absurdly cumbersome with the surprisingly graceful.

For a few seconds the creature hung motionless, save for the laboured strokes of its mighty wings, about halfway up the side of the castle's edifice. The newly visible moon and stars were part obscured by its bulky, ragged-edged silhouette. Then the shape continued its ascent, took a heading towards Taklakameer and soared away.

The door Jennesta had passed through opened. General Kysthan emerged, escorted by a small contingent of her personal guard. He looked pale.

'You have word of our quarry?' she asked.

'Yes and . . . no, Majesty.'

'I'm in no mood for riddles, General. Just tell me straight.' She patted the side of her leg impatiently with the coiled whip.

'I've had a message from Captain Delorran.'

Her eyes narrowed. 'Go on.'

The General fished a square of folded parchment from his tunic pocket. Despite the cold, he was sweating. 'What Delorran has to say may not immediately seem like news your Majesty would wish to hear.'

With a deft flick of her hand, Jennesta unwound the whip.

The night was moonlit and starry. A gentle breeze pleasantly tempered its warmth.

He stood at the door of a grand lodge. There were sounds inside.

Stryke looked around. Nothing troubled the genial countryside and it did not feel threatening. In itself that was almost beyond his comprehension. The normality seemed disturbing.

Hesitantly, he reached out to try the door.

Before he could, it opened.

Light and noise blasted him. A figure was outlined by brightness. He couldn't see its features, only an inky contour. It came toward him. His hand went to his sword.

The shape became the female orc he had met before. Or imagined. Or dreamt. She was just as handsome, just as proud, and her eyes held the same tender steel.

Stryke was taken aback. She was, too, but less so.

'You've returned,' she said.

He stammered some banal reply.

She smiled. 'Come, the festivities are well underway.'

He let her usher him into the great hall.

It was crowded with orcs, and only orcs. Orcs feasting at long tables laden with food and drink. Orcs engrossed in good-natured conversa-

tion. Orcs laughing, singing, enjoying raucous horseplay and rough games.

Females made their way through the company bearing tankards of ale and horns of ruby wine, baskets of fruit and platters of tender meats. A fire burned in the middle of the floor on slate blocks, with joints of game and hunks of fowl roasting over it on spits. Smoke suffused with dancing sparks drifted up to a hole in the roof. Perfumed woods released their aromas to mingle with the myriad other smells scenting the air. Among them, Stryke thought he detected the sweetly pungent odour of crystal.

At one end of the hall, adult males lounged on skins of fur, drinking and roaring at ribald jokes. At the other, boisterous adolescents engaged in sham combat with wooden swords and muffle-ended staves. Drummers beat jaunty rhythms. Squealing youngsters chased each other through the throng.

Many revellers greeted Stryke warm-heartedly, despite him being a stranger.

'Are you celebrating.' She snatched a flagon from a tray held high by a passing server, and drank from it. Then she passed it to him.

Stryke took a deep draught. It was mulled ale, flavoured with honey and spices, and it tasted wonderful. He drained the cup.

The female moved closer to him. 'Where have you been?' she asked.

'That's not an easy question.' He put his flagon down on a table. 'I don't know if I'm sure of the answer myself.'

'Again you shroud yourself in mystery.'

'I see you *as a mystery, and this place.'*

There's nothing mysterious about me, or this place.'

'I know it not.'

She shook her head in good-natured pique. 'But you're here.'

'That means nothing to me. Where is *here?'*

'I see you're no less eccentric than when we first met. Come with me.'

She led him across the hall to another, smaller door. It opened to the back of the lodge. The cooler air outside had a sobering effect, and closing the door deadened most of the clamour.

'See?' She indicated the calm night-time landscape. 'All is as you'd expect.'

'As I would have expected once, perhaps,' he replied. 'Long ago. But now . . .'

'You're talking giddiness again,' she cautioned.

'What I mean is, is it like this . . . everywhere?'

'Of course it is!' A second passed as she made a decision. 'I'll show you.'

They walked to the end of the lodge. When they turned its corner they came to a stand of horses. Most were war chargers, magnificent, immaculately groomed animals with elaborate, gleaming tackle. The female selected two of the finest, a pure white and a pure black stallion.

She told him to mount. He hesitated. She climbed on to the white, her movements fluid, dextrous, as though born to the saddle. He took the black.

They rode off. At first she led, then he caught up and they galloped through the velvety countryside together.

Silver moonlight dusted the boughs of trees and painted the meadows with spurious frost. It bathed the upper slopes of rolling hills, as though snow had fallen, despite the temperate climate.

Burnished rivers and shimmering lakes were fleetingly sighted. Flocks of birds took wing at the approach of pounding hooves. Swarming insects lit the heart of brooding forests with their mottled fireglow. All was fresh, vibrant, teeming.

Above hung a glorious array of stars, crystalline in the virgin night sky.

'Don't you see?' she called. 'Don't you see that all is as it should be?'

He was too intoxicated by the undefiled air, by the sense of innate rightness, *to reply.*

'Come on!' *she cried, and urged her horse to greater effort.*

Her mount surged ahead of him. He spurred his own ride to match the pace.

They raced, exhilarated, the wind buffeting their faces. She laughed at the sheer joy of it, and so did he. It was a long time since he had felt quite so alive.

'Your land is wondrous!' he shouted.

'Our *land!' she returned.*

He looked to the way ahead.

The way ahead was barren.

It was cold. The trail was rocky. Nothing stirred. The moon and stars were visible, but dingy in the clouded sky. Stryke was riding alone at the head of the column.

The chill hand of fear caressed his spine.

What in the name of the gods is happening to me? he thought. *Am I going insane?*

He tried to be rational. He was exhausted and under pressure. They all were. All that had happened was that he'd fallen asleep in the saddle. Fatigue had conjured the pictures in his mind. They were vivid and realistic, but only pictures. Like a story the wordsmiths told around winter fires.

It would be comforting if he believed that.

He unclipped his canteen and took a gulp of water. As he replaced the stopper, he caught a familiar bouquet on the breeze. A whiff of pellucid. He shook his head, half convinced the smell had carried over as a sort of olfactory memory from his dream. Then it came again. He looked around.

Coilla and Alfray were riding behind him. Their faces were tired and passive. His gaze travelled beyond them, down the lines of sleepy grunts. He saw Jup, slumped with weariness. A place or two further back, near the column's end and riding alone, was Haskeer. He seemed furtive, turning his head in an obvious attempt to avoid scrutiny.

Stryke swung his horse out. 'Take the lead!' he barked at Alfray and Coilla.

They reacted and at least one said something. He didn't hear it, and ignored them anyway. His attention was focused on Haskeer. He galloped his way.

When he reached him, the rich odour of burning crystal was unmistakable, and the sergeant was making a ham-fisted job of trying to conceal something.

'Give it up,' Stryke said, icy menace in his voice.

With lazy insolence, Haskeer opened his hand to reveal the tiny clay pipe he'd been hiding. Stryke snatched it.

'You took this without permission,' he growled.

'You didn't say we couldn't.'

'I didn't say you could either. You're on your last warning, Haskeer. And think on this.' Lightning fast, Stryke leaned in and swung his fist at the sergeant's head. It landed on his temple with a meaty smack. The blow knocked Haskeer clean off his horse. He hit the ground heavily.

The column stopped. Everybody was watching.

Haskeer groaned and got unsteadily to his feet. For a moment it looked as though he might retaliate, but he thought better of it.

'You'll walk till you learn some discipline,' Stryke told him, gesturing for a trooper to take the reins of Haskeer's mount.

'I haven't slept,' Haskeer complained.

'Never leave off bellyaching, do you, Sergeant? *None* of us have slept, Wolverine, and none of us are going to till I say. Got it?' Stryke turned to the rest of the band. 'Anybody else feel like defying me?'

They let silence answer for them.

'Nobody touches the crystal until, and if, I say so!' he told them. 'I don't' care how much there is, that's not the point. It might be all we've got to bargain for our lives with *her*.

Jennesta. Particularly if we don't get that fucking cylinder back, which right now looks pretty unlikely. Understood?'

Another eloquent silence spoke for them.

Coilla eventually broke it.

'Looks like we'll get to find out about the cylinder any time now,' she said, nodding at what was coming into sight as they rounded a bend.

A vast outcrop of granite sat by the trail, squat and contorted, as though melted by inconceivable heat. It was an unmistakable landmark even to those who had never set eyes on it before. Whether by chance or some design of the gods, the likeness it bore was true enough to have been carved by a titanic sculptor.

'Demon's Claw,' Stryke declared, though none of them needed telling. 'We'll be in Black Rock in less than an hour.'

11

Stryke knew that if the Wolverines were to function properly, if they were to survive, he had to put the disturbing dreams out of his mind. Fortunately, the prospect of a raid into enemy territory was more than enough to keep him occupied.

He ordered a temporary camp to be struck while they prepared for their assault on Black Rock. Several troopers were sent to rendezvous with the forward scouts spying the land. The rest of the Wolverines set about checking their kit and honing their weapons.

Stryke decided that no fires were to be lit, in order not to betray their position. On this, Alfray asked him to think again.

'Why?' Stryke said.

'We've got a problem with Darig. He took a leg wound when we fought the Unis. Fact is, it's in a worse state than I thought. Gangrenous. I need a fire to heat my blades.'

'It's got to come off?'

Alfray nodded. 'He loses the leg or he loses his life.'

'Shit. Another wounded trooper to move. We don't need it, Alfray.' He nodded at Meklun. 'How's he?'

'No improvement, and there are signs of fever now.'

'At this rate we won't need to worry about Jennesta. All right, a fire. But small, and covered. Have you told Darig?'

'He's guessed, I think, but I'm about to spell it out to him. It's a damn shame. He's one of the youngest in the band, Stryke.'

'I know. Anything you need?'

'I've got herbs that might dull the pain a bit, and a little alcohol. Probably not enough. Can I try some crystal?'

'Have it. But it won't block the pain that much, you know.'

'At least it should take his mind off it. I'll get to work on an infusion.'

Alfray went back to his patient.

Coilla took the field surgeon's place. 'Got a minute?'

Stryke grunted that he had.

'You all right?' she said.

'Why ask?'

'Because you've not been yourself lately. Kind of distant. And then piling into Haskeer back there—'

'He's been asking for it.'

'You can say that again. But it's you I'm talking about.'

'We're in a mess. What do you expect, a song and a dance?'

'I just thought that if you're—'

'Why the touching concern for my state of health, Corporal?'

'You're our commander, it's in my interests. All our interests.'

'I'm not going to crack, if that's what you think. I'll get us through this.'

She didn't reply.

He took a different tack. 'Heard about Darig?'

'Yes. It stinks. What are we going to do about the kobolds?'

Stryke was grateful that she wanted to talk about tactics. It made him feel more comfortable. 'Hit them when they least expect it, of course. That might be in what's left of the night, it might be at daybreak.'

'Then I want to get up there with the scouts and check the lay-out for myself.'

'Right. We'll go together.'

'Black Rock's big, Stryke. Suppose the kobolds we're after are right in the middle of it?'

'From what I've heard, the raiding parties camp around the main settlement. They keep the females and young at the core. The raiders can come and go more easily like that, as well as guard the place.'

'That sounds a dangerous set-up. If we're walking into some kind of defensive ring—'

'We just have to be careful how we do it.'

She regarded him with troubled eyes. 'You know this is insane, don't you?'

'Can you think of another way?'

For the briefest instant, he hoped she was going to say yes.

An hour flew by while the Wolverines busied themselves with the countless tasks needed to make a fighting unit combat-ready.

With everything in hand, Stryke went to the makeshift bender used as a medical tent. He found Alfray tending an oblivious Meklun, stretched at the far end of the shelter, a damp cloth resting on his forehead. Most of the remaining space was taken up by Darig, also lying but somewhat more animated. A vacant grin on his face, eyes glazed, he rolled his head from side to side, mumbling incessantly. In the flickering candlelight, Stryke saw that the blanket covering him was twisted and blotched with sweat.

'Just in time,' Alfray said. 'I need some help.'

'He's ready?'

Alfray looked down at Darig. He was giggling.

'I've given him enough crystal to poleaxe a regiment. If he's not ready now he never will be.'

'Mahogany elbows bushels of songbirds tied with string,' Darig announced.

'Take your point,' Stryke said. 'What do you want me to do?'

'Get somebody else in here. It'll take two to hold him down.'

'Pretty string,' Darig added. *'Pretty . . . smitty . . . pring.'*

Alfray crouched next to the patient. 'Take it easy,' he soothed.

Stryke peered out of the tent and saw Jup nearby. He beckoned him. The dwarf jogged over and sidled in.

'You're in luck,' Stryke told him drily. 'You get to hold one of the bits that's coming off.' He nodded at the grunt's legs.

The tent was about as crowded as it could get. Jup edged gingerly to the end of the trooper's bed. 'Wouldn't do to step on him,' he explained.

'Don't think he'd notice,' Alfray said.

'There's a weasel in the river,' Darig confided knowingly.

'He's been given some crystal as a painkiller,' Stryke explained.

Jup raised an eyebrow. *'Some?* To use an old dwarf expression, I'd say he's ripped out of his crust.'

'And it won't last forever,' Alfray reminded them, a mite testily. 'Let's get on with it, shall we?'

'The river, the river,' Darig chanted, saucer-eyed.

'Take hold of his ankles, Jup,' Alfray instructed. 'Stryke, bear down on his arms. I don't want him moving when I start.'

They did as they were told. Alfray pulled aside the blanket, revealing the infected leg. The angry wound was drenched in pus.

'Gods,' Jup muttered.

Alfray dabbed gently with a cloth. 'Not too pretty, is it?'

Stryke wrinkled his nose. 'Or very sweet-smelling. Where are you going to cut?'

'Here, across the thigh, well above the knee. And the trick is to do it fast.' He finished cleaning the affected area and wrung the cloth in a wooden bowl. 'Hang on and I'll get what I need.'

He ducked out of the tent. A small fire was burning in a pit a couple of paces away. 'You!' he snapped at a passing grunt. 'Stand here and hand me what I want when I tell you.' The trooper nodded and padded over.

Alfray tore the damp cloth into two pieces and gave him one. He used the other to grasp the hilt of a long-bladed knife protruding from the fire. Its blade glowed cherry-red. A hatchet he left in the flames. With his foot, he nudged the business end of a shovel in beside it.

Back in the tent, he knelt again, pulling from his jerkin pocket a scrap of thick, sturdy rope, about equal to a hand's span.

Darig smiled beatifically. 'Pig's riding the horse, pig's ridin*mumph*.'

'Bite!' Alfray ordered, jamming the chunk of rope into the trooper's open mouth.

'Now?' Stryke said.

'Now. Hold him tight!'

He brought the scalding blade into play. Darig's eyes widened and he began struggling. Jup and Stryke strained against his writhing limbs.

With several rapid, skilful strokes, Alfray excavated the wound. He folded aside flaps of skin and began digging through the flesh beneath. Darig struggled the harder, and spat out the rope. His agonised yelling had Meklun stirring restlessly, but was short-lived; Alfray rammed the restraint back in. Holding it in place with the heel of his palm, he carried on working one-handed. In short order he had the bone exposed.

Darig groaned and passed out.

Tossing the knife aside, Alfray bellowed, *'Hatchet!'*

It was passed in over Stryke's head, stock wrapped against the blistering, near-white heat of its cleaving end.

Alfray grasped it two-handed and raised it high. He aimed, took a breath and brought it down with all his might. The blow landed with a muffled *thunk*, dead on target. Stryke and Jup felt the grunt's body buck under the impact. But the leg was only half severed.

Darig snapped back into consciousness, a wild expression on his face, and resumed thrashing. He spat out the gag again and commenced shrieking. No one had a hand free to stop him.

'Hurry!' Stryke urged.

'Hold him still!' Alfray demanded. He disengaged the axe and lined up another swing.

The second blow also struck true, and if anything had greater force behind it. This almost finished the job, save the last remaining threads of sinew and skin. A third weighty chop parted them, carrying the cleaver through the horse blanket Darig lay on and into the hardened earth below.

The screaming continued. Stryke ended it by landing a smart punch to the side of Darig's head, knocking him cold.

'We've got to stem the flow of blood,' Alfray told them, pulling away the amputated leg. 'Get me that shovel.'

The spade was carefully delivered. Its flat was crimson-coloured, and when Alfray blew on it, a patch shone sparkly yellow-white for an instant. 'Should be hot enough,' he decided. 'Keep holding him. This is going to be another rude awakening.'

He laid the shovel against the stump. The tangy odour of burnt flesh filled the air as the heat did its work and cauterised. Darig was dragged into wakefulness once more, and emptied his lungs in protest, but the shock and blood loss had taken their toll. The clamour he sent up was faint compared to the noise he'd made moments before.

Jup and Stryke kept pressing down as Alfray sprinkled alcohol over his handiwork, then applied dressings smeared with healing balms.

Darig fell to low, repetitious muttering, and his breath took on a regular, if shallow rhythm.

'His breathing's even,' Alfray pronounced. 'That's something.'

'Will he pull through?' Jup wondered.

'I'd give him a fifty-fifty chance.' He bent to the amputated leg and rolled it in a square of fabric. 'What he needs now,' he said, lifting his load, 'is rest and good nourishment to help rebuild his strength.' He tucked the bloody bundle under his arm.

'That's a tall order,' Stryke told him. 'We're only carrying iron rations, remember, and I can't spare anybody to hunt.'

'Leave that to me,' Alfray said, 'I'll take care of it. Now get out, the pair of you. You're disturbing my patients.' He shoved at them.

Stryke and Jup found themselves outside the tent, staring at the lowered flap.

•

The last of the night would soon give way to dawn.

Stryke had mustered a group of twenty for the raid, including the scouts already positioned on the outskirts of Black Rock. A skeleton crew would be left to guard the camp and the wounded. Needing to talk to Alfray about this, he made his way to the medical tent.

Meklun was as far gone as ever. Darig was sitting up. His eyes were bleary and his skin pale, otherwise he seemed to be doing well after such a short time. And the effects of the pellucid had all but worn off. Alfray was serving him a platter of stew from a black iron cauldron.

'Got to keep your strength up,' he ordered, handing over the steaming dish.

Darig spooned a tentative mouthful. His uncertain expression vanished at the first bite and he tucked in with relish. 'Hmmm, meat. Tasty. What is it?'

'Er, don't worry about that now,' Alfray told him. 'Just eat your fill.'

Stryke caught his eye. 'Needs must,' Alfray mouthed, then looked away, uncharacteristically sheepish. They sat in slightly awkward silence as Darig cleared his plate.

Then Haskeer stuck his head into the tent and provided a distraction. 'Something smells good,' he said, staring hopefully at the cauldron.

'It's for Darig,' Alfray replied hurriedly. 'It's . . . special.'

Haskeer looked disappointed. 'Pity.'

'What do you want?' Stryke asked pointedly.

'We're waiting for the order to move, chief.'

'Then wait a bit longer. I'll be out soon.'

The sergeant shrugged, gave the cooking pot a last, hankering glance and left.

'If the stew's special in the way I think it is,' Stryke remarked, 'you should have given him some.'

Alfray smiled.

Darig looked from one to the other, baffled.

'Rest now,' Alfray said, taking his shoulders and easing him back to a recumbent position.

'It might be a good idea if you stayed to look after him and Meklun,' Stryke suggested.

'There are grunts who can do that. Vobe or Jad, for instance. Or Hystykk. They're capable.'

'Just thought you'd prefer to be here with them.'

'I'd rather be in on the action.' Alfray's furrowed chin jutted stubbornly. 'Unless you think I'm getting too *old* for that kind of—'

'Whoa! Age is nothing to do with it. Only giving you the choice, that's all. Come. Glad to have you.'

'All right. I will.'

Stryke made a note to tread carefully with Alfray when it came to the question of age. He was getting damn prickly about it.

'I'll finish here and follow on,' Alfray added.

As Stryke went out, Darig stirred. 'Sir?' he ventured. 'Is there any more of that stew?'

The band had gathered fifty paces distant. By the time Stryke reached them, Alfray had caught up with him.

'Report, Coilla,' Stryke ordered briskly.

'According to our scouts, the group we're after seem to be at the western edge of Black Rock. Direct heading from here, in other words.'

'How can we be sure it's them?'

'We can't. But it looks that way. I've been up there, and I saw a bunch of kobolds corralling war lizards. Seemed to me they were a raiding party, not long back.'

Stryke frowned. 'Doesn't prove it's the same one.'

'No,' she agreed. 'But unless you can come up with a better way of knowing, that's all we've got.'

'Even if it ain't them, I say we get in there and kick arse anyway,' Haskeer offered.

Some of the band muttered agreement.

'If they *are* the ones we're looking for,' Jup said, 'it's a bit of luck to find 'em camped outside Black Rock proper.'

'Though we'll still have the whole population down on our necks if we put a foot wrong,' Alfray cautioned. He turned to their commander. 'Well? Do we go in?'

'We go in,' Stryke decided.

12

They left the horses behind and set out for the forward observation point on foot.

The blades of their weapons had been blackened with damp charcoal lest they catch a glint from the waning moon. Senses alert for sight or sound of trouble, the band moved stealthily.

A change took place in the terrain. It became pulpy underfoot as the margins of the plains gave way to marshland.

Dawn was breaking as they arrived, the sun a bloody-red harbinger of another overcast, rain-sodden day.

The silent rendezvous with the scouts took place on the crest of a small hill, crowned with a modest copse, from which they could see but not be seen. As the sun climbed they watched Black Rock emerge from the clinging mist.

A jumble of single-storey buildings, crude wooden huts of various shapes and sizes, stretched as far as they could see in the unclear air. The scouts indicated a pair of huts almost directly below their viewing point, set some way apart from the settlement proper. One was small, the other much larger and similar in dimensions, if not in ornamentation, to an orc longhouse. Between and beyond them was a corral in which a herd of kirgizils was penned, recumbent and motionless in the way of lizards. They looked sluggish, no doubt suffering from the relentless drop in temperature that all parts of the land were enduring. Stryke wondered how much longer the kobolds could continue using them.

He leaned to one of the scouts and whispered, 'What's been happening, Orbon?'

'There were a few bandits around until about an hour ago. Most went into the big hut. One went into the smaller building. We've seen no movement since.'

Stryke motioned Coilla and Haskeer over. 'Take four grunts and get down there. Orbon, you're one of them. I want to know the lie of the land and the kobolds' deployment. If there are guards, deal with 'em.'

'What if we're spotted?' Coilla asked.

'Be damn sure you're not! Otherwise, it's every orc for himself.'

She nodded, attention half on selecting a pair of knives from her arm sheath.

'And you behave yourself,' Stryke warned Haskeer darkly.

The sergeant's face was a picture of offended innocence.

Coilla quickly picked the other troopers to go with them and the group made its way down the incline.

They progressed from tree to tree. When there were no more to shelter behind they headed for a line of bushes, the last hiding place before the level clearing. Crouching low, they scrutinised the way ahead.

From this angle they could see four kobold guards. They wore furs against the night's chill. Two of the wiry creatures were at the side of the big hut, two beside the smaller. None was moving.

Swiftly deciding a strategy, Coilla conveyed it to the others via sign language. Her plan was that she would go to the right with two grunts, toward the small hut, Haskeer and his grunts to the large hut on the left. The gesticulations ended with her drawing a finger across her throat.

Tensely, they awaited their opportunity, and the open ground to be crossed meant that when it came they would have to move fast. Several minutes went by. Then in conjunction both sets of guards were vulnerable. One pair engaged in conversation, half turned away from the hill. Their fellows at the large hut began a patrol, backs to the orcs.

Haskeer and Coilla broke cover and ran. The grunts fanned out behind them.

A knife gripped between her teeth, the other in her hand, Coilla moved as lightly and swiftly as she could. She was little more than halfway across the clearing when the guards finished talking and parted.

Coilla froze, signalling the others to do the same.

Without looking their way, one guard went to the end of the hut and turned its corner. The other still faced away from Coilla, but was slowly turning as he scanned his turf.

She glanced at the larger hut. The guards there were oblivious to what was happening. Haskeer's group must have been further back; she didn't see them.

A fraction of a second had gone by. There were perhaps thirty paces between her and the turning guard. It was now or never. She drew back her arm and hurled the knife with all her force. The momentum bent her forward at the waist and expelled the breath she held.

The throw was true, catching her target squarely between its shoulder blades. A muffled *thock* marked the impact. The kobold went down without a sound.

Coilla dashed forward, the grunts at her side. They arrived just as the second guard came back round the corner. The grunts piled into the startled creature, denying it time to draw a weapon. It was dealt with quietly and brutally.

The bodies were dragged out of sight. Coilla and the others

hid themselves as best they could and looked to the big hut. They saw Haskeer's group creeping up on their prey.

Around the larger building the ground had been more thoroughly trampled by kirgizils and the going was muddier. Never the most graceful of orcs, but often the most over-confident, Haskeer managed to get one of his boots stuck in the slime. In pulling it free, with a loud sucking sound, he lost balance and pitched headlong. His sword went flying.

The kobold he was sneaking toward spun around. Its jaws gaped. Haskeer scrabbled for his sword. It was out of reach, so he grabbed a rock and pitched it. The missile struck the creature's mouth, bringing a spray of blood and broken fangs. Then the grunts rushed in and finished the job with daggers.

Haskeer snatched his sword, tumbling forward. He skidded as much as sprinted at the remaining sentry. The kobold had its own weapon drawn, and fended off the first blow. Knocking the scimitar aside with his second, Haskeer drove his blade deep into the guard's chest.

Again, bodies were hauled away and concealed.

Panting, Haskeer looked to Coilla, and exchanged a triumphant thumbs-up with her. A few further signs established that their next move would be checking the huts.

The one Haskeer's group had reached was without windows. Its door was not a door as such, but rather an open entrance covered by a rush hanging. He led the way to it and they positioned themselves, ready for trouble. Very carefully, Haskeer edged the curtain aside a little, vigilant for the tiniest sound. The frail dawn allowed in enough light for him to see.

What he saw was kobolds. Their sleeping forms covered the floor, and each cot in a line against the far wall was shared by heaps of them. Weapons were scattered everywhere.

Haskeer held his breath, fearful of waking the overwhelming force. He began to withdraw slowly. A kobold stretched out near the door stirred fitfully in its sleep. Haskeer went rigid, and stayed that way until he was absolutely sure it was safe to move again. Then he gently replaced the curtain and silently expelled a relieved breath.

He backed off three paces. The curtain stirred. Haskeer and the grunts flattened themselves to the wall on either side of the door.

A dishevelled kobold came out of the hut, too drowsy to pay much attention to its surroundings. It staggered a couple of steps and pawed at its groin. A vacantly blissful expression on its face, and swaying gently, the creature let loose a hissing stream of urine. Haskeer pounced, locking his arm around the creature's neck. There was a brief struggle. The kobold's gush of water splashed uncontrollably. A muscular jerk of Haskeer's forearm snapped the bandit's neck.

The orc sergeant remained stock still, holding up the limp body, listening for any further movement. Satisfied, he dragged the corpse to the spot where their other victims were dumped, cursing soundlessly all the while at the piss soaking his boots. After dropping the body he continued grumbling as he rubbed them on the back of his breeches.

Apart from size, the hut Coilla's group were investigating differed from the larger building in two respects. It had a door, and at the side, a window. Coilla ordered the grunts to keep a lookout while she tiptoed to it. Stooped beneath the opening, which had neither shutter nor blind, she tried to gauge any noises from inside. Once attuned, she heard a rhythmic, wheezy sound that took a moment to identify as snoring.

She slowly raised her head and looked in.

The single room had three occupants. Two of them were kobold guards, sitting on the floor with their backs against the wall and legs outstretched. Both seemed to be asleep, and one was the source of the snoring.

But it was the third occupant that drew her attention.

Tied to the room's only chair was a being at least as short as the kobolds, though of much chunkier build. Its rough hide had a green tinge. The large pumpkin-shaped head appeared out of proportion with the rest of the body, and the ears jutted outward slightly at an angle. There was something of the vulture about its neck. The elongated eyes had excessively fleshy lids, with black elliptical orbs against white surrounds shot through with yellow veining. Its pate and face were hairless, save for whiskery sideburns of reddish-brown tufts of fur, turning flaxen.

It wore a simple grey robe, the worse for being obviously long unwashed. Its feet were shod in suede ankle boots, with tarnished buckles, that had also seen better days. Where skin showed, on the face and hands, which were not unlike an orc's, it was wrinkly like a serpent's. Coilla reckoned the creature was very old.

As the thought occurred, the gremlin looked up and saw her.

His eyes widened. But he made no sound, as she feared he might. They stared at each other for a few seconds, then Coilla dropped out of sight.

With signs and whispers she conveyed her discovery to the grunts, and ordered them to stay while she reported. As they hid, she signalled Haskeer. He left his own troopers behind and joined her for the jog back to the hill.

By the time they rejoined the rest of the band, Stryke was growing anxious.

'We took care of all the guards we came across,' Haskeer blurted. 'And that big hut's full of the whole fucking raiding party by the looks of it. The little bastards.'

'Any sign of the cylinder?'

Haskeer shook his head.

'No,' Coilla concurred. 'But what I saw in the smaller hut was interesting. They've got a prisoner in there, Stryke. A gremlin. He looked pretty old, too.'

'A gremlin? What the hell's that about?'

Coilla shrugged.

Haskeer was getting impatient. 'What are we waiting for? Let's whomp 'em while they're sleeping!'

'We're going to,' Stryke told him. 'But we're doing it right. The cylinder's the reason we're here, remember. This is our only chance of finding it. And I don't want that prisoner hurt.'

'Why not?'

'Because our enemy's enemy is our friend.'

The concept seemed alien to Haskeer. 'We have no friends.'

'Ally, then. But I want him alive, if possible. If the cylinder *isn't* here, he might be able to tell us where to look. Unless any of you have worked out how to understand that kobold gibberish.'

'We should be moving,' Jup urged, 'before the bodies are found.'

'Right,' Stryke agreed. 'This is how we're doing it. Two groups. Me, Coilla and Alfray will join the grunts already at the small hut. I want to be sure of the prisoner. Haskeer and Jup, you take everybody else and surround the big hut. But don't do anything till I get there. Got that?'

The sergeants nodded, but avoided looking at each other.

'Good. Let's go.'

The Wolverines divided into their assigned groups and flowed down to the settlement. They met no resistance and saw no movement.

Once Stryke's party had joined with the grunts left on guard, they positioned themselves outside the smaller hut. They could see Jup and Haskeer's group doing the same.

'Stand ready for my order,' Stryke instructed in a hushed tone. 'Coilla, let's see that window.'

She went ahead, staying low, and he followed. After peeking through the opening she beckoned him to look. The scene was as before; two lounging kobold guards, spark out, and their bound prisoner. This time the gremlin was unaware of being watched and didn't look up. Coilla and Stryke crept back to the others.

'Time to take a gamble,' Stryke whispered. 'Let's do this fast and quiet.'

He rapped on the door and ducked to the side, out of sight. A long half-minute passed as they waited tensely. Stryke wondered if things had gone sour, and wouldn't have been surprised if the entire kobold nation had appeared and fallen on their necks. He scanned the terrain, saw nothing, then knocked again, a little louder. After a few more seconds crawled by they heard the scrape of a bolt.

The door opened and one of the kobolds stuck its head out. It was done casually enough to indicate it wasn't expecting trouble. Stryke seized the creature by its neck and savagely tugged it aside. The other Wolverines poured into the hut.

Stryke killed the squirming kobold with a single dagger-thrust to its heart. Dragging the body behind him, he quickly entered the building. The second sentry was already dead. It hadn't even had a chance to rise, and the rigour of violent death was frozen on its face. Stryke dropped the first guard's corpse next to it.

Coilla had her hand over the mouth of the trembling prisoner. With the other she held a knife to his throat.

'Make a sound and you follow them in death,' she promised. 'If I take my hand away, will you keep quiet?'

The gremlin nodded, eyes wide with fear. Coilla removed her hand, but kept the knife near enough to underline her threat.

'We've no time for a polite chat,' Stryke told the captive. 'Do you know about the artefact?'

The gremlin seemed confused.

'The *cylinder*?'

Looking from one grim orc face to another, then down to

the slaughtered kobolds, the gremlin returned his gaze to Stryke. Again, he nodded.

'Where is it?'

The gremlin swallowed. When he spoke, his voice had a gravelly, bass quality. But it was tempered by the higher notes of age-stretched vocal cords, and terror. 'It is in the long-house with those who sleep.'

Coilla gave him a hard look. 'You'd better not be lying, ancient one.'

Stryke pointed at a grunt. 'Stay with him. The rest of you come with me.'

He led them across to the long-house.

The band armed themselves with their preferred weaponry for close-quarter fighting. Most chose knives. Stryke favoured a sword and knife combination. Haskeer settled on a hatchet.

As they'd already discovered, there was only one door. They clustered around it, Stryke, Coilla, Haskeer, Jup and Alfray to the fore.

Despite being on the edge of a township housing unknown numbers of a hostile race, certainly hundreds, Stryke was aware of a strange quietness that amounted to a kind of serenity. He put it down to the sense of calm he often felt before combat, the unique feeling of being centred, of being whole, that only the nearness of death engendered. The air, for all its impurities, had never smelt quite so sweet.

'Let's do it,' he growled.

Haskeer ripped aside the cloth.

The Wolverines piled into the hut, laying about them with unstoppable ferocity, hacking, slashing, stabbing everything in their path. They trampled the kobolds, kicked them, bayoneted them with swords, slashed their throats, pummelled their bodies with axes. A deafening cacophony of screams, squeals and foreign-tongued curses rose from their victims to add to the chaos.

Many of the creatures died without rising. Others got to their feet only to be instantly cut down. But some, further into the packed room, did manage to stand and mount a defence. The slaughter became vicious hand-to-hand combat.

Facing a wildly slashing scimitar, Stryke ran through its owner with such force that his sword tip penetrated the wall beyond. He had to apply his boot to the kobold's chest to prise the blade free. Without pause, he sought fresh meat.

Belying his advancing years, Alfray deftly felled a bandit to his right, switched tack and skewered another to his left.

Coilla dodged a spear-wielding assailant, slashed bare its knuckles and buried both her daggers in its chest.

Haskeer slammed his ham-like fist on top of a kobold's head, shattering its skull, then turned and swiped his hatchet into the next foe's stomach.

Fencing with a hissing bandit clutching a rapier, Jup knocked the weapon aside and sent his blade into the kobold's brain via its eye.

The frenzy continued unabated. Then, as suddenly as the carnage had begun, it ended. None of the enemy was left standing.

Stryke ran a hand across his face, clearing it of sweat and blood. 'Hurry!' he barked. 'If that doesn't bring more of 'em, nothing will. *Find that cylinder!*'

The band began a frantic search of what had become a charnel house. They rummaged through the bodies' clothing, rooted in straw on the floor, tossed aside the possessions of the vanquished.

As Stryke reached for a corpse it proved less dead than he thought, lashing out at him with a wickedly jagged-edged cleaver. He planted his sword on its chest and fell on it with all his weight. The kobold convulsed, gurgled, died. Stryke resumed his ransacking.

He was starting to think it had all been in vain when Alfray cried out.

Everybody stopped and stared. Stryke pushed his way through them. Alfray pointed at a mutilated kobold. The cylinder was looped into the creature's belt.

Stryke knelt and eagerly disengaged it. He held it up to the light. It looked complete. Unopened.

Haskeer was smirking, gleefully triumphant. 'Nobody takes from orcs!'

'Come on!' Stryke hissed.

They poured out of the place and ran to the other hut.

If anything, the gremlin looked in even more of an agitated state. But he couldn't take his eyes off the cylinder.

'We have to get out of here!' Jup urged.

'What do we do with him?' Haskeer asked, pointing at the quailing gremlin with his sword.

'Yes, Stryke,' Coilla said, 'what about him?'

Haskeer had a typically straightforward solution. 'I say we kill him and get it over with.'

Alarmed, the gremlin cowered.

For the moment, Stryke was undecided.

'This cylinder is of great significance!' the gremlin suddenly exclaimed. 'For orcs! With my knowledge, I can explain it to you.'

'He's bluffing!' Haskeer reckoned, brandishing his sword menacingly. 'Finish it, I say!'

'After all,' the gremlin added tremulously, 'that's why the kobolds kidnapped me.'

'What?' Stryke said.

'To make sense of it for them. That's why they brought me here.'

Stryke studied the captive's face, trying to decide whether he was telling the truth. And if it made any difference to them if he was.

'What do we *do*, Stryke?' Coilla demanded impatiently.

He made up his mind. 'Bring him. Now let's get the hell out of here.'

13

The Wolverines wasted no time getting away from Black Rock settlement. They dragged the gremlin after them, still bound and at the end of a rope. By the time their rapid route march was over, the aged creature was panting from the effort of keeping pace.

Stryke issued orders to break camp and prepare for a quick exit.

Haskeer was jubilant. 'Back to Cairnbarrow, at last. I tell you, Stryke, I didn't think we were going to do it.'

'Thanks for trusting me,' his commander replied coolly.

The sarcasm was lost on Haskeer. 'We'll be heroes when we turn up with that thing.' He nodded at the cylinder in Stryke's belt.

'It isn't over yet,' Alfray warned him. 'We have to get there first, and that means crossing a lot of hostile territory.'

'And there's no telling how Jennesta's going to react to the delay,' Jup added. 'The cylinder and pellucid's no guarantee we'll come out of this with our heads.'

'Gloom merchants,' Haskeer sneered.

Stryke thought that was rich coming from him, but decided against pointing it out. After all, this was supposed to be a joyful occasion. He wondered why he didn't feel that way.

'Shouldn't we hear what this one has to say?' Coilla said, indicating the gremlin. He sat on a tree stump, exhausted and frightened.

'Yes,' Haskeer agreed, 'let's get it over with or we'll have another free-loader to drag around with us.'

'Is that what you think of our wounded comrades?' Alfray flared.

Stryke held up his hands to silence them. 'That's enough. I don't want us standing here bickering when a couple of hundred kobolds come looking for revenge.' He addressed their involuntary guest. 'What's your name?'

'Mmm . . . Mmoo . . .' The elderly gremlin cleared his throat nervously and tried again. 'M-M-M . . . *Mobbs*.'

'All right, Mobbs, what was that about the kobolds kidnapping you? And what do you know of this?' He tapped the cylinder.

'You have your life in your hands, gremlin,' Alfray cautioned. 'Choose your words with care.'

'I'm just a humble scholar,' Mobbs said, and it sounded like a plea. 'I was going about my business north of here, in Hecklowe, when those wretched bandits seized me.' An edge of indignation crept into his voice.

'Why?' Coilla asked. 'What did they want from you?'

'I have made languages my life's work, particularly dead languages. They needed my skills to decipher the contents of the artefact. I believe it to be a message carrier, you see, and—'

'We know that,' Stryke interjected.

'Therefore it is not the cylinder itself that is of interest but rather the knowledge it may contain.'

'Kobolds are stupid,' Alfray stated bluntly. 'What use would they have of knowledge?'

'Perhaps they were acting for others. I know not.'

Haskeer scoffed.

But Stryke was intrigued enough that he wanted to hear more. 'I've a feeling your story isn't one to be told in a hurry, Mobbs. We'll get ourselves into the forest and hear the rest. And it better be good.'

'Oh, *come on*, Stryke!' Haskeer protested. 'Why waste time when we could be heading for home?'

'Getting ourselves hidden from another kobold attack isn't wasting time. Do as you're told.'

Haskeer went off in a sulk.

The camp was cleared, the wounded made ready to travel and Mobbs placed on the horse pulling Meklun's litter. All traces of their presence erased, the Wolverines made haste for the shelter of Black Rock Forest.

They reached their goal three hours later.

The forest was fully mature. Its towering trees spread a leafy ceiling far overhead, filtering the already weak sunlight, making ground-level shadowy and moist. Crunching on a brittle carpet of brown mulch, they set up a temporary camp. Grunts were assigned to keep their eyes peeled for signs of trouble.

For security, no fires were lit. So their first meal of the day was another austere ration; wedges of dense black bread, solid plugs of cured meat, and water.

Stryke, Coilla, Jup and Haskeer sat with Mobbs. Everybody else gathered around and looked on. Alfray came back from checking the wounded and pushed through the lounging troopers.

'Darig's not too bad,' he reported, 'but Meklun's fever's got worse.'

'Do what you can for him,' Stryke said. Then he, and the whole band, turned their attention to Mobbs.

The gremlin had refused food and taken only a little water.

Stryke reckoned fear had dulled his appetite. Now their scrutiny was making him even more uncomfortable.

'You've nothing to fear from us,' Stryke assured him, 'as long as you're honest. So no more puzzles.' He held up the cylinder. 'I want to hear exactly what you know about this thing, and why it's worth your life.'

'It could be worth *yours*,' Mobbs replied.

Coilla frowned. 'How so?'

'That depends on how much you value your heritage, and the destiny denied you.'

'These are empty words, meant to postpone his death,' Haskeer thundered. 'Stick 'im, I say.'

'Give him his due,' Jup said.

Haskeer glared at the dwarf. 'Trust *you* to take his side.'

'I'll decide if there's meaning in his words,' Stryke stated. 'Make yourself plain, Mobbs.'

'To do that, you need to know something of our land's history, and I fear history is something we are all losing.'

'Oh yes, tell us a story,' Haskeer mouthed acerbically. 'We've all the time in the world, after all.'

'Shut up,' Stryke intoned menacingly.

'I for one know something of Maras-Dantia's past,' Alfray put in. 'What are you trying to say, gremlin?'

'With respect, most of what you think you know, what many of us believe to be so, is only a mishmash of legends and myths. I have devoted myself to understanding the true course of events that led us to the present sorry situation.'

'Humans have brought us to our present state,' Stryke declared.

'Yes. But that was a fairly recent development in historical terms. Before then, life in Maras-Dantia had remained unchanged since time out of mind. Of course there was always enmity between the native races, and ever-shifting alliances often led to conflict. But the land was big enough for all to live in harmony, more or less.'

'Then the humans came,' Coilla said.

'Aye. But how many of you know that there were *two* influxes of that wretched race? And that at first relations between them and the elder races were not hostile?'

Jup looked sceptical. 'You jest.'

'It is a fact. The first immigrants to arrive through the Scilantium Desert were individuals and small groups. They were pioneers looking for a new frontier, or fleeing persecution, or simply wanting to make a fresh beginning.'

'*They* were persecuted?' Haskeer exclaimed. 'Your tale beggars belief, wrinkled one.'

'I tell you only the truth as I have found it, unpalatable as it may be.' The gremlin sounded as though his pride had been hurt.

'Go on,' Stryke urged.

'Although their ways seemed mysterious to the native population, and still do to most of us, those early incomers were left in peace. A few gained some respect. Hard to believe now, is it not?'

'You can say that again,' Coilla agreed.

'Tiny numbers of the outsiders even bred with members of elder races, producing strange hybrid offspring. But this you know, as I believe you are followers of the fruit of one such union.'

Coilla nodded. 'Jennesta. Followers isn't quite the right word.'

Stryke noted the spleen in her voice.

'That comes later in the story,' Mobbs told them, 'if you will allow me to return to it.' A vague expression clouded his features. 'Now, where was I . . .?'

'The early incomers,' Alfray prompted.

'Oh yes. As I said, the first wave actually got on with the

elder races quite well. At least, they gave more cause for curiosity than concern. The second wave was different. They were more a flood, you might say.' He gave a snorting little laugh at his own witticism. The orcs remained granite-faced. 'Er, yes. This second and larger inflow of humans was different. They were land grabbers and despoilers, and at best they saw us as a nuisance. It wasn't long before they began to fear and hate us.'

'They showed contempt,' Coilla murmured.

'Yes, and no more so than in renaming our land.'

'Centrasia,' Haskeer spat. He voiced it like an obscenity.

'They treated us like beasts of burden, and set to exploiting Maras-Dantia's resources. You know about that; it continues to this day, and grows more fevered. The rounding-up of free-roaming animals for their meat and hides, the overgrazing . . .'

'The fouling of rivers,' Coilla added, 'the levelling of forests.'

'Putting villages to the torch,' Jup contributed.

'Spreading their foul diseases,' Alfray said.

Haskeer looked particularly aggrieved at the last point.

'Worse,' Mobbs went on, 'they ate the magic.'

A stir went through the band, a murmur of agreement at the outrage.

'To we elder races, our powers diminishing, that was a final insult. It sowed the seeds of the wars we have endured ever since.'

'I've always been puzzled why the humans don't use the magic they've taken against us,' Jup commented. 'Are they too stupid to employ it?'

'I think it possible that they are simply ignorant. Perhaps they are not taking our magic for themselves but wasting it.'

'That's my feeling.'

'The bleeding of the earth's magic is bad,' Stryke said, 'but their overturning of the natural order of the seasons is much worse.'

'Without doubt,' Mobbs agreed. 'In tearing the heart out of the land, the humans interfered with the flow of energies sustaining nature's balance. Now the ice advances from the north as surely as humans pour in from the south. And all this has happened since your father's father's time, Stryke.'

'I never knew my father.'

'No, I know you orcs are raised communally. That isn't my point. I'm saying all of this has happened to Maras-Dantia in fairly recent times. The coming of the ice has only really begun in my lifetime, for example, and despite what you may think, I am not *that* old.'

Stryke couldn't help noticing Alfray giving Mobbs a fleeting, sympathetic glance.

'In my time I have seen the purity of the land ravished,' the gremlin recalled. 'I have seen the treaties races built smashed and realigned by the Manis and Unis.'

'And the likes of us forced to fight for one of those factions,' Coilla remarked, her depth of resentment apparent.

Mobbs sighed ruefully. 'Yes, many noble races, the orcs included, have been reduced to little more than serfdom by the outsiders.'

Coilla's eyes were blazing. 'And suffered their intolerance.'

'The two factions are indeed intolerant of us. But perhaps no more so than they are of each other. I am told that the more zealous of them, particularly among the Unis, regularly burn their own kind at the stake for something they call *heresy*.' He saw their curious expressions. 'It is to do with breaking the rules about how their god or gods are to be served, I believe,' he explained. 'Elder races have been known to behave in similar ways, mind. The history of the pixie clans, to take one example, is not without persecution and bloodshed.'

'And there's a race that can't afford to lose anybody,' Haskeer pronounced, 'seeing as how they're such notorious butt bandits.'

'What with that and their fire-starting abilities,' Jup pitched in, 'I don't know how they've survived this long. All that friction . . .'

The band roared with bawdy laughter. Even Haskeer cracked a grin.

Mobbs's green hide took on a pink hue of embarrassment. He cleared his throat in an attempt at delicacy. 'Er, quite.'

Coilla seemed less amused than the rest, and impatient. 'All right, we've had a history lesson. What about the cylinder?'

'Yes, get to the point, Mobbs,' Stryke said.

'The point, Commander, is that I believe this artefact has its origins long, long before the events we have just discussed. Back to the earliest days of Maras-Dantia, in fact.'

'Explain.'

'We spoke of symbiotes; those rare hybrids produced from unions between elder races and humans.'

'Like Jennesta.'

'Indeed. And her sisters, Adpar and Sanara.'

'They're mythical, aren't they?' remarked Jup.

'They are thought to exist. Though where they are, I have no idea. It is said that while Jennesta is a balance of the two races, Adpar is more purely nyadd. No one knows much about Sanara.'

'Real or not, what have they to do with the cylinder, beyond Jennesta laying claim to it?' Stryke asked.

'Directly, nothing that I know of. It is their mother, Vermegram, of whom I am thinking. You know the stories of how mighty a sorceress she was, of course.'

'But not as great as the one said to have slain her,' Stryke commented.

'The legendary Tentarr Arngrim, yes. Though little is known of him either. Why, even his race is in doubt.'

Haskeer sighed theatrically. 'You repeat stories made up to frighten hatchlings, gremlin.'

'Perhaps. I think not. But what I am saying is that I believe this artefact dates from ancient times, the golden age when Vermegram and Tentarr Arngrim were at the height of their powers.'

Jup was puzzled. 'I never understood how Vermegram, if she did exist, could possibly have been the mother of Jennesta and her sisters. Having lived so long ago, I mean.'

'It is said that Vermegram's life was of incredible longevity.'

'What?' Haskeer said.

'She was *long-lived*, blockhead,' Coilla informed him. 'So Jennesta and her sisters are also incredibly old. Is that it, Mobbs?'

'Not necessarily. In fact, I think Jennesta is probably no older than she appears to be. Remember, Vermegram's death and whatever fate befell Arngrim occurred not that long ago.'

'That must mean Vermegram was an ancient crone when she birthed her brood. Are you saying she stayed fertile into her dotage? That's insane!'

'I don't know. All I *would* say is that scholars are agreed she possessed magic of remarkable potency. Given that, anything is possible.'

Stryke slipped the cylinder free of his belt and laid it at his feet. 'What had she to do with this thing?'

'The earliest annals that mention Tentarr Arngrim and Vermegram contain hints about what I believe to be this cylinder. Or rather, what it contained: knowledge. And knowledge means power. A power many have given their lives to possess.'

'What kind of power?'

'The stories are vague. As best as I can grasp it, it is a . . . key, let us call it. A key to understanding. If I am right, it will throw light on many things, not least the origin of the elder races, including orcs. All of us.'

Jup stared at the cylinder. 'Whatever's inside this little thing would tell us all that?'

'No. It would *begin* to tell you. If my reasoning is correct, it would set you on that path. Such knowledge does not come easy.'

'This is horse shit,' Haskeer complained. 'Why don't he talk in plain language?'

'All right,' Stryke intervened. 'What you're saying, Mobbs, is that the cylinder contains something important. Given how much Jennesta wants it, that hardly comes as a surprise. What are you getting at?'

'Knowledge is neutral. It is generally neither good nor bad. It becomes a force for enlightenment or evil depending on who controls it.'

'So?'

'If Jennesta has command of this knowledge it's likely no good will come of it, you must know that. It could be better used.'

'You're saying we shouldn't return the cylinder to her?' Coilla asked.

Mobbs didn't answer.

'You *are*, aren't you?' she persisted.

'I have lived for many seasons and seen many things. I would die content if I thought my one cherished wish might come true.'

'Which is?'

'You do not know, even in your heart? My dearest wish is that our land be returned to us. That we could go back to the way things were. The power of this artefact is the nearest we may ever get to a chance of that. But just a *chance*. It would be the first step in a long journey.'

The passion of his words quietened them all for a moment.

'Let's open it,' Coilla said.

'What?' Haskeer exclaimed, leaping to his feet.

'Aren't you curious about what we might find inside? Don't you wish, too, for a power that might free our land?'

'Like fuck I do, you crazy bitch. Do you want to get us all killed?'

'Face it, Haskeer; we're as good as dead anyway. If we go back to Cairnbarrow, that cylinder and the pellucid will count for nothing as far as Jennesta's concerned. Any of you think otherwise and you're fooling yourselves.'

Haskeer turned to the other officers. 'You've more sense than she has. Tell her she's wrong.'

'I'm not sure she is,' Alfray replied. 'I think the minute we screwed up our mission we signed our own death warrants.'

'What have we got to lose?' Jup added. 'We have no home now.'

'I'd expect that of *you*,' Haskeer gibed. 'Your place was never with orcs anyway. What do you care if we live or die?' He looked to Stryke. 'That's right, isn't it, Captain? We know better than a female, a has-been and a dwarf, don't we? Tell them.'

Every eye was on Stryke. He said nothing.

'*Tell* them,' Haskeer repeated.

'I agree with Coilla,' Stryke said.

'You . . . you can't be *serious*!'

Stryke ignored him. What he saw was Coilla smiling, and few faces in the band showing disapproval.

'Have you all gone fucking *mad*?' Haskeer demanded. 'You, Stryke, of all orcs; I didn't expect this of you. You're asking us to throw everything away!'

'I'm asking that we open this cylinder. Everything else we've thrown away already.'

'Stryke's just saying we should look,' Jup said. 'We can reseal it, can't we?'

'And if the Queen discovers we've tampered with it? Can you imagine her wrath?'

'I've no need to imagine it,' Stryke told him. 'That's one reason we should seize any chance to change things for ourselves. Or perhaps you're happy with the way they are?'

'I *accept* the way things are, because I know we *can't* change anything. At least we've got our lives, and now you want to waste them.'

'We want to *find* them,' Coilla said.

Stryke addressed the whole band. 'For something this important, something that touches all of us, we're going to do what we've never done before. We're going to have a show of hands. All right?'

Nobody objected.

He held up the cylinder. 'Those who think we should leave this be and return to Cairnbarrow, raise your hand.'

Haskeer did. Three grunts joined him.

'Those who say we should open it?'

Every other hand went up.

'You're outvoted,' Stryke declared.

'You're making a big mistake,' Haskeer muttered grimly.

'You're doing the right thing, Stryke,' Coilla assured him.

Right or not, the relief he felt was almost physical. It was as though he was doing something honest for the first time in as long as he could remember.

But that didn't stop the icy tingle of fear that caressed his spine as he looked at the cylinder.

14

As the band looked on in silence, Stryke took a knife to the cylinder's seal. Having cut through it, he prised off the cap. There was a faint whiff of mustiness.

He pushed his fingers inside. Their clumsiness made for a moment of awkward fumbling before he slipped out a rolled parchment. It was fragile and yellowing with age. This he handed to Mobbs. The gremlin accepted it with a mixture of eagerness and reverence.

Stryke shook the cylinder. It rattled. He held it up and looked into it.

'There's something else in here,' he said, half to himself.

He patted the tube's open end on his palm. An object slid out.

It consisted of a small central sphere with seven tiny radiating spikes of variable lengths. It was sandy-coloured, similar to a light, polished wood. It was heavier than it looked.

Stryke held it up and examined it.

'It's like a star,' Coilla decided. 'Or a hatchling's toy of one.'

He thought she was right. The object did resemble a crude representation of a star.

Mobbs had the parchment unrolled on his lap, but was ignoring it. He stared awestruck at the object.

'What's it made of?' Alfray wondered.

Stryke passed it to him.

'It's no material I know,' the field surgeon pronounced. 'It's not wood, nor bone.'

Jup took it. 'Could it be fashioned from some kind of stone?' he asked.

'Something precious?' Haskeer ventured, interest overtaking his resentment. 'Carved from a gem maybe?'

Stryke reached for it. 'I don't think so.' He squeezed it in his fist, gently at first then applying all his strength. 'Whatever it is, it's tough.'

'How tough can it be?' Haskeer grunted. 'Give it here.'

He raised the object to his mouth and bit it. There was a crack. A spasm of pain creased his face and he spat out a bloody tooth. *'Vuckk!'* he cursed.

Stryke snatched the star and wiped it on his breeches. He inspected it. There wasn't a mark. '*Very* tough then, if your fangs can't make an impression.'

Several band members sniggered. Haskeer glared at them.

Mobbs's attention was torn between the object and the parchment. His expression was intense, excited, as his gaze went from one to the other.

'What do you make of it, scholar?' Stryke asked.

'I think . . . I think this is . . . it.' The gremlin's hands were shaking. 'What I hoped for . . .'

'Don't keep us in the dark,' Coilla demanded impatiently. 'Tell us!'

Mobbs indicated the parchment. 'This is written in a language so old, so . . obscure, that even I have difficulty understanding it.'

'What *can* you make out?' she persisted.

'At this stage, merely fragments. But I believe they confirm my suspicions.' He was jubilant, in a Mobbs kind of way. 'That object . . .' he pointed to the star in Stryke's hand, '. . . is an instrumentality.'

'A *what*?' Haskeer said, dabbing at his mouth with a grubby sleeve.

Stryke gave the thing to Mobbs. He accepted it gingerly. 'An instrumentality, in the old tongue. This is tangible proof of an ancient story hitherto thought a myth. If the legends are true, it could have been handled by Vermegram herself. It may even have been created by her.'

'For what purpose?' Jup asked.

'As a totem of great magical power, and of great truth, in that it hints at a mystery concerning the elder races.'

'How so?' Stryke demanded.

'All I really know is that each instrumentality is part of a larger whole. One fifth, to be precise. When this is united with its four fellows, the truth will be revealed. I have no idea what that means, to be honest. But I would stake my life on this being the most significant object any of us has ever seen.'

He spoke with such conviction that all were held by his words.

Jup pricked the bubble. 'How could it be united with the others? What happens if they are? *Where* are they?'

'Mysteries within mysteries and unanswered questions. It has always been so for any student of these matters.' Mobbs sniffed, matter-of-factly. 'I have no answers to your first two questions, but something I overheard from my captors might be a clue to the location of another instrumentality. *Might*, I say.'

'What was it?' Stryke asked.

'The kobolds were not aware that I have a rudimentary grasp of their language. I thought it useful not to reveal the fact. Consequently they spoke freely in my presence, and several times referred to the Uni stronghold called Trinity. They were convinced that the sect holding sway there had incorporated the legend of the instrumentalities into their religion.'

'Trinity? That's Kimball Hobrow's redoubt, isn't it?' Coilla remarked.

'Yes,' Alfray confirmed, 'and he's notorious for being a fanatic. Rules his followers with a rod of iron. Hates elder races, by all accounts.'

'You think they might have one of these . . . stars at Trinity, Mobbs?' Stryke said.

'I do not know. But the odds are fair. Why else would the kobolds be interested in the place? If they are gathering the instrumentalities, either for themselves or somebody else, it would be logical.'

'Just a minute,' Jup interrupted. 'If these instrumentalities are so powerful—'

'*Potentially* powerful,' Mobbs corrected him.

'All right, they promise power. That being the case, why isn't Hobrow searching for them? Why aren't others?'

'Quite likely they don't know the legends of their power. Or perhaps they know enough of the legends to realise an instrumentality is a revered object, but don't know that it's necessary to unite them. Then again, who is to say that Hobrow or others are *not* looking? Such an aim is best served by secrecy.'

'What about Jennesta?' Coilla said. 'Is she likely to know about the legend of the five stars, Mobbs?'

'I cannot say. But if she is so anxious to get this one, quite possibly she does.'

'So she could have searches underway too?'

'It is what I would do in her position. But remember, orcs, that I told you the power the instrumentalities offer would not be easily gained. That does not mean you should give up.'

'Give up?' Haskeer blustered. 'Give up *what*? You're not going on this insane quest, are you, Stryke?'

'I'm thinking about several ways we could jump.'

'You know what chasing another of these star things means, don't you? Desertion!'

'We must be listed as deserters already, Haskeer. It's been over a week since we should have returned to Cairnbarrow.'

'And whose fault was *that*?'

For a brace of heartbeats, those looking on didn't know how Stryke would take the accusation. He surprised them.

'All right, blame me. I can't argue with that.'

Haskeer pressed a little further. 'I wonder how much you *wanted* to put us in this position. Particularly as now you're trying to push us into making things worse.'

'I didn't set out to make life harder for us. But now it's happened, it's happened. We should make the best of it.'

'By swallowing these stories of myths and legends? They're tales for the hatcheries, Stryke. You can't believe this gryphon shit.'

'Whether I do or not isn't the point. What matters is that Jennesta does. That gives us a powerful bargaining counter. This star could mean the difference between us living or dying. I'm not sure it's enough, knowing Jennesta. But if we had more than one, even all five . . .'

'So you think it's better to set off on this brainless quest than go back and throw ourselves on the Queen's mercy?'

'She *has* no mercy, Haskeer. Can't you get that through your head? Or does it take my fists to do it?'

'But you want to make this move on the word of an old gremlin.' He jabbed his finger at Mobbs, who flinched. 'How do you know he's telling the truth? Or that he isn't just plain crazy?'

'I believe him. Even if I didn't, we can't go back. Look, if you and the ones who voted with you, Jad, Finje, Breggin, if you want to go, then do it. But there's safety in numbers.'

'You want to break up the band?'

'No, I don't.'

'You only got us to vote on the cylinder, Stryke, not turning renegade.'

'Fair point. Though I reckon we're renegades already. You just haven't realised it.' He faced the assembled Wolverines. 'You've heard what's been said. I want to go after another star, and Trinity looks the best bet. I won't pretend it'll be anything but rough. But then we're orcs, and that's what we do best. If any of you don't want to come, if you'd prefer to go back to Cairnbarrow or anywhere else, you'll be given rations and a horse. Make yourselves known now.'

No one, not even those who had voted with Haskeer, came forward.

'So, are you coming?' Stryke asked him.

After a pause, he replied moodily, 'Don't have much choice, do I?'

'Yes, you do.'

'I'm coming. But if things go against my liking, I'll leave.'

'All right. But mark this. We might not be part of Jennesta's horde any more, but that doesn't mean discipline isn't going to hold in this band. It's what makes everything work. If you've got a problem with that, we'll take another vote. On who's going to be leader.'

'Keep your leadership, Stryke. I just want to get out of this mess with my head.'

'You have taken the first step of a long and perilous journey,' Mobbs told them all. 'You cannot go back. You are outlaws now.'

The sobering atmosphere that brought down was cut into by Stryke. 'Let's get ready to move.'

'To Trinity?' Coilla said.

'To Trinity.'

She smiled and went off.

Alfray left to check his patients. The rest of the band dispersed.

Mobbs looked up at Stryke and asked hesitantly, 'What about . . . me?'

Stryke regarded him for a few seconds, an unreadable expression on his face. 'I don't know whether we should thank you for helping us break away or kill you for turning our lives upside down.'

'I think you had already started to do that before you met me, Stryke.'

'I think perhaps we had.'

'What *are* you going to do with me?'

'Let you go.'

The gremlin gave a little bow of gratitude.

'Where will you go?' Stryke said.

'Hecklowe. I still have business to finish.' His eyes took on a shine. 'A trunk full of writing tablets was found in a cellar there. Tax records, apparently, from the . . . You don't find this quite as fascinating as I do, do you, Stryke?'

'Each to his own, Mobbs. Can we escort you part of the way?'

'I am for Hecklowe, you for Trinity. They are in opposite directions.'

'We'll let you have a horse and some victuals for the journey.'

'That is generous.'

'You may have given us back our freedom, it's little enough in exchange. Anyway, we have spares, not least Darig's. He won't be needing one for a while. Oh, and you might as well keep that.' He nodded at the parchment in Mobbs's hand.

'Truly?'

'Why not? We have no need of it. Do we?'

'Er, no, indeed not. It has no bearing on the function of the instrumentalities. I thank you for it, Stryke. And for freeing me from the kobolds.' He sighed. 'I would love to accompany you, you know. But at my age . . .'

'Of course.'

'But I wish you and your Wolverines all good luck, Stryke. And if you'll take the counsel of an old gremlin . . beware. Not only because you have made many enemies on all sides by your recent actions, but also because your search for the instrumentalities may well lead you into conflict with others on the same mission. With so much at stake, your rivals will stop at nothing to gain the prize.'

'We can look after ourselves.'

Mobbs regarded the orc's massive chest, imposing shoulders, muscular arms and proudly thrusting jaw. He read the determination in the craggy face, the flint in the eyes. 'I have no doubt you can.'

Haskeer returned, hefting a saddle one-handed. He dropped it nearby and began arranging his kit.

'What route will you take to Hecklowe?' Stryke wanted to know.

Mobbs cracked a thin smile. 'Not through this forest, that is for certain. I will go west, in order to leave it as quickly as possible, then turn north to skirt it. It's a longer way—'

'But much safer. I understand. We'll ride to the forest's edge with you.'

'Thank you. I shall make ready.'

He walked off clutching the parchment.

'That could be a mistake too,' Haskeer commented. 'He knows too much. What if he talks?'

'He won't.'

Before Haskeer could offer any more unwanted advice, Alfray arrived, his face troubled.

Without preamble he announced, 'Meklun's dead. The fever took him.'

'Shit,' Stryke said. 'But it's not a surprise.'

'No. At least his suffering's over. I hate losing them, Stryke. But I did my best.'

'I know.'

'Question now is, what do we do with him? Given the fix we're in.'

'A funeral pyre's going to be like a beacon for kobolds and any other race looking for trouble. We can't risk it. This once, forget tradition. Bury him.'

'I'll get it done.'

As Alfray made to leave, he glanced at Haskeer and stopped. 'You all right?' he enquired. 'You look a bit off-colour.'

'I'm *fine*,' Haskeer replied sharply. 'I'm just sick of what's happening to this band! Now leave me alone!'

He turned his back on them and stormed off.

Jennesta stared at the necklace of snow leopard's teeth.

It had arrived with an impertinent message from the captain that Kysthan had sent after the Wolverines. Despite his orders, Delorran had taken it upon himself to extend the deadline she had decreed. The necklace was a reminder of how minions would resort to insubordination the moment they were out of sight. And of the punishment she would inflict for the transgression.

She slipped the necklace into the pouch in her cloak and gazed at the sky. The flock of dragons was no more than a distant speckle of black dots now. They were off on yet another patrol, searching for her quarry.

The wind changed and brought the odour of something unpleasant her way. She looked at the gibbet set in the middle of the courtyard.

General Kysthan's body hung from it, swaying gently.

Decomposition was setting in. Soon birds of prey as well as dragons would be circling above her castle. But she would leave the carcass there for a while yet. It served as an example to others who might fail her. In particular it would be a warning to the one she was about to receive.

She watched as the dragons were completely swallowed by the overcast sky.

Then several of her orc bodyguards approached, escorting another of their kind. He was young, or at least youngish, being perhaps thirty seasons old. His physique spoke of a warrior, rather than the general his abnormally clean and tidy uniform indicated.

Naturally he couldn't resist a sidelong glance at the suspended corpse.

He clicked his heels smartly and gave a bobbing head bow. 'My lady.'

She waved away the guards. 'At ease, Mersadion.'

If he relaxed at all, it was imperceptible.

'I'm told you're ambitious, energetic, and more politically adept than Kysthan was,' she said. 'You've also risen well in the ranks. Having been a soldier in the field until recently could prove to both our advantages. That you are not still there is due entirely to me. Be sure that having made you, I can break you.'

'Ma'am.'

'What did you think of Kysthan?'

'He was . . . of an older generation, my lady. One with which I have not a great deal of sympathy.'

'I do hope you're not going to begin our working relationship with mealy words, General, or it won't last long. Now try the truth.'

'He was a fool, Your Majesty.'

She smiled. An act which, had Mersadion known her better, would not have reassured him even to the limited extent it did. 'I picked you for preferment because I understand foolishness is *not* one of your weaknesses. Do you know the situation concerning the Wolverines?'

'The warband? All I know is that they've gone missing, presumed dead or captured.'

'Presumed nothing. They're absent without leave, and they

have an item of great value that belongs to me.'

'Isn't Captain Delorran searching for them already?'

'Yes, and he's overdue. You know this Delorran?'

'A little, my lady, yes.'

'What's your opinion of him?'

'Young, headstrong, and driven by his hatred of the Wolverines' commander, Stryke. Delorran has long harboured resentments about Stryke. But he's an orc you'd expect to obey orders.'

'He's gone beyond the time limit I set for his return. This displeases me greatly.'

'If Delorran's late returning it must be for a good reason, ma'am. A warm trail left by the Wolverines, for example.'

'He sent a message to that effect. Very well. For the moment I won't add him and *his* band to those regarded as outlaws. But every day the Wolverines are absent the more it looks as though they've gone renegade. Your first assignment, and it's by far the most important, is to take command of the search for them. It's vital to get back the artefact they've stolen.'

'What is this artefact, ma'am?'

'That you don't need to know, beyond its description. I have other assignments for you, related to the recovery of this item, but my orders about those will be passed to you in due course.'

'Yes, Your Majesty.'

'Serve me well, Mersadion, and I'll reward you. Further advancement will be yours. Now take a good look at your predecessor.' A note of menace crept into her voice. 'Be clear that if you fail me you will share his fate. Understood?'

'Understood, my lady.'

She thought he took that well. He looked respectful of the threat but not overawed by it. Perhaps she could work with this one, and not have to submit him to the kind of death she had in mind for Stryke. And when he finally returned, Delorran.

★

Delorran surveyed the charred remains of the tiny makeshift village.

Most of the foliage that had hidden the depression where the settlement was located had been destroyed by fire. Only skeletal trees and the stumps of burnt bushes were left.

He sat astride his horse, his sergeant mounted beside him, as the grunts investigated the ruins.

'It seems the Wolverines leave destruction everywhere they go,' Delorran commented.

'That's their job, isn't it, sir?' the sergeant replied.

Delorran gave him a disdainful look. 'This wasn't a military target. It looks like a civilian camp.'

'But how do we know the Wolverines had anything to do with it, sir?'

'It would be too great a coincidence if they hadn't, given that their trail led straight here.'

A trooper ran to them. The sergeant leaned over and heard his report, then dismissed him.

'The bodies in the burnt-out huts, sir,' the sergeant related. 'They're orcs. All women and young ones, apparently.'

'Any signs of what killed them?'

'The bodies are too far gone for that, sir.'

'So, Stryke and his gang have sunk low enough to slay their own kind now, and defenceless ones at that.'

'With respect, sir . . .' the sergeant ventured carefully.

'Yes, Sergeant?'

'Well, these deaths could have been due to any number of things. It could have been the fire. We have no proof that the Wolverines—'

'I have the proof of my own eyes. And knowing what Stryke's capable of, it doesn't surprise me at all. They're renegades now. Maybe they've even gone over to the Unis.'

'Yes, sir.' It was a muted, less than enthusiastic response.

'Get the company together, Sergeant, we've no time to

waste. What we've seen here gives us even more reason to catch these bandits, and put a stop to them. We're pushing on.'

They could do no more for Meklun than commend his spirit to the gods of war and bury him too deep for scavenging animals.

Having escorted Mobbs from Black Rock Forest, the Wolverines headed south-west on the first leg of their journey to Trinity. This time, their course would take them between Weaver's Lea and Quatt, the dwarves' homeland. The most direct route put Weaver's Lea directly in their path, but bearing in mind the trouble they'd had with the roadblock near there earlier, Stryke was determined to approach the human settlement with caution. His plan was to bypass it and make for the foothills of the Carascrag Mountains. Then they'd turn due west in the direction of Trinity. That would greatly lengthen the journey, but he thought it a price worth paying.

As the day wore on they sighted a sizeable herd of gryphons. The animals were heading north, travelling at speed with the loping, jerky movement peculiar to their species. An hour or two later a far-off group of dragons was spotted, soaring high above the western horizon. That the beasts enjoyed a freedom threatened by the turmoil engulfing the land somehow made it seem sweeter. The parallel with the Wolverines' liberation was not lost on Stryke.

Typically, Haskeer failed to appreciate any similarity, and continued to complain as they rode.

'We don't even know what this star thing is, or what it does,' he moaned, repeating a point already made numerous times before.

Stryke's patience was wearing thin, but he took another shot at explaining. 'We know Jennesta wants it, that it's important to her, which in itself gives it power. That's all you need to hold on to.'

Haskeer effectively ignored that and kept the questions

coming. 'What do we do even if we find the second star? What about the other three? Suppose we never find them? Where do we go? Who do we ally ourselves with when all hands are turned against us? How can—'

'For the god's sake!' Stryke flared. 'Stop telling me what we *can't* do. Concentrate on what's possible.'

'What's possible is that we'll all lose our heads!' Haskeer yanked on his horse's reins and rode back down the column.

'I don't know why you wanted him to stay, Stryke,' Coilla remarked.

'I'm not sure myself,' he sighed. 'Except I don't like the idea of breaking up the band, and whatever else you can say about the bastard, at least he's a good fighter.'

'We might be needing that particular skill,' Jup said. 'Look!'

A column of thick black smoke was rising from the direction of Weaver's Lea.

15

Mobbs was happy.

He had been liberated from the kobolds. The orcs that had rescued him had spared his life, despite their fearsome reputation. Given the choice, he could think of more suitable guardians of an instrumentality, but at least it looked as though they weren't going to hand it to Jennesta. To Mobbs's way of thinking, that seemed the lesser of two evils. And he hoped he had been able to impress on the orcs that their future course of action should be designed to help all the elder races. He even had a fascinating historical document as a souvenir of his adventure. Perhaps some good would come from his ordeal after all.

But the last couple of days had seen more than enough excitement for a humble scholar, particularly one of his age, and he was glad to be out of it.

It was more than six hours since the orcs had taken him to the edge of Black Rock Forest and pointed him north. All he had to do was keep the forest on his right, and when it came to an end veer east for the coast and then along to Hecklowe. What he hadn't bargained on was the forest being so large and the journey so long. Or perhaps it just seemed that way to an old academic unused to travelling. The first time he had made this journey, going the other way, he was the kobolds' captive, and they had brought him blindfolded in a covered wagon.

He was a little worried that he might run into the kobolds again, or some other group of brigands, particularly as he was far from being a good rider and unlikely to outrun them. In fact, as a member of such a small race, his feet did not reach the horse's stirrups. All he could do was trust in the gods and make as fast a pace as he was able.

But the world had a way of imposing its troubles on him. An hour or two before, he had noticed a column of black smoke behind him, in the south. If he had his bearings correctly, it was coming from the area of Weaver's Lea. Every so often he glanced over his shoulder. The pillar of smoke seemed no more distant and ever higher.

He was thinking about what its cause might be when he became aware of movement to his left.

The land in that direction was hilly, and dotted with patches of trees seeded from the main forest by birds and the wind. So he couldn't make out what was approaching other than that it appeared to be a party of horse riders. He assumed it wasn't kobolds because they rode not horses but kirgizils. His fading eyesight wouldn't let him make out more and he grew apprehensive. All he could do was stay on his trail and hope they passed without seeing him.

It was a forlorn hope.

The riders turned from their parallel heading, put on a spurt of speed and made for the path he was travelling. He clung to the belief that he had not been spotted until they climbed the slight rise leading to his track, emerging ahead of and behind him.

Then he saw that they were orcs. He felt relief. This must be the band that had freed him, Stryke's band, probably back to ask more about the instrumentality. Or perhaps to escort him through this troubled region.

Mobbs pulled back on the reins and halted. The orcs trotted to him.

'Greetings,' he hailed. 'Why have you returned?'

'Returned?' one of them said. He bore the facial tattoos of a sergeant.

Mobbs blinked. He didn't recognise the one who had spoken. None of the others looked familiar either. 'Where's Stryke?' he asked jauntily. 'I can't see him.'

The looks on their faces showed it was the wrong thing to say. He was confused. An orc with captain's tattoos steered his horse through the troopers. Again, Mobbs didn't remember seeing him before.

'He mistook us for the Wolverines,' the sergeant reported, nodding at Mobbs. 'He mentioned Stryke.'

Delorran drew level with the gremlin and studied him, hard-eyed. 'Perhaps all orcs look the same to him,' he said. There was no trace of humour in his voice, and certainly no warmth.

'I can assure you, Captain, that—'

'If you know Stryke's name,' the Captain cut in, 'you must have encountered the Wolverines.'

Mobbs sensed danger. Somehow he knew that admitting to it put him in a difficult position. But he couldn't see how to deny it.

While he dithered, the Captain's patience visibly stretched. 'You've had contact with them, yes?'

'It's true I did run into a band of orc warriors,' Mobbs finally replied, choosing his words prudently.

'And what?' Delorran pressed. 'Passed the time of day? Chatted about their exploits? Aided them in some way, perhaps?'

'I cannot see what aid an old gremlin like myself, and a lowly scholar at that, could possibly offer such as yourselves.'

'They're not like ourselves', the Captain snapped. 'They're renegades.'

'Really?' Mobbs put on what he hoped was a convincing show of surprise. 'I had no idea of their . . . status.'

'Perhaps you were more successful in learning where they were going?'

'Going? You don't know, Captain?'

Delorran drew his sword. Its menacing tip hovered at Mobbs's chest. 'I've not time to waste, and you're a bad liar. Where are they?'

'I . . . I don't . . .'

The blade pricked the gremlin's matted robe. 'Talk now or never again.'

'They . . . they mentioned that they might be going . . . going to . . . Trinity,' Mobbs imparted reluctantly.

'Trinity? That hotbed of Unis? I *knew* it! What did I tell you, Sergeant? They've not only deserted, they've turned traitors, the bastards.'

The sergeant looked Mobbs over. 'Suppose he's lying, sir?'

'He's telling the truth. Look at him. It's all he can do not to piss himself.'

Mobbs rose in the saddle to his full, modest height, ready to deliver a dignified rebuttal of the insult.

Without warning, Delorran drove his sword into the gremlin's chest.

Mobbs gasped and looked down at the blade. Delorran tugged it free. Blood flowed freely. Mobbs looked at the orc officer, incomprehension written all over his face. Then he toppled from the saddle.

The alarmed horse bucked. Reaching out for its reins, the sergeant steadied it.

Delorran noticed a saddlebag that had been concealed by the gremlin's robe. He flipped it open and began rifling. It held little more than the rolled parchment. Delorran realised that it was very old, but could otherwise make no sense of it.

'This might have some bearing on the object we're looking for,' he admitted lamely. 'Perhaps we could have questioned him more closely.'

The sergeant thought his superior looked faintly embarrassed. Naturally he didn't draw attention to it. Instead he glanced at the gremlin's body and contented himself with, 'Bit late to put that right now, sir.'

The irony was lost on Delorran. He was staring at the column of smoke.

By evening, the Wolverines were much nearer the pillar of smoke, which now showed white against the darkness. They were close to Weaver's Lea, and expected to reach it at any time. As they rode, they spoke in hushed tones.

'Something big's going on around here, Stryke,' Jup said. 'Shouldn't we try avoiding Weaver's Lea altogether?'

'There's no way of reaching Trinity without going *somewhere* near the place.'

'We could turn back and not go to Trinity at all,' Alfray suggested. 'Regroup and think again.'

'We're committed,' Stryke told him, 'and wherever we go, we'd have to expect trouble.'

The exchange was cut short by the return of an advance scout.

'The settlement's just on the other side of a rise about half a mile further along, sir,' he reported. 'There's trouble there. It'd be best to dismount when you reach the hill and approach on foot.'

Stryke nodded and sent him back.

'The gods know what we're walking into,' Haskeer grumbled.

But the complaint wasn't delivered in his usual acerbic style and Stryke ignored it. He passed on an order for silence in the ranks and the band resumed its journey.

They got to the rise without hindrance, dismounted and climbed to join the waiting scouts.

Weaver's Lea stretched out below them. It was a sizeable human community, and typical in consisting mainly of cottages, most built of part stone, part wood. There were some larger buildings; barns, grain stores, meeting halls and at least one place of worship, bearing a spire.

But the most striking thing about the town was that much of it was on fire.

A few figures could be seen, outlined by the blaze, running to and fro. Here and there they were trying to douse the flames, but their efforts looked futile.

'There should be many more humans about than this,' Coilla reckoned. 'Where are they?'

The scouts shrugged their shoulders.

'There's no point in hanging around here waiting to be spotted,' Stryke decided. 'We'll circle this and push on.'

An hour later, having topped a higher range of hills, they found out what had happened to all the humans.

In a valley below, two armies faced each other.

An engagement was near, and had probably only been delayed by nightfall. The number of torches and braziers twinkling like a swath of stars on either side indicated that the conflict was major.

'A Uni and Mani battle,' Jup sighed. 'Just what we needed.'

'How many would you say there were?' Coilla said. 'Five or six thousand a side?'

Stryke squinted. 'Hard to tell in this light. Looks like at least that many to me.'

'Now we know why Weaver's Lea was burning,' Alfray concluded. 'It must have been the opening shot.'

'So what do we do, Stryke?' Coilla wanted to know.

'I'm not keen on backtracking and risking another clash with the kobolds, and trying to get round a field of battle in the dark's too chancy unless we want to run into raiding parties. We'll stay put here tonight and look at the situation tomorrow.'

Unable to move on, unwilling to go back, they watched the unfolding scene below.

When dawn broke, most of the band were sleeping. A roar from the battlefield roused them.

In the cold light of morning, the size of the armies could be clearly seen, and they were easily as large as Coilla had estimated.

'Not long before they meet now,' Stryke judged.

Jup rubbed sleep from his eyes. 'Human against human. No bad thing from our point of view.'

'Maybe not. I just wish they weren't doing it now, and here. We've enough problems.'

Somebody pointed to the sky. Several dragons were approaching at a distance.

'So the Manis have help,' Alfray said. 'From Jennesta, you think, Stryke?'

'Could be. Though she's not the only one with command of them.'

Haskeer came out with, 'Well, wouldn't you know it. Both armies have dwarves in their ranks.'

'So?' Jup responded.

'Says it all, doesn't it? Your kind will fight for anybody with enough coin.'

'I've told you before: I'm not responsible for every dwarf in the land.'

'Makes me wonder how much their loyalty's to be valued when it goes to the highest bidder. For all we know, you . . .'

A coughing fit broke the invective. Red-faced, he barked and hawked.

'You all right, Haskeer?' Alfray asked. 'That doesn't sound too good to me.'

Haskeer caught his breath and responded angrily. 'Get off my back, sawbones! I'm fine!' He resumed coughing, though less violently.

Stryke was about to put in a word when a grunt's yell distracted him.

The band turned and looked down the hill behind them. A group of mounted orcs were approaching the foot of the rise. They outnumbered the Wolverines by about three to one.

'A search party?' Coilla wondered.

'For us? Could be,' Stryke said.

'Maybe they've been sent to reinforce the Mani side in the battle,' Jup suggested.

The newcomers were nearer. Stryke cupped his eyes and concentrated on them. 'Shit!'

Coilla looked at him. 'What's the matter?'

'The officer leading them. I know him. He's no friend.'

'He's an orc, isn't he?' Alfray reasoned. 'We're on the same side, after all.'

'Not when it comes to Delorran.'

'Delorran?' Alfray exclaimed.

'You know him too?' Coilla said.

'Yes. He and Stryke have a lot of . . . history.'

'That's one way of putting it,' Stryke granted. 'But what the hell's he doing here?'

It was no mystery to Alfray. 'It's obvious, isn't it? Who better to hunt you down than somebody who hates you enough not to give up?'

The search party halted. Delorran and another orc rode forward a little further and stopped too. The second orc raised a war banner and moved it slowly from side to side.

They all understood the signal. Coilla articulated it. 'They want to parley.'

Stryke nodded. 'Right. You'll come with me. Get our horses.'

She ran off to obey the order.

Stryke leaned over to Alfray and slipped him the star. 'Guard this.' Alfray put it in his jerkin. 'Now signal that we're going down to talk.'

The Wolverines' own standard was lying in the grass nearby. Alfray unfurled it and sent the message.

'Get Darig to a horse,' Stryke added.

'What?'

'I want him ready, I want you *all* ready, in case we need to move fast.'

'I don't know if he's in a fit state to ride.'

'It's that or we leave him, Alfray.'

'Leave him?'

'Just do as you're told.'

'I'll double with him on my horse.'

Stryke thought about that for a moment. 'All right. But if he slows you, dump him.'

'I'll pretend you didn't say that.'

'Remember it. It could be the difference between us losing one life or two.'

Alfray looked far from happy, but nodded agreement. Not that Stryke believed he'd do it.

'If this Delorran is such an enemy,' Jup said, 'are you sure it's wise for you to go?'

'It has to be me, Jup, you know that. And it's under truce. Stand ready, all of you.'

He went to Coilla. They mounted and began riding down the hill.

'Leave the talking to me,' he told her. 'If we have to get out fast, don't hesitate, just do it.'

She gave an almost imperceptible nod.

They reached Delorran and what they could now tell was his sergeant.

Stryke spoke first. He kept it even and cool. 'Well met, Delorran.'

'Stryke,' he responded through clenched teeth. Even a basic civility seemed an effort for him.

'You're a long way from home.'

'Let's cut the niceties, shall we, Stryke? We both know why I'm here.'

'Do we?'

'If you want to play out this farce to its bitter end, I'll tell you. You and your band are absent without leave.'

'I hope you're going to let me explain why.'

'The reason's obvious. You've deserted.'

'Is that a fact?'

'And you have something belonging to the Queen. I've been sent to get it back. By any means necessary.'

'*Any* means? You'd take up arms against fellow orcs? I know we've had our differences, Delorran, but I'd have thought even you—'

'I've no scruples when it comes to traitors.'

Stryke bridled. 'So we've gone from deserters to traitors, have we? That's quite a jump.' There was steel in his tone.

'Don't play the innocent with me. What else would you call it when you fail to return from a mission, steal Jennesta's property and side with the Unis?'

'That's some set of charges, Delorran. But no way have we gone over to the Unis or anybody else. Use your head. We couldn't approach them without being cut down, even if we wanted to.'

'I should think they'd welcome an orc fighting unit with open arms. Probably be good for recruiting others as treacherous as you. But I'm not here to bandy words. I judge you by your actions, and slaughtering a camp of orc females and hatchlings tells me all I need to know.'

'*What?* Delorran, if you're talking about what I think you are, the orcs in that camp died from disease. We just torched it to—'

'Don't insult me with your lies! My orders are clear. You'll hand over the artefact, and your band will lay down their weapons and surrender.'

'Like hell we will,' Coilla said.

Delorran shot her a look of fury. 'You exercise little discipline over your subordinates, Stryke. Not that it surprises me.'

'If she hadn't said it, I would. If we've got something you want, come and get it.'

Delorran reached for his sword.

'And if you want to violate a flag of truce, go ahead,' Stryke added, raising a hand to his own blade.

They glared at each other.

Delorran didn't draw his sword. 'You've got two minutes to think about it. Then give up or put up.'

Stryke turned his horse without a word. Coilla, after a parting scowl at Delorran, joined him. They galloped back up to the band.

Swinging from his saddle, Stryke outlined the exchange. 'They've got us marked as traitors, and they think we massacred those orcs in the camp we torched.'

Alfray was shocked. 'How could they think we'd do *that*?'

'Delorran's ready to believe anything about me, as long as it's bad, and in about a minute and a half they'll be coming up here to take us. Dead or alive.' He looked to the gathered Wolverines. 'It's crunch time. Surrender and we face certain death, either at Delorran's hands or when he takes us back to Cairnbarrow. If I'm to meet my death it's going to be here and now, with a sword in my hand.' He scanned their faces. 'How say you? Are you with me?'

The band let him know they were. Even Haskeer and the trio who supported him were game for a fight, although their assent was a little less enthusiastic than the others.

'All right, we're prepared to make a stand,' Jup said. 'But look at the situation we're in; a battle about to start behind us and a determined force of hardened warriors ahead. What the fuck do we do?'

A few other voices were raised, wanting to know the same thing.

'We strengthen our position if we hold off their first attack,' Stryke told them. 'And it's coming any second.'

At the bottom of the hill, Delorran's force was massing for a charge.

'Mount up!' Stryke shouted. He waved his sword at a couple of grunts. 'Help Darig on to Alfray's horse. Alfray, I want you to the back of our defences. Move! All of you!'

The band scrambled for their horses and filled their hands with weapons. Stryke retrieved the star from Alfray and remounted.

Delorran's band was galloping up to them, with perhaps a third of the group holding back as reserves.

Stryke voiced a final thought. 'It goes against the grain to meet our own kind in battle. But remember they believe we're renegades and they'll kill us if they get the chance.'

The time for talk was over. Stryke raised his arm, brought it down hard and yelled, 'Now . . . *charge*!'

The Wolverines turned their horses and swept down to meet the first wave.

They might have been outnumbered, despite the reserve left behind, but they had the advantage of defending higher ground.

Blades clashed, horses milled and shied, blows were delivered and returned. The air was filled with the sound of steel impacting steel as swords met shields.

For Stryke and the others, fighting their own race was a unique and disturbing experience. He hoped it didn't curb their determination. He wasn't sure if it affected Delorran's troop.

But it could have been significant that after five minutes of intense swordplay the attackers began to fall back without major injuries on either side.

As they retreated down the hill, Stryke shouted, 'Their hearts weren't in it! If I know Delorran, he'll be giving them hell for that effort. We can't expect it so easy when they come back.'

Sure enough, they watched as Delorran addressed his band, and it didn't look like a gentle lecture.

'We can't hold them off forever,' Coilla stated grimly.

Jup glanced down at the battlefield behind them. The two sides were slowly advancing towards each other. 'Nor do we have anywhere to run.'

Delorran's group prepared to attack again, this time with the entire force.

Stryke made a decision. It bordered insanity, but he saw no other way.

'Listen to me!' he bellowed at the Wolverines. 'Trust the order I'm going to give, and follow me!

'We're going to charge them again?' Coilla asked.

Delorran's troop was thundering up the rise.

'Trust me!' Stryke repeated. 'Do as I do!'

The enemy was nearer and gathering speed. There was no doubt of their greater resolve. They advanced to a point no more than a short spear throw away.

Stryke's gaze flicked to the battlefield. *'Now!'* he yelled.

Then he turned his horse and spurred it to the top of the rise.

In seconds he had reached the crest and was down the other side.

'Oh no . . .' Jup moaned.

Haskeer was slack-jawed, unable to take in what was happening. He wasn't alone. None of the rest of the band moved.

Delorran was almost on them.

It was Coilla who seized the initiative. 'Come on!' she roared. 'It's our only chance!'

She brought her horse around and followed Stryke.

'Shit!' Haskeer cursed. But he did the same, along with the other Wolverines.

Alfray, with Darig hanging on, even managed to raise their banner.

As they reached the hill's summit, Stryke was already well down the other side.

In the valley below, the two armies were approaching each other with increasing speed. Humans ran with pikes and spears. Cavalry charged.

The gap between them was closing fast. Like bats out of hell, the Wolverines headed for it.

Delorran and his troops arrived at the top of the hill.

The fact that there was a battle going on in the valley below came as a shock to them. Horses were suddenly reined in, and would have been even if Delorran hadn't thrown up a hand to halt them.

They gazed down, astonished, as the charging orcs made straight for the point where the front lines of the two opposing armies were about to meet.

'What do we do, sir?' the sergeant said.

'Unless you've got a better idea,' Delorran replied, 'we watch them commit suicide.'

16

The angle the Wolverines were racing down was so acute they slid as much as rode.

Coilla turned in her saddle and looked back up the hill. She saw the rest of the band close behind. Above, their pursuers had stopped and were watching them. She goaded her horse and drew parallel with Stryke.

'What the hell are we doing?' she bellowed.

'We just go through!' he mouthed over the wind whipping at their faces. 'They won't be expecting it!'

'They're not the only ones!'

The opposite armies were moving closer by the moment.

Stryke pointed downward. 'But we have to keep going! And we don't stop even when we reach the other side!'

'*If* we reach the other side!' she yelled at him.

With a jarring thud they bumped on to the flat, the other Wolverines close behind. Stryke glanced over his shoulder. The band were still together. Alfray, with Darig hanging on grimly, was at the rear, but holding his own.

Now they were on the level the going was faster. The drawback was losing the vantage point they had had on higher ground. From this angle the armies looked a lot closer together, and the increasingly narrow space between them was harder to gauge. Stryke spurred his already lathering horse and called out for the others to keep pace.

Onward, onward, into the valley of death they rode.

They hurtled towards the killing field, the roar of thousands of battle-crazed combatants filling their ears.

Then they were between the advancing lines. Enemies to the left of them, enemies to the right.

A blur of bodies and indistinct faces flashed by. Stryke was dimly aware of heads turning, arms pointing, inaudible shouts aimed in their direction. He prayed that the element of surprise and the confusion of imminent battle would give the Wolverines some kind of edge. And he hoped that the band could benefit from neither army being sure whose side these unexpected intruders were on. Though once they were identified as orcs, he knew the Unis would assume they were here to support the Manis.

They were less than a quarter of the way across the battlefield when arrows and spears began winging their way. Fortunately the two hordes were still far enough apart that the missiles fell harmlessly short. But the soldiers were covering ground at even greater speed. If they flagged for a moment, the Wolverines would be dashed by lethal tides on either side. Here and there, knots of warriors faster on their feet, or mounted on horses with a clear path, were already rushing to block the band's progress.

A group of footsoldiers, armed with pikes and broadswords, ran forward just ahead of Stryke. He rode through them, knocking them aside. Coilla and the band trampled the rest. The orcs were lucky. Had the ground troops been less taken by surprise, and more organised, they could have put a stop to the Wolverines' flight there and then.

Arrows were landing nearer. A spear cut the air between the rump of Stryke's horse and the snout of the one behind.

Individual soldiers dashed in right and left to harry the galloping orcs. They lashed out in their turn, cutting down Unis and Manis indiscriminately.

A black-garbed human ran forward and leapt at Coilla's horse, grabbing its reins. He hung on, pulling down with all his weight. Her horse faltered and wheeled, bunching up the Wolverines behind her. More humans were running from all directions to join the fray.

She plucked free a knife and slashed at the face of the man slowing her. He screamed and fell. The following orcs rode over him. Coilla dug in her heels. The band put on a burst of speed and outpaced the running soldiers.

On the flank of the column and more vulnerable, Haskeer swung his axe, to one side then the other, cracking the skulls of pikemen trying to unseat him. Roaring, he made his getaway.

The Wolverines rode on, the view to either side choked with endless twin seas of charging human warriors.

Stryke knew the band was losing momentum. He feared they'd be overwhelmed at any second.

Seen from atop the hill, the band's progress across the valley resembled a handful of tiny black pearls rolled by a giant. Delorran and his troopers watched as the vice closed in to crush them.

'The *lunatics*,' Delorran exclaimed. 'They'd rather throw their lives away than face my justice.'

'They're finished right enough, sir,' his sergeant agreed.

'We can't linger here and risk being seen. Make ready to leave.'

'What about the artefact, sir?'

'Do *you* want to go and get it?'

The Wolverines' way across the battlefield was about to be blocked. Hundreds of humans, Uni and Mani, were converging ahead of them, from left and right.

'Come!' Delorran barked.

He turned his horse and led his troopers down their side of the hill.

In the valley, Stryke saw humans running forward to obstruct the band's path. He kept going, barrelling into them, lashing out with his sword. A brace of heartbeats later the rest of the Wolverines smacked into the human wall and began carving through it. More chaos ensued as the two sides also started fighting each other.

The scene tipped from confusion into bloody anarchy.

Jup came close to being pulled from his horse by a small mob of Unis with spears. His wild slashing held them off, but he would have been dragged down if a knot of other Wolverines hadn't joined in beating off the attackers. He and they resumed the dash.

Alfray kept pace with the others, but because of his passenger inevitably fell back. They too were targeted for an attack, this time by Manis who had by now abandoned any idea that the orcs were there to aid them. He gave as good an account of himself as he could. But carrying a wounded comrade hampered him, as did bearing the Wolverines' banner, which proved less effective a weapon than a broadsword would have done in the circumstances. And no other Wolverines were near enough to help.

Alfray and Darig were almost out of the mobs' grasp when Darig caught the full force of a spear thrust.

He cried out.

Alfray slashed down at the spear carrier, gouging a chunk out of his shoulder. But as far as Darig was concerned, the damage was done.

He swayed in the saddle, head lolling.

Alfray was too busy fending off other attackers to pay Darig much heed. Then another mounted warrior confronted him and Alfray's horse reared. Darig toppled. As soon as he hit the ground, a mass of humans rushed in. Their swords, axes, spears and knives rose and fell.

Alfray cried out in rage and despair. With a single blow he struck down the cavalryman blocking his way. A quick glance at the mob around Darig confirmed that there was nothing he could do. Spurring on his horse, he escaped another onslaught by the skin of his teeth. He joined the tail end of the Wolverines, fighting their way through the bottleneck at the edge of the battlefield. By now he was convinced they wouldn't make it.

Behind them, the armies met and melded in savage conflict.

The start of the battle full-blown proved a boon. The two sides' preoccupation with killing each other, and preserving their own lives, meant the Wolverines were a lesser priority.

Two more minutes of furious slaughter, stretched to infinity, saw the band off the battlefield. They galloped at high speed across the sward and up the opposite bank.

As they climbed, Coilla looked back. A group of humans, twenty or thirty strong, was riding after them. From their appearance, she took them for Unis.

'We've got company!' she yelled.

Stryke already knew as much. *'Keep going!'* he shouted.

When they got to the top of the valley side they found beyond a sweeping slope leading to grassy flatlands dotted with woods. They kept moving. Their pursuers bobbed over the hill behind them, riding just as swiftly.

The going was softer on this side of the valley. Clods of earth were kicked up by the hooves of hunters and hunted.

A grunt yelled. Everybody looked skyward.

Three dragons were gliding in from the direction of the battlefield.

Stryke had to assume they were after his band. He led the Wolverines in the direction of trees, gambling on cover.

'Heads down!' Jup cried.

A dragon swooped. They felt a blast of heat at their backs. The dragon soared low over their heads and climbed to rejoin its fellows.

The band looked to their rear and saw the pursuing humans had been decimated. Charred corpses of men and horses littered the ground. Some still burned. Several humans, blazing head to foot, tottered and fell. A few hadn't been hit, but they'd had the heart knocked out of them as far as the chase was concerned. Their horses halted, they simply stared at the fallen, or watched dumbly as the orcs slipped from their grasp.

Stryke wondered if the carnage was intentional or not. You never knew with dragons. They were an imprecise weapon at the best of times.

As if in answer, they came in for another attack. The band strained their mounts to reach the fringes of the wood

A great jagged shadow covered them. The dragon's scalding breath flamed a vast swath of grass a couple of yards to their right. They goaded their shying horses harder still.

Another dragon dived, its mighty wings flapping. A down-rush of air battering them, they raced to the wood.

They reached it with stragglers, including Alfray, barely making the shelter in time. The dragon unleashed its scalding breath, igniting the trees overhead with a roar. Burning branches fell, smouldering leaves and sparks showered down.

Maintaining their pace, the Wolverines drove deep into the wood. Through gaps in the curtain above their heads they caught glimpses of their flying antagonists keeping pace.

At length the sightings grew rarer. Eventually the dragons were apparently eluded. The band slowed but kept moving. They stopped when they reached the wood's far limit.

Concealed within the treeline, they spotted the dragons again, passing overhead in a circling reconnaissance. Not daring to break cover, the band dismounted and guards were posted to watch for any humans that might be following. As far as they could tell, none were. They settled, weapons to hand, waiting for a chance to break cover.

Gulping a long draught from his water sack, Haskeer hammered back the stopper and commenced complaining. 'That was one hell of a risk we took back there.'

'What else could we have done?' Coilla said. 'Anyway, it worked, didn't it?'

Haskeer couldn't argue with that and contented himself with some moody scowling.

His temper wasn't shared by most of the others. The grunts in particular were jubilant about getting away with it, and Stryke had to bark at them to keep the racket down.

Alfray was less joyful. His thoughts lay with Darig. 'If I'd just hung on to him, perhaps he'd still be here now.'

'There was nothing you could do,' Stryke told him. 'Don't scourge yourself with what might have been.'

'Stryke's right,' Coilla agreed. 'The wonder is there weren't more lost.'

'Even so,' Stryke murmured, half to himself, 'if anyone's to be blamed for the waste of lives, perhaps it's me.'

'Don't start getting sappy,' Coilla warned him. 'We need you clear-headed, not wallowing in guilt.'

Stryke took the point and dropped the subject. He reached into his pocket and brought out the star.

'That odd-looking thing's caused us so much trouble,' Alfray said. 'It's turned our lives upside down. I hope it's worth it, Stryke.'

'It could be our furlough from serfdom.'

'Perhaps. Perhaps not. I think you've been looking for any excuse to break away for some time.'

'In truth, haven't we all?'

'That could be so. But I'm more wary of change at my age.'

'This is a time of change. Everything's changing. Why not us?'

'Huh, change,' Haskeer sneered. 'There's too much . . . talk of . . .' He appeared breathless and swayed unsteadily. Then he went down like a felled ox.

'What the *hell*?' Coilla exclaimed.

They gathered around him.

'What's the matter?' Stryke asked. 'Has he taken a wound?'

After a quick examination, Alfray replied, 'No, he hasn't.' He laid a hand on Haskeer's forehead, then checked his pulse.

'So what's wrong with him?'

'He's got a fever. Know what I think, Stryke? I reckon he's got the same thing Meklun had.'

Several of the grunts backed away.

'He's been hiding this, the fool,' Alfray added.

'He's not been himself for the last couple of days, has he?' Coilla remarked.

'No. All the signs were there. And here's another thought, and it's not a pleasant one.'

'Go on,' Stryke urged.

'I was suspicious of what it was that killed Meklun,' Alfray admitted. 'Because although his wounds were bad, he could have recovered. I think he picked up something at that encampment we torched.'

'He didn't go near the place,' Jup reminded him. 'He *couldn't.*'

'No. But Haskeer did.'

'Gods,' Stryke whispered. 'He said he didn't touch any of the bodies. He must have lied.'

Coilla said, 'If Haskeer got the disease there, and passed it on to Meklun, couldn't he have given it to the rest of us too?'

There was a murmur of unease from the band.

'Not necessarily,' Alfray told her. 'Meklun was already weakened by his wounds, and open to the infection. As for the rest of us, if we were infected, you'd expect to see the signs by now. Does anybody feel unwell?'

The band chorused no or shook their heads.

'From what little we know about these human diseases,' Alfray went on, 'the greatest risk of infection seems to be in the first forty-eight hours or so.'

'Let's hope you're right,' Stryke said. He looked down at Haskeer. 'Think he'll pull through?'

'He's young and strong. That helps.'

'What can we do for him?'

'Not much beyond trying to keep his fever down and waiting for it to break.'

'Another problem,' Coilla sighed.

'Yes,' Stryke agreed, 'and we don't need it.'

'It's a good thing for him we don't follow his own suggestion about what to do with the wounded. Remember his idea about Meklun?'

'Yeah. Ironic, isn't it?'

'What now, chief?' Jup wondered.

'We stick to the plan.' He indicated the dragons circling above. 'As soon as they've gone, assuming they *do* go, we push on to Trinity.'

It was several hours before the coast was clear.

The dragons, having flown over the wood numerous times, finally headed north and disappeared. Stryke ordered Haskeer to be put over a horse and tied in place. A grunt was assigned to lead it. Cautiously, the band set out in the direction of Trinity. Stryke estimated the journey would take about a day and a half, assuming no obstacles.

With Weaver's Lea behind them, they were free to take a more or less direct route. But now that they were in the south, that part of Maras-Dantia where humans had established themselves in greatest numbers, they had to be even more cautious. Wherever possible they sought the shelter of timberland, blind valleys and other naturally protective areas. Though the further south they travelled, the more evidence they saw of human habitation, and of despoliation.

On the morning of the second day, they came to what had been a small forest, now almost completely felled. Much of the wood had been removed, but large amounts had simply been left to rot. The severed stumps were overgrown with mosses or brown with fungi. Which meant the felling was at least several months old.

They marvelled at the destruction, and the amount of effort needed to achieve it. And they grew more wary, knowing that such devastation required many hands to accomplish.

Several hours later they discovered the use the wood had been put to.

They reached a river, its course running south-west toward the Carascrag mountain range. As rivers were the most reliable navigational aids, they followed it. Soon they noticed that the water flowed deep and was turning sluggish.

Rounding a bend, they found out why.

The river became an enormous, shimmering lake, covering many acres of previously open country. It had been created by a massive wooden dam, constructed they felt sure with trunks taken from the denuded forest. The dam both appalled and impressed them. Standing higher than the tallest pine, it consisted of a barrier six trunks in depth, running a distance a good archer would be sore put to match with an arrow's flight. The timbers had been fitted with a high standard of precision, then lashed with what must have been miles of cable-thick twine. Mortar sealed the joins. On either bank, and emerging from several places in the river itself, were vast angled props, adding to the dam's stability.

Despite the great structure, scouting parties found no sign that humans were present. There having been no let-up in their journey since the previous day, Stryke ordered a halt and posted lookouts.

Once Alfray attended Haskeer's fever, which had grown worse, he joined the other officers to discuss their next move.

'This capturing of the water means we must be near Trinity,' Stryke reasoned. 'They'd need that much to serve a large population.'

'It represents power, too,' Alfray suggested. 'The power that controlling the water supply brings.'

'Not to mention the power it represents in terms of the number of hands needed to build such a thing,' Stryke said. 'The humans of Trinity must be highly organised as well as numerous.'

'Yet they ignore the *magical* power they damaged by perverting the river's course,' Jup told them. 'Even I can sense the negative energy here.'

'And *I* sense a major problem,' Coilla said, bringing the conversation to more immediate matters. 'Trinity's a fanatical Uni stronghold. Word is they aren't exactly crazy about elder races there. How the hell are we going to get in to try for the star? Or are you planning a suicide mission, Stryke?'

'I don't know what we're going to do. But we'll follow basic military strategy; get as near as we can, try to find ourselves a hiding place and assess the situation. There has to be a way, we just don't know what it is yet.'

'What if there isn't?' Alfray asked. 'What if we can't get near the place?'

'Then we'll have to rethink everything. Maybe we'll negotiate with Jennesta for the one star we have, in exchange for some kind of amnesty.'

'Oh yes, of course,' Coilla remarked cynically.

'Or it could be that this is the beginning of a new life for us, as outlaws. Which, let's face it, is what we are anyway.'

Jup looked troubled. 'That doesn't sound an appetising prospect, chief.'

'Then we'll have to do our best to avoid it, won't we? Now get some rest, all of you. I want us back on the road to Trinity in no more than an hour.'

17

They spotted Trinity in late afternoon.

Hidden by the cover of vegetation, eyes peeled for patrols, the Wolverines took in the distant settlement. The town was an enclave, completely surrounded by a high timber wall, with lookout towers.

The Carascrag Mountains loomed above and beyond it, steely blue with saw-jagged peaks. Shimmering air played over the mountains, heated by thermals rising from the Kirgizil desert on the far side of the range.

A well-used road led to a pair of huge gates that served as Trinity's main entrance. They were closed. The township was surrounded by fields of crops so extensive they almost reached the band's hiding place. But the yield looked frail and stunted.

'Now we know what they need all that water for,' Coilla said.

'For all the good it does them,' Jup replied. 'Look at how mean the crops are. These humans are stupid. They can't see that messing with the earth magic affects them as well as us.'

'How in damnation are we going to approach the place, Stryke?' Alfray wanted to know. 'Let alone get in?'

'We might have one piece of luck on our side. We haven't

seen any humans yet. Most of them were probably drawn to the battle at Weaver's Lea.'

'But they wouldn't have left the settlement undefended, would they?' Coilla reminded him. 'And if most of the population *is* there, they'll be back at some point.'

'I meant it might help, not that it solved our problem.'

'So what to do?' Jup wondered.

'We scout for somewhere to hide and made a base camp. Coilla, take three grunts and work your way on foot around the township left to right. Jup, pick your three and do the same the other way. Note anything that'll do as a hiding place, and remember it has to be suitable for the horses as well as us. Got that?'

They nodded and moved off to obey their orders.

Stryke looked to Alfray. 'How's Haskeer?'

'About the same.'

'Trust the bastard to make a nuisance of himself even when he's unconscious. Do what you can for him.' He turned to the remainder of the band. 'The rest of you keep yourselves alert and combat-ready.'

They settled down to watch and wait.

'I'm not sure about this,' Jup whispered.

Concealed by bushes, they stared over at the yawning tunnel mouth cut into the bluff.

'What worries me is that there's only the one entrance,' Alfray said, 'and I don't know how spooked the horses might be in there.'

'It's all we could come up with,' Coilla repeated, a little exasperated.

'Coilla's right,' Stryke decided. 'We'll have to make the best of it. Are you *sure* it's disused?'

She nodded. 'A couple of the grunts went quite a way in. It's been abandoned.'

'We'd be rats in a trap if the humans knew we were hiding there,' Jup opined.

'That's a risk we'll have to take,' Stryke told him. He checked that the way was clear. 'Right, get in there fast. Horses first.'

The band swept over to the mine-shaft entrance. Not all the horses went into the black maw willingly and had to be forced the last few yards.

Inside it was dank and much cooler than the open air.

The daylight let them see dimly perhaps thirty paces along the tunnel, at which point it became lower and narrower. After that, all was pitch darkness.

'We stay away from the mouth,' Stryke decreed, 'and I want no lights used unless absolutely necessary.'

Coilla shivered. 'I won't be going far enough in to need one. Give me open skies any time.'

Jup touched the rough-hewn wall. 'What do you think they dug this for?'

Bent over applying a damp cloth to Haskeer's forehead, Alfray ventured, 'Gold, probably. Or some other of the earth's booty they think precious.'

'I've seen this kind of thing before,' Jup said, tapping some stones with the tip of his boot. 'I reckon they were going for the black rocks they burn as fuel. Wonder how long it took them to exhaust the seam?'

'Not very, knowing humans,' Coilla suggested. 'And I think you're right, Jup. I'd heard that Trinity was founded here because there's so much of the black rock to be dug in these parts.'

'Again the land is raped,' Jup muttered. 'We should have breached that dam and given them something to think about.'

'We would have had a job doing it,' Stryke told him. 'An army would be hard put to bring it down. But that's not our concern at the moment. What we need to do is find Trinity's weak point.'

'If it has one.'

'We won't find out sitting here, Jup.'

'So what's your plan?' Coilla asked.

'One thing we need to avoid is having too big a group of us out there, particularly in daylight. So I want to take a look around myself, along with you and Jup.'

Coilla nodded. 'Suits me fine. I'm not keen on living like a troglodyte.'

'The rest will stay here, out of sight,' Stryke ordered. 'Post a couple of guards, Alfray, and one or two more out there in the undergrowth, to warn of anyone approaching. And try to keep those horses quiet. Come on, you two.'

Coilla and Jup followed him from the shaft.

They darted for the first available cover and headed in the direction of the township. Moving cautiously for perhaps half a mile, keeping low, they were going through one of the cultivated fields when Coilla grabbed Stryke's arm. *'Down!'* she hissed, tugging him groundward.

The trio burrowed into the corn. Twenty yards away stood the first humans they'd seen at Trinity. A small group of women, dressed simply and mostly in black, were working in an adjacent field. They were picking a crop of some kind, loading the harvest into baskets borne by mules. Two armed men, bearded and also black-garbed, stood guard as the women worked.

A finger to his lips, Stryke motioned Coilla and Jup to follow him. Their route took them quietly around the toilers. Several more detours then proved necessary to avoid other heads they spotted bobbing above the crops.

Crawling on their hands and knees, they came unexpectedly to a track of compacted earth with a shingle surface. Peeping out from the shelter of the corn, they realised it was the road leading to Trinity's gates. As there were no humans in sight in the fields opposite, they prepared to cross. Coilla was about to lead off when they heard the rumble of approaching wagons. They ducked back and watched.

A procession of vehicles came into view. The first was an open carriage, drawn by a pair of fine white mares. In the front sat the driver and another human, both heavily armed, both dressed in black. There were two other people in the back. Again, both wore black. One was obviously another guard, this time armed with a bow. But the man sitting next to him, on a higher seat, was the most arresting.

He was the only one wearing a hat, a tall, black piece of headgear that Stryke thought was called a stovepipe. Even seated it was obvious that the man was tall, and his build was thin and wiry. He had a weathered face ending in a pointed chin adorned with greying whiskers. The mouth was a thin, featureless slit, the eyes dark and intense. It was a forceful face, unaccustomed to smiling.

The carriage passed.

It was followed by three wagons drawn by teams of oxen. Each wagon was steered by a black-garbed human, with an accompanying guard. The wagons carried passengers, so crammed there was standing room only. All were dwarves.

Stryke noticed Jup's preoccupied reaction to this as the wagons trundled on toward the township's gates.

Jup let out a breath. 'Imagine what Haskeer would have made of *that*.'

'They weren't prisoners, were they?' Coilla said.

Stryke shook his head. 'I'd say they were working parties. What interests me more was that human in the back of the carriage.'

'Hobrow?'

'He certainly had the bearing of a leader, Coilla.'

'And dead-fish eyes,' Jup added.

They watched the convoy's procession to the gates. Guards appeared at the top of the township's wall. The gates swung slowly open, affording a brief glimpse of the scene within as the carriage and wagons entered. Then the gates were pushed shut again. They heard the sound of a weighty crossbar being dropped into place.

'That's it, isn't it?' Jup announced. 'Our way in.'

Stryke missed his point. 'What do you mean?'

'Do I have to spell it out? They're using dwarves in there. I'm a dwarf.'

'That's a risky plan, Jup,' Coilla responded.

'Can you think of a better one?'

'Even if we could get you in,' Stryke said, 'what would you expect to achieve?'

'I'd gather information. Check the layout and defences. Maybe even get some idea where they keep the star.'

'Assuming Mobbs was right about them having one,' Coilla reminded him.

'We'll never find out unless we get somebody in there.'

'We don't know what kind of security they have,' Stryke pointed out. 'Suppose all the dwarf workers are known to them?'

'Or known to each other,' Coilla put in. 'How would they react to a stranger in their ranks?'

'I didn't say it wouldn't be dangerous,' Jup stated. 'But I think it's fair to assume that the humans are unlikely to know the dwarves by name. Everything I've heard about this place, and everything we know about humans, tells me they've nothing but contempt for the elder races. I can't see them bothering to learn names.'

Coilla frowned. 'That's a big assumption.'

'It's a chance to be taken. The other thing, about the dwarves themselves noticing a stranger, might not be such a problem. You see, those dwarves were from at least four different tribes.'

'How do you know?' Stryke wondered.

'The way they dress, mostly. Neckerchiefs of certain colours, a particular cut of jerkin, and so on. They all indicate a tribal origin.'

'What are the signs you wear to indicate your tribe?' Coilla said.

'I don't. You have to get rid of them when you go into Jennesta's service. That's so there's no problem identifying our allegiance. But I can easily put that right.'

Stryke was still doubtful. 'It's an awful lot of ifs and maybes, Jup.'

'Sure, and I haven't mentioned the toughest problem yet. They must have *some* kind of security here as far as workers coming and going is concerned. Probably a simple head-count.'

'Which means we couldn't just mix you in with the other dwarves. Assuming we could find a way of doing it.'

'Right. I'd have to be *swapped* for one of them.'

Coilla gave him a quizzical look. 'How the hell are we going to do that?'

'Offhand, I don't know. But if we can, there are a couple of things in our favour. First, I don't think a new face would arouse too much suspicion as far as the other dwarves are concerned, because they're being drawn from different tribes. Second, the humans can't tell us apart anyway. They usually can't when it comes to elder races, you know that.'

'And?' Coilla prompted.

'The humans wouldn't be expecting a hostile dwarf to want to get in there.'

Stryke shook his head slowly. 'Don't take this the wrong way, Jup, but your race does have a reputation for . . . blowing with the wind, let's say. Humans know that dwarves fight for all sides.'

'No offence taken, Stryke. You know I've long stopped

apologising for the ways of my kind. But let's say they wouldn't expect a *lone* dwarf to be insane enough to infiltrate the place. And remember that in some ways humans are like elder races in seeing what they expect to see. They're using dwarves. I'm a dwarf. Hopefully they wouldn't think much further than that.'

'Hopefully,' Coilla echoed in a slightly mocking tone. 'Humans are bastards but that doesn't make them half-wits, you know.'

'I'm aware of that.'

'So what are you going to do about your rank markings?' She pointed at the tattoos on his face.

'Garva root. You grind it up with water and add just a little clay for colouring. That'll cover 'em, and it's good enough to match my skin.'

'Unless anybody takes a *close* look,' Stryke said. 'You'd be taking a hell of a lot of chances.'

'I know. But will you agree to the plan in principle?'

Stryke pondered it for a moment. 'I can't see another way of doing it. So . . . yes.'

Jup smiled.

Combat instinct had the three of them craning to check their surroundings. There were no humans in sight.

Coilla sounded a note of caution. 'Don't get too excited. We still have to work out the practicalities. Like how we'll swap you for one of the workers.'

'Any ideas?' Stryke asked.

'Well, assuming the dwarves are brought in and out every day, and that's a big if in itself, maybe we could ambush one of those wagons. Then we'd take out a passenger and Jup could mingle with the workers in the confusion.'

'No. Too much to go wrong, and it'd alert the humans to some kind of trickery.'

'You're right,' she conceded, 'it wouldn't work. What about you, Jup?'

'All I can think of would be to go to the source of the dwarf workers. I mean, they have to come from somewhere, and I'd bet it isn't too far away. It wouldn't make sense bringing them great distances. Somewhere around here there must be a village or pick-up point.'

'That makes sense,' Stryke agreed. 'So to find it, we'd just have to trail those wagons the next time they leave.'

'Exactly. We'd have to do it on foot, of course, but those wagons move pretty slow.'

'Then let's hope you're right about the pick-up point being near.' He turned the notion over in his mind for a second. 'We'll do it. Coilla, get back to the others and tell them what's happening. Then come back here with a couple of grunts and we'll wait for the wagons to come out.'

'You do realise this is insane, don't you?' she said.

'Insanity's something we're getting quite good at. Now go.'

She smiled thinly and snaked into the field.

The wagons carrying the dwarves left Trinity at dusk. There was no sign of the carriage this time.

Stryke, Coilla, Jup and two troopers waited for the carts to pass and get a head start, then followed, keeping low and under cover. When the fields of crops petered away they had to be more inventive in staying out of sight, but they had enough experience to manage that. Fortunately the trio of laden wagons moved ponderously enough to make trailing them no problem.

Eventually the wagons left the path and struck out across open countryside. The orcs tracked the little convoy for about two miles in the direction of the Calyparr Inlet. Just as Stryke was beginning to worry that they'd be led all the way to the inlet itself, the wagons turned into a glade and halted.

The orcs watched as the wagon tailgates were lowered and

the dwarves dismounted. They began leaving, in groups and singly, in different directions.

'So it's a meeting point, not a village,' Stryke said.

'They must be drawing labour from the whole area,' Jup suggested. 'That's better for us. One of them is much less likely to be missed in this situation.'

Circling round, the wagons started their journey back to Trinity. The orcs kept their heads down as the transports passed, moving faster now they'd rid themselves of their load. Several dwarves, too, passed nearby without seeing them.

'So far, so good,' Stryke judged. 'Now we wait until morning and hope there's another pick-up.'

He allotted turns as lookouts and they settled down to their vigil.

The night passed uneventfully.

Shortly after daybreak, dwarves began drifting in to the meeting place. Jup tied a rusty-red bandanna around his neck, the emblem of an obscure and distant tribe. Then he smeared the garva root paste over his cheeks, covering the tattoos. Stryke had feared that it wouldn't look convincing, but it worked remarkably well.

'What we need now is a worker on his own,' he said, 'and we need him at a distance from the glade.'

They all looked out for a likely candidate. One of the grunts nudged Stryke and pointed. A lone dwarf was wading through long grass over to their right.

Jup began to move. 'I'll do it.'

Stryke laid a hand on his arm. 'But—'

'It has to be me, Stryke. You can see that, can't you?'

'All right. Take Coilla with you, to cover your back.'

They set off, creeping low through the cover.

The others watched the dwarf they'd targeted moving towards the glade. At the same time they kept an eye on the other workers converging on the pick-up.

Suddenly the lone dwarf went down and there was a brief rustling in the grass. A moment later Jup popped up in his victim's stead and began walking in the direction of the waiting wagons.

The orcs watched intently, ready to break cover and rush to his aid if anything went wrong. Jup moved with a relaxed, unhurried stride.

'He's doing a good job of looking casual, I'll give him that,' Stryke commented.

There was a movement in the grass nearby and Coilla reappeared. 'Is he there yet?'

'Nearly,' Stryke reported.

Jup reached the glade, which now had several dozen other dwarves milling around in it. It was a moment of tenseness; the first test of many. But neither the dwarves nor the wagon drivers paid him any particular attention. A few minutes later they began to mount the wagons. Having stood apart from the others, Jup now had to come into close contact with them. This was when his disguise proved either passable or worthless.

The orcs looked on with bated breath.

Mingling with the crowd, Jup climbed aboard a wagon. There was no uproar, no hue and cry. The wagons' tailgates were secured. Whips cracked over the oxen and the convoy moved off.

Keeping very still, the orcs watched the convoy pass. A moment later, the coast clear, they followed. There was no deviation in the route back to Trinity.

But as the wagons rolled on to the road leading to the township's gates, the orcs saw more humans working in the fields than there had been yesterday. Again, they were mostly women, and there were a larger number of guards protecting them.

The Wolverines had to be even more careful to avoid being seen, and there was a limit to how near the wall they could get.

But they found a vantage point, crouching in a field of wheat, from where they could follow the wagons' progression.

As before, guards appeared on the walls above and scanned the arrivals. A moment later the vast gates began creaking open. Again, there was a tantalising glimpse of the interior. The wagons moved forward and entered. Black-clad men rushed to shut the gates.

They closed with a booming crash.

Stryke hoped it didn't mark a death knell for Jup.

18

The great gates slammed behind Jup with a terrible finality.

Without obviously appearing to do so, he looked around. The first thing he saw was several dozen guards, dressed uniformly in black and all bearing arms.

What he could make out of Trinity was formal to the point of severity. The place seemed to be arranged in a way that would have satisfied the most pedantic military commander. All the buildings were neatly positioned in rows. Some were cottages, made of stone with thatched roofs, of a size to house a family. Others were larger, barracks-like buildings, fashioned from timber. Without exception they were pristine in appearance. Further on, towers and spires of equal correctness poked above the rooftops. Arrow-straight roads and lanes cut through the concise landscape. Even the trees, of which there were a few, had been marshalled into regimented lines.

There were humans, men, women and children, going about their business in the stifling orderliness. Like the guards, the men were dressed in uncompromised black. Those of the women and children who weren't wore clothes of bland plainness.

No sooner had he taken in the scene than Jup and his fellow

dwarves, none of whom had spoken to him, or to each other in most cases, were herded off the wagons.

It was another moment of truth. Now he'd find out if the humans kept a list of their guest workers' names. If they did, what followed was likely to be unpleasant, and almost certainly terminal.

As seemed fitting in a place obsessed by symmetry, the dwarves were mustered into tidy columns beside the wagons that had brought them. Then to Jup's relief men went along the lines, finger-jabbing each dwarf in turn as they counted them. The human on Jup's line moved his lips in the process, but passed him by without a second look.

Jup was wondering what happened next when there was a flurry of activity at the door of one of the buildings that resembled a barracks. The man he, Stryke and Coilla had seen the day before in his carriage, and whom they assumed to be Kimball Hobrow, appeared at the entrance.

His eyes were just as chill, his expression no less unsmiling. Jup wondered, as he had the previous day, how old the man might be. This closer look was hardly more telling than his first fleeting glimpse, but Jup reckoned him to be about middle-aged in human terms, though he always found it hard to tell when it came to that race. It was rumoured there was some kind of formula for working it out, similar to the one used for dogs and cats, but he was damned if he could remember it.

One thing of which there was no doubt, however, was Kimball's charismatic presence. He radiated an aura of authority, of power, and not a little menace.

The settlers fell silent and parted to let him through. He made his way to a wagon and climbed on to the seat. It added to his already commanding height, making him an even more imposing figure. He scrutinised the dwarves. Despite himself, Jup shrank a little under that penetrating gaze.

Hobrow raised his hands in a gesture that called for quiet,

though as there had barely been a sound since he appeared, this was hardly necessary.

'I am Kimball Hobrow!' he boomed. It came across as a profound statement rather than mere information. His voice was bass and silken, belying the slender frame it came from.

'Some of you are new here,' Hobrow continued.

Jup was glad to hear that. It made his position a bit more tenable.

'Those of you who have been here before will have heard what I'm about to say,' Hobrow went on, 'but it bears repeating. You'll do as you're told and remember at all times that you're guests, allowed here so my people can devote themselves to more important tasks.'

We're going to be shovelling shit for them, Jup thought. What a surprise.

Hobrow scanned his audience with those beguiling eyes, in a pause obviously intended to hammer home his point.

'There are certain things we permit here and certain things we don't,' he said. 'We allow you to work hard at the labours for which you're being well rewarded. We allow you to show deference to your betters. We allow you to express respect for our belief in the one true Supreme Creator.'

So much for the stick, Jup reflected. What about the carrot?

'We don't allow laziness, insolence, insubordination, lax morals or profane language.'

Gods, Jup realised, that *was* the carrot.

'We don't tolerate alcohol, pellucid or any other intoxicant. You'll not speak to any citizen without first being spoken to, and you'll obey without question any order given to you by a custodian or a citizen. You will at all times abide by the laws of this place, which are the laws of our Lord. Transgress and you'll be punished. Like the Supreme Being, what I've given I can take away.'

He ran his steely eyes over them again. Jup noticed that few if any of his fellow dwarves met that disturbing gaze. He tried to avoid it himself, if only so he wouldn't attract attention.

Hobrow plucked off his hat, revealing a shock of ebony hair touched with silvery grey. 'We'll now offer up a prayer for our endeavours,' he announced.

Jup looked to the others. Such dwarves as had hats were doffing them too. Following their example, and Hobrow's, he bowed his head, feeling foolish and conspicuous. Why this was necessary, he didn't know. He didn't go through such a performance when he needed to speak to his gods. Whether they listened surely had nothing to do with whether you wore a hat or not.

'Oh Lord who created all things,' Hobrow began, 'we humbly beseech You to heed our prayer. Bless the labours of these lowly creatures, oh Lord, and help us raise them from their ignorance and savagery. Bless too the efforts of we Your chosen, that we might best serve and honour You. Strengthen our arm in pursuit of our mission as instruments of Your wrath, oh Lord. Let us be Your sword and You our shield against the unrighteous and the blasphemers. Keep pure our race and smite without mercy our enemies and Yours. Make us truly thankful for the infinite bounty You bestow upon us, Lord.'

Without another word, Hobrow replaced his hat, climbed down from the wagon and headed back for the building he had come from. A knot of followers walked respectfully in his wake.

'Bit keen, isn't he?' Jup remarked to the dwarf next in line.

This unsmiling individual ignored the comment. He did look Jup up and down, but without too much curiosity.

I'm going to love it here, Jup thought.

A guard, or custodian as Jup supposed he had to call him, took Hobrow's place on the wagon's seat. Several of his fellows hovered in the background.

'You new ones, stay here to be given your duties,' the man said. 'Those of you who know your duties, go to your places of work.'

Most of the dwarves streamed off in different directions.

'Be back here at dusk for your transport away!' he shouted after them.

Jup and four others were left. Now that he was no longer part of a crowd he felt more vulnerable. The other four moved in nearer to the custodian. Not wanting to stand out, he did the same.

'You heard the master's words,' the custodian told them. 'Make sure you heed them. We have ways of punishing those who don't,' he added menacingly. He consulted a sheet of parchment. 'We need three more on the rebuilding in Central Square. You, you and you.' He pointed to a trio of dwarves. 'Follow him.'

One of the other custodians beckoned and they went off with him.

The man went on to the next item on his list. 'One needed to help dig the new cesspit on the south side.'

Jup decided it would be just his luck to pull that job.

'You.'

The custodian indicated the other remaining dwarf. He didn't look like a beam of sunshine as a guard took him off.

As the last one left, Jup began to feel uncomfortable. It crossed his mind that they *had* realised his true intentions, and that this was a trap, designed to get him alone. The custodian stared at him.

'You look strong,' he said.

'Er, yes, I suppose I am.'

'You'll call me *sir*,' the custodian informed his cuttingly. 'All humans are sir to your kind.'

'Yes . . . sir,' Jup corrected, doing his best to suppress the resentment he felt at having to kow-tow to an incomer.

The custodian consulted his parchment again. 'Another pair of hands are wanted at the arboretum kilns.'

'The what?' Jup quickly added, 'Sir.'

'The hothouse. We're growing plants there that need warmth. Your job's helping to feed the fires that heat—' He dismissed him with a careless wave. 'It'll all be explained.'

Jup followed the custodian he'd been assigned to. The man was silent, and the dwarf didn't try to start a conversation.

What Jup had hoped for was a job that gave him enough freedom to slip off and spy out this place. He didn't know if that was what he'd got. But judging by the way they took security so seriously here, he doubted it. There might not be anything to show for this day other than callused hands. And maybe a lost head.

With Jup a couple of paces to the human's rear, they walked along one of the precise avenues, passing buildings in all major respects identical. At the road's end they turned right into another, which exactly resembled the one they'd just left. Jup was finding all the uniformity a bit disturbing.

They turned again. This time, the walkway was distinguished by something different: the largest building Jup had seen in Trinity so far. It stood a good four or five times higher than the surrounding houses, and was built of granite slabs.

What distinguished it apart from its size was a great oval above the double oak doors. The oval, a window, was equivalent in size to two or three humans laid head to foot. More remarkable, it was filled with glass. Jup had only ever seen glass once before, at Jennesta's palace, and knew it to be a rare and expensive material whose creation was difficult. This glass was blue-tinted, and bore at its centre a representation, uncoloured, of the Uni X motif. He assumed it was a place of worship. His escort was watching him looking at it, so he dropped his gaze and pretended indifference.

Jup pondered the fact that what he had to do must be done

within the day. Because although the body of the dwarf he'd replaced would be well hidden by the band, there was a distinct risk of him being reported missing and questions asked.

They passed the temple, turned again and came to another large and extraordinary structure. It was smaller than the temple, but much more eccentric in appearance. The outer walls, of brick-sized stone slabs, were no taller than Jup. Or at least their brick part was no taller. Above the low walls extended a curtain of plain glass, in wood-frame squares, that met a flat roof. The building was box-shaped, at least two-thirds fashioned from glass, and the glass was misty with condensation. All Jup could make out through it was a jumble of jagged shapes and a faint hint of greenness.

Tacked to one end of the building was an extension of stone and wood, containing no glass at all. It was this that the custodian made for.

When they entered, a blast of heat hit them.

Jup registered the fact that there was no wall between this structure and the house of glass, what they called the arboretum presumably, that abutted it. A humid atmosphere pervaded the whole interior. The hothouse was stocked with plants large and small. They stood in containers on the floor and were stacked on shelves. Some were in flower, many weren't. There were tall, slender-stalked varieties, short bushy ones and others that looked like climbers. He didn't recognise any of them.

In the building Jup had entered, which was whitewashed, there were three large kilns, like oversized open grates, set against the far wall. All had fires roaring in them. Heaps of wooden logs and a copious pile of the black fuel stones were being used to feed the flames. Jup could see how at least some of the fruits of the mining and tree-felling were being used.

Across the top of the grates ran a wide clay gully, from which steam rose. The gully, an open pipe, entered the building through a hole in the wall. It channelled water that the grates heated and passed into enclosed pipes which snaked around the hothouse.

It was a clever arrangement. Jup admired its ingenuity, but had no idea why it should be necessary.

There were two dwarves in the room, one shovelling the black rocks into the grates, the other tossing in logs. They were sweating and grimy. A human was present too, sitting in a chair near the door, as far from the heat of the kilns as possible. When Jup and his human came in, he stood up.

'Sterling,' he greeted Jup's custodian.

'Istuan,' the custodian returned. 'New one for you,' he added, jabbing a thumb at Jup but not bothering to look at him.

Istuan didn't take much of a look either. 'About time,' he grumbled. 'We're finding it hard keeping up the temperature with only two.'

Jup liked the 'we.'

Sterling bade his farewells and left.

'There are water tanks out the back,' Istuan explained without preamble. 'They feed the channel above the kilns in here.' He pointed. 'The water has to be kept hot at all times so the plants are happy.'

He ran through the set-up mechanistically, as though addressing a stupid pet.

'What kind of plants are they, sir?' Jup asked.

Istuan looked startled that the pet could talk. That expression was quickly overtaken by suspicion. 'None of your concern. All you need to know is that the temperature can't be allowed to drop. If it does, you get a whipping.'

'Yes, sir,' Jup responded, acting suitably cowed.

'Your job's to keep the fuel stockpiles up, check the water levels in the tanks and to take over banking these kilns when the others need relieving. Understand?'

Jup nodded.

'Now take a spade and start bringing in some fuel from out

there,' the custodian ordered, indicating a door in the side wall.

The door led outside to an enclosed yard. There were small mountains of wood and burning-stones, and a pair of round wooden tanks, similar to very large barrels, mounted on legs, that supplied the water. He set to replenishing the fuel supply.

It was back-breaking work, and as neither his fellow dwarves or the custodian went in for much in the way of conversation, Jup undertook it in silence.

About an hour into the job, the custodian stood up and stretched. 'I've got a report to make,' he informed them. 'Don't slack, and keep those fires steeped.'

Once he'd gone, Jup tried getting the other dwarves to talk.

'Strange plants,' he said.

One shrugged indifferently. The other didn't even bother doing that. Neither spoke.

'Never seen anything quite like them,' Jup persisted. 'They're obviously not vegetables.'

'They're herbs or something,' one of them finally revealed. 'For medicines . . .'

'Is that so?' He approached the plants for a closer look.

'You can't go in there,' the other dwarf piped up sharply. 'It's forbidden.'

Jup spread his hands out submissively. 'All right. Just curious.'

'Don't be. Just do the work and earn your coin.'

Jup returned to his chores and no further words were exchanged until the custodian came back. He sent Jup to check the water levels in the tanks with a measuring stick.

As it happened, they were low enough to need refilling, which proved a stroke of luck. It meant the custodian and the dwarves had to go for fresh supplies. Warning Jup to keep the fires banked, the man and the dwarves set off in a wagon.

As soon as they had left, Jup investigated the plants. He still couldn't identify any, which wasn't surprising as it was a subject he had little interest in, but decided it might be useful to take some samples to show the band. Selecting three plants at random, he carefully stripped off some leaves. It occurred to him that anybody leaving Trinity could well be searched, so he took off one of his boots and lined it with the leaves.

Knowing this could be his only chance, he made up his mind to take a bigger risk. He fed a plentiful supply of fuel into the kilns, hoping it would keep them going for the amount of time he thought he needed. Then he went to the door, opened it carefully and peered into the street. There was no one around. He slipped out.

When he was being escorted in he'd seen other dwarves on the streets, presumably carrying messages or running errands. So he walked with purpose, hoping any humans he encountered would think he was acting under orders.

He'd already made up his mind where to go, though it was a long shot. His reasoning was that if the instrumentality had been included in the Unis' religious practices, the logical place to keep it was the temple. He headed that way.

Jup didn't need to be told that dwarves wouldn't be welcome in such a human holy place. Nor that the penalty for being caught there would be dire. But he saw no point in taking the risk of getting into Trinity if he didn't try to do the job he had come for.

As before, the doors of the temple were closed. There could be humans in there. The place could be filled with them for all he knew.

He took a deep breath, strode to the entrance and turned the handle. The door opened. He looked in. The place was empty. Quickly, he slipped inside.

The interior of the temple was simple to the point of plainness, but its austerity had a kind of elegance. Its effect derived from the use of a number of different kinds of wood, rather than more obvious adornments. Rows of benches faced an elementary altar. The ceiling was high and vaulted.

Most striking was the blue oval window over the doors, which now that he was inside Jup could see had a twin above the altar. This second window was tinted ruby and also had the Uni emblem set at its heart. The light from outside struck the design, throwing an elongated X across the polished pine floor.

He crept along the aisle to the altar. This too was basic; a modest white cloth covering, a metal Uni symbol, a pair of wooden candlesticks, a silver goblet. And a cube of the precious clear glass.

It held the star.

Jup had assumed that if they ever found another instrumentality it would be identical to the one they already held. This turned out to be only partly true. The object he gazed at was of the same size and spiky appearance. But whereas the other was sandy-coloured, this was green, and the arms extending from the central core numbered five, not seven, and were differently arranged.

He hesitated. His instinct was to smash the glass and take the star, in the hope that he could smuggle it out of the township. His good sense told him this was a bad, quite possibly suicidal, idea.

His decision was postponed when he heard voices outside. More than one human was approaching the doors. Jup had seen no other exit. Near panic, he looked for a hiding place. There was nowhere except the back of the altar. He all but fell behind it as the doors opened.

Stretched full-length on the floor, he dared to peek around the side.

Kimball Hobrow entered, removing his hat as he strode in. Two equally grave-looking humans followed him. They walked up the aisle, and for a moment Jup thought they knew he was there and were coming for him. He bunched his fists, determined to make a fight of it.

But they stopped short of the altar and sat themselves on the first row of benches. Jup's next thought was that they were going to perform an act of worship. He was wrong about that too.

'How does the matter of the water progress, Thaddeus?' Hobrow asked one of the duo.

'All done. We could begin drawing from our own protected supplies today, if necessary.'

'And the essences? They'll take to the waters without betraying themselves?'

'Once introduced they're not obvious. Until they have their effect, of course. We run the final test in two days.'

'See that you do. I'll have no delays.'

'Yes, master.'

'Take heart, Thaddeus. The Lord's scheme proceeds well, and once we've triumphed here we'll spread the scourge much farther afield. The day of our race's deliverance is at hand, brethren. As is ridding ourselves of the Mani pestilence.'

Jup had no idea what they were talking about, but it didn't sound good.

Then Hobrow suddenly stood and made his way to the altar. Jup tensed. He couldn't see Hobrow properly, but had the impression that he was looking at the star, or possibly even handling its container. The dwarf was relieved when the zealot turned to face his cohorts.

'We mustn't lose sight of the fact that the crusade to Scratch is of equal importance. Are we up to strength on that front, Calvert?'

At mention of the trolls' homeland, Jup's ears pricked.

'The battle at Weaver's Lea was ill-timed,' the second man answered, a little nervously, Jup thought. 'It drew too many away from the plan. It'll be a couple of weeks before we have enough men.'

Hobrow wasn't pleased. 'That won't do. The ungodly have what must be ours. The Lord will not be frustrated.'

'We can't open hostilities there with less than a full compliment, master. It invites disaster.'

'Then bring in more of the non-humans to free our own for this work. Let nothing stand in the way of the plan, brethren. We'll speak again on the morrow. Now go about your duties and trust in the Lord. We do His work and will prevail.'

Hobrow's men departed. But Hobrow himself stayed. He returned to the bench, clasped his hands and lowered his head.

'Give me the strength I need, Lord,' he intoned. 'We're eager to carry out Your plan, but You must give us what we need to do it. Bless our efforts to cleanse this land, that your chosen may harvest it unmolested.'

Jup was worried about the time passing. If Hobrow took much longer he was in trouble.

'Shower Your diving blessings, too, on our mission to the heathen non-human nest at Scratch. Let us gain that which they have and which we need to do Your bidding. Keep firm my resolve, oh Lord, and let me not waver in your service.'

Hobrow stood, turned away and left the temple.

Jup forced himself to wait a moment before leaving his hiding place. With trepidation, he opened the doors a crack. There was no sign of anyone nearby and he left the building, making as much haste getting back to the hothouse as he could without actually running. All the way he puzzled over what he'd just heard.

There was a moment of suspense when he arrived, as he couldn't be certain if the others had returned. Or whether another custodian had visited in his absence.

In the event, the building was empty. But the fires had burnt dangerously low. He shovelled fuel on to them like a maniac.

The task was barely complete when he heard the sound of a wagon outside.

Istuan came in and cast a critical eye about the room. Jup steeled himself against the accusation he more than half expected.

'You've worked up a fine sweat there,' the custodian said. It was as near a compliment as he'd yet paid him.

Jup smiled thinly and nodded, too breathless to speak.

He was assigned the back-breaking work of transferring the water from the wagon to the tanks. After that, there were other strenuous chores. He didn't mind. It gave him time to think. One conclusion he came to was that what needed to be achieved wouldn't be done today after all. But at least he knew where the star was kept, and he had some other information, although it made little sense to him.

The work continued in virtual silence until dusk. Then Istuan told them to make their way to the main gate to be picked up. They were allowed to go unaccompanied.

On the way, Jup's fellow workers were no less taciturn. In the main avenue leading to the gates they were passed by Hobrow in his carriage. Sitting next to him was a human female. No longer a child but not yet a woman, she was dressed a little more flamboyantly than any other human Jup had seen in Trinity. In build she was chubby, almost fat. Her hair was honey blonde and her eyes china blue. But it seemed to Jup that her scowling face spoke of greed and bad temper. She had an unpleasant mouth.

When proud Hobrow and the haughty child-woman had gone by, Jup asked his companions who she was.

'Hobrow's daughter,' the more voluble one replied, then cracked the first smile he had favoured Jup with. Not that it contained much humour.

'What's funny?' Jup said.

'Her name. It's Mercy.'

They arrived at the main gates. The other dwarves were there and the wagons were waiting. All were counted and, as Jup feared, they were searched. But it consisted of no more than the patting of clothes and a quick delve into pockets. Nobody, thank the gods, wanted to look in his boots. At least it confirmed his hunch that smuggling out the star wasn't a very smart idea.

Some coins were dropped into his hand and he climbed aboard a wagon.

The opening of the gates was the most comforting thing he'd seen all day.

They arrived at the [illegible] [illegible] [illegible] [illegible] [illegible]
[illegible] [illegible] [illegible] [illegible] [illegible] [illegible] [illegible] [illegible]
[illegible] [illegible] [illegible] [illegible] [illegible] [illegible] [illegible]
[illegible] [illegible] [illegible] [illegible] [illegible] [illegible] [illegible]
[illegible] [illegible] [illegible] [illegible] [illegible] [illegible] [illegible]
[illegible] [illegible] [illegible] [illegible] [illegible] [illegible] [illegible]
[illegible]

[illegible] [illegible] [illegible] [illegible] [illegible] [illegible] [illegible]
[illegible]

[illegible] [illegible] [illegible] [illegible] [illegible] [illegible] [illegible]
[illegible]

19

Safely installed in their mine-shaft hideaway, Jup related the day's events to the Wolverines. Alfray was busy examining the plant samples.

'You've done well, Jup,' Stryke praised, 'but I'm not keen on you going back in there. Apart from anything else, there's too high a chance that the dwarf you killed might be reported missing.'

'I know that. Believe me, I'm not happy about it myself, chief. But if we want that star, I can't see how else to do it.'

'Finding it's one thing, getting it out is another,' Coilla said. 'What's the plan?'

'I was wondering if I could get it over the wall to you somehow,' Jup suggested.

Stryke was unimpressed. 'Not practical.'

'What about making a copy of the star and swapping it for the real one?' Coilla pitched in.

'Nice idea. But that wouldn't work either. We haven't got the skill to make even a half-convincing copy. Nor do we have anything that comes anywhere near the kind of material we'd need.'

'The one I saw in Trinity's is different to ours, too,' Jup reminded them. 'We'd have to do it from what I could remember. Even if we could copy it, that doesn't solve the problem of getting the original out.'

'No, it doesn't,' Stryke agreed. 'I think the only way is a more direct approach. Of the kind we do best.'

'You don't mean we should storm the place?' Coilla said. 'A handful against an entire township?'

'Not exactly. But what I have in mind would put a lot on you, Jup. It's much more dangerous than anything you've done so far.'

'What are you getting at, Stryke?'

'I'm thinking of you getting hold of the star then us getting hold of you.'

'What?'

'It's simple really. All being well, tomorrow you and the star will be together behind the walls at Trinity and we'll be outside. Is there any way you could let us in?'

'Shit, Stryke, I don't know . . .'

'Did you notice any way in or out apart from the main gates? Anything we missed on our reconnaissance?'

'Not that I saw.'

'It'd have to be the main gates then.'

'How?'

'We'll agree a time. You'll have to get away from the hothouse, grab the star—'

'And get to the gates and open them for you. That's asking a hell of a lot, Stryke. Those gates are massive, and they're guarded.'

'I didn't say it'd be easy. You'd have to deal with the guards and get those gates unbarred. We'd be waiting close by to help open them. Then it's a quick getaway. If you think it's too risky, we'll try to come up with something else.'

'Well, there were only two guards by the gates when I left

tonight, so I suppose it wouldn't be impossible overcoming them. All right, let's go for that.'

Alfray joined them, frowning, the plant samples in his hand. 'Well, what you've brought us adds another twist to things, Jup.'

'Why? What are they?'

'I know two of the three types, although they're quite rare.' He held up a leaf. 'This is wentyx, which you can find in a few places down here in the south.' He indicated another. 'This one, the vale lily, tends to grow more in the west, though you could spend years looking for it.' He showed them the third sample. 'This is new to me, and I suspect it's something the humans brought with them to Maras-Dantia. But I'd guess it does the same thing these others do.'

'Which is what?' Stryke asked.

'Kills. The two I know are among the most lethal plants in existence. The vale lily yields berries that always prove fatal even in tiny amounts. With the wentyx you have to boil the stalk for a residue that's even more potent, if anything. The gods know how dangerous the one I can't identify is. And the first two have something else in common. They're so potent that large quantities of water hardly dilutes them. Does what Hobrow has in mind seem clearer now?'

Jup was stunned. 'Hell, yes. They're growing these things for poisons to kill elder races with.'

Alfray nodded. 'Massacre, more like. This explains the dam. Hobrow's protecting Trinity's own water supply so they'll be safe when they poison the other sources.'

'I saw wells in Trinity.'

'Then the reservoir's a further guarantee for them.'

'Or else it's the reservoir they'll poison,' Stryke said. 'If you control the major water supply for a whole area, then let it be known that any of the races can use it—'

'Or just leave it unguarded,' Coilla added, 'knowing they'll come and draw from it. Particularly if there's a drought, which isn't impossible seeing how the weather's been so unpredictable in recent seasons.'

'Either way, the result's likely to be the slaughter of every race but humans in these parts,' Alfray said.

Jup recalled something. 'Hobrow said that if it works here, they'll try it on a wider scale. They go in for a lot of purity-of-the-race stuff in Trinity, certainly if the way they treat dwarves is anything to go by. How much purer can you get if there *are* no other races?'

'It's an insane plan,' Alfray judged. 'Think about it. The first to drink the water would die, and that would warn off others. How can these Unis believe it would work?'

'Maybe they're too blinded by hatred to see things straight,' Stryke said. 'Or it could be they think enough would be killed to make it worthwhile.'

'The *bastards,*' Coilla seethed. 'We can't let them get away with it, Stryke.'

'What can we do? Things are going to be hard enough for Jup tomorrow without another near-impossible task.'

'We're just going to walk away from this?'

'From what Jup says, that plant house is a fair distance inside Trinity. There's no way we're going to get to it, particularly if the alarm's gone out about the missing star. All we can do is spread the word among local elder races and hope they can act on the warning.'

She wasn't happy. 'It doesn't seem much.'

'What if I can do anything while I'm in there, Stryke?' Jup asked. 'Without putting the star in peril, that is?'

'Then good luck. But the star's your first priority. The power the stars promise could do a lot more good for Maras-Dantia than us throwing away our lives to stop this scheme.'

'Have any of you wondered where Hobrow got his star?' Alfray wanted to know.

Stryke had. 'Yes. But I remember what Mobbs said. It's possible that the humans came upon it by chance, the gods know how, and just haven't an idea of what it's for.'

'Any more than we have,' Coilla put in.

'Hobrow's enough of a tyrant to go after the other stars if he knew their power, and to use it,' Jup informed them.

'Wiping out whole races seems to back that,' Coilla agreed, more than a little cynically.

'All right, there's not much else we can do tonight,' Stryke decided.

Jup turned to Alfray. 'How's Haskeer?'

If Alfray was surprised at Jup asking after the health of his antagonist, he didn't show it. 'Fair. I'm hoping his fever's going to break soon.'

'Pity he's out of it. Irritating fucker he may be, but we could use him tomorrow.'

They talked a while longer about tomorrow's plans, and the expedition Hobrow planned to Scratch particularly intrigued them. But in the end they settled down to catch what sleep they could with more questions than answers.

Getting into Trinity the next day proved no harder than before.

Jup presented himself at the pick-up point, boarded a wagon and was delivered to the township. This time he took especial notice of the number of guards manning the gates. There were five. His heart sank. But he consoled himself with the thought that perhaps more were assigned at busy times like this.

One thing Jup did differently for his second visit was to conceal a knife in his boot. His reasoning was that as they hadn't searched him coming in yesterday, they wouldn't today. In the event, his gamble paid off.

This time, there was no lecture from Hobrow. And when

the dwarves were told to report to their places of work, Jup didn't check with the custodians. He simply went with the two other dwarves assigned to the hothouse. Istuan told Jup what to do, which was a rerun of his previous day's duties, and Jup got on with it.

The time agreed for Jup to be at the gates was midday, which he reckoned was in about four hours. Which meant he needed to be out of the arboretum well before that. As he worked, his mind and eye kept returning to the small jungle of plants in the adjacent glassed area. He didn't favour leaving Trinity without at least trying to do something about them. As Stryke had said, that was all right as long as it didn't endanger gaining the star. He thought it worth the additional risk.

The plan he had for getting away from the hothouse and to the temple was basic, direct and by necessity brutal. He pondered it as he lugged the wood and black burning-stones to the piles that fed the kilns. Time dragged, as it often did when a particular moment was anticipated, but he knew that when it came to it things would move fast enough. He carried on shovelling the fuel, working up a sweat and casting shifty glances at the toxic nursery.

When he judged the moment near, he left the furnace room by way of the back door, ostensibly to check the tank's water levels.

Jup didn't want to use his knife against fellow dwarves unless he had to, no matter how treacherous they might seem. So he selected a sturdy timber bough, concealed himself behind the door and waited.

Several long minutes passed before a voice was raised inside. The words were unclear, but he was obviously being called for. He ignored it.

The door opened and one of the dwarves came out.

Jup waited for the door to close again, then stepped forward and rapped the dwarf smartly across the back of the head with his improvised bludgeon. His victim went down. Jup dragged him out of sight.

He returned to his hiding place and renewed the vigil. There were no warning shouts before the door opened a second time. Then not one but two figures exited.

Jup found himself facing Istuan and the other dwarf. He laid into them. The dwarf went down first, and without too much effort, if only because he had no weapon to defend himself with.

But the custodian put up a fight.

'You filthy little freak!' he bellowed, swinging his own club, which unlike Jup's improvised version was designed for the purpose.

They stood toe to toe and exchanged grunting blows. Jup's concern was that the human would cry out loudly enough to bring help. He had to finish this quickly.

The custodian proved no easy prey, however, and one of his swings caught Jup's arm. It was a painful but not crippling strike, and it spurred him to greater effort. He powered into Istuan, battering at him in search of an opening. Another swing by the human gave him his chance. Jup ducked and brought his club up to connect heavily with the custodian's chin.

Istuan gasped and the weapon fell from his loosened fingers. Jup quickly followed through with a swinging blow to his head, knocking him cold.

Tossing aside the piece of timber, he took up a two-handed axe used to chop the logs. A single swipe severed the pipe carrying water from the tanks into the furnace room.

He rushed through the door. The water in the open gully above the kilns was already drying up. Snatching one of the stoking shovels, he loaded it with glowing coals. He turned, ran the few paces to the hothouse and tossed the coals into the jumble of plants. This he repeated several times, with both hot coals and flaming logs, until the plants in the hothouse began to burn and the wooden shelving caught.

His hope was to kill two birds with one arrow. The fire should create a diversion, and destroying the plants might scupper Hobrow's plan, or at least delay it.

Satisfied the blaze had taken, he checked the street and left, firmly slamming the door behind him. As he hurried past the glass end of the structure he saw smoke inside, and pinpoints of yellow flame. He set off for the temple, careful not to break into a run no matter how much he wanted to.

He wondered how long he had before the alarm was raised.

Glancing at the sky showed the sun was near its highest point. The Wolverines would now be in position. He hoped he wasn't going to disappoint them.

Moving as fast as he dared, he tried not to dwell on the enormity of the task he'd agreed to.

Jup turned into the avenue of the temple. Almost as soon as he did, the doors opened and a crowd of humans flooded out, presumably from attending a service. He froze, shocked at this sudden profusion of the species.

Conscious that standing in the road and staring was likely to attract attention, he snapped out of his paralysis and resumed walking. Very slowly, with his head down. He went past the place of worship, staying on the other side of the road, careful not to obstruct any of the departing worshippers scattering in all directions. Very few took much notice of him. For the first time he appreciated how being regarded as a member of a lowly race had its advantages.

He rounded a corner, making out that he was heading somewhere else. As the worshippers thinned he turned back and walked towards the temple again.

The street outside was clear now, except for a few humans moving off with their backs to him. He decided on a direct approach and damn the consequences. Marching straight to the temple doors, he shoved them open.

Much to his relief, the building was deserted.

He ran to the small glass case, grabbed it and dashed it against the altar, shattering it. Snatching up the star, he stuffed it into his pocket and fled.

Outside, he noticed smoke rising from the next street where the hothouse was located. Behind him, somebody shouted. He looked over his shoulder.

Four or five custodians were running his way.

He ran too. There was no point in trying to avoid attention now.

They chased him through the streets, yelling and waving their fists. Others joined in. By the time he turned the last corner and saw the gates, a howling mob was at his heels.

That wasn't all he saw. For a start there were more guards than he had anticipated. He counted eight. There was no way he was going to overpower that number single-handed. Two, certainly; three, possibly; four, maybe. Twice that number, never.

The other thing he saw was Hobrow's carriage. His daughter, Mercy, was sitting in it alone. Hobrow was standing some way off, talking to a custodian.

It gave him an idea. A desperate one, admittedly, but he could see no other choice.

Hobrow and the guards, alerted by the cries of the pursuing mob, turned and looked his way. Several of the custodians were already drawing weapons and starting to move in Jup's direction.

Jup put on a spurt of speed and ran for all he was worth. He made a beeline for the carriage. The guards raced forward to cut him off. Hobrow himself, seeing Jup's intention, also began to run.

Heart pounding, Jup reached the carriage just a few paces ahead of Hobrow and the custodians. He leapt on to it. Mercy

Hobrow squealed. Jup grabbed her, ripped the knife from his boot and held the blade to her throat.

Hobrow and the guards were clambering on to the carriage.

'Hold it!' Jup yelled, pressing the knife closer to the trembling girl's pinky-white flesh.

'Let her go!' Hobrow demanded.

'Another step and she dies,' Jup said.

The holy man and the dwarf locked gazes. Jup inwardly prayed for him not to call his bluff. The girl might have been a pretty unpleasant example of humanity, and the offspring of a ruthless dictator, but she was little more than a child for all that. Given the choice, he would rather not harm her.

'My daddy will *kill* you for this,' Mercy promised. It was all the more chilling a threat coming from the lips of one so young.

'Button it,' Jup sneered.

'You monster!' she wailed. 'You stunted ogre! You . . . *eyesore*! You—'

He let her feel the keenness of his blade. She gulped and shut up.

'Open the gates!' he said.

The mob had halted and were watching in silence. Their weapons half raised, the custodians stared. Hobrow pinned Jup with his searing gaze.

'Open them,' Jup repeated.

'There's no need for this,' Hobrow told him.

'Open the gates and I'll let her go.'

'How do I know you will?'

'You'll just have to take my word for it.'

Hobrow's expression turned meaner, his tone took on a harsher edge. 'How far do you think you're going to get out there?'

'That's my problem. Now are you going to open those gates or do I spill her blood?'

The preacher's fury was building. 'You harm one hair on that child's head—'

'Then open the gates.'

Hobrow fumed silently for a moment and Jup wondered what his daughter's life was worth to him. Then the holy man turned and gave the custodians a curt order. They ran to lift the crossbar. Others pulled open the gates.

For Jup it was another moment of truth. If the Wolverines weren't out there his chances of escaping were down to near zero.

The reins of the horses in one hand and the knife at Mercy's neck in the other, he edged the carriage through the gates and out into the road.

There was no sign of the Wolverines. That didn't worry him unduly. He hadn't expected to be able to see them.

Then, as he moved into the open, the band appeared from the cover of the long grass.

'Get off,' he told the girl.

She stared at him, wide-eyed.

'Get off!' he barked.

She winced and jumped down from the carriage, then started running back toward her father's outstretched arms.

Now she was free, the humans had no constraint. Yelling and screaming, they charged. Jup cracked the reins and started to move.

As they spilled through the gates, the wave of humans got their first sight of the Wolverines. They thought they were going to lynch a dwarf, not engage in a minor battle. The suddenness of the orcs' appearance, and the ferocity of their onslaught, threw the humans into disarray. Further discord was sewn by Coilla picking off the guards in their towers with her bow. Three grunts peppered the crowd with arrows.

Led by Stryke, the remainder of the band beat back the mob, which broke ranks and fled for the safety of the enclave.

Hobrow could be heard shrieking orders and vowing revenge.

Stryke jumped up beside Jup. 'They'll be getting horses! Let's move!'

Coilla and several other band members leapt aboard; the rest jogged along beside the speeding carriage.

'Did you get it?' Stryke said.

Jup grinned. 'I got it!'

The Wolverines raced from Trinity with their prize.

20

Amid the chaos, Kimball Hobrow was beside himself with rage.

Custodians were scrambling for horses and climbing to re-man the walls. Citizens armed themselves for the chase. The wounded were being tended, the dead dragged clear of the gates. A team of fire fighters carted water to the blazing arboretum.

Mercy Hobrow, tearful and petulantly angry, tugged at her father's frock coat and wailed. 'Kill them, Daddy! Kill them, *kill them*!'

Hobrow raised his arms, fists clenched, and bellowed over the confusion. 'Track them down, brethren! As the Almighty is your guide and your sword, find them and smite them!'

Heavily armed riders galloped out of the gates. Wagonloads of citizenry, bristling with weapons, careered through to join the hunt.

A dishevelled custodian, ashen-faced, ran to Hobrow. 'The temple!' he cried. 'It's been desecrated!'

'Desecrated? How?'

'They've taken a relic!'

A deeper fury creased the preacher's face. He reached out

and grasped the man's coat, pulling him close with maniacal strength. His eyes blazed.

'*What* have they taken?'

The Wolverines had left their horses with Alfray and a trooper in a copse several fields distant. Haskeer, semi-conscious and groggy with fever, was there too, lashed to his steed.

Abandoning the carriage, the band wasted no time mounting. As they rode off, a massive posse appeared on the road from Trinity.

Stryke had earlier decided that they'd head due west toward the Calyparr Inlet. This gave them the advantage of an open run, and once they reached it, a terrain varied enough to hide them.

The pursuers were disorganised and still recovering from the shock of the unexpected. But they were also tenacious. For several hours they hunted the band doggedly, rarely losing sight of them. Then the less able or less energetic began to fall back, with the overladen wagons the first to be lost.

By the end of the day only a comparative handful of diehards were still on the Wolverines' trail. Some high-speed, devious riding on the band's part eventually shook them off, too.

Having reached the vicinity of the inlet, riders and horses near exhaustion, Stryke allowed the pace to drop to a canter.

Coilla was the first to speak since the chase began. 'Well, that's one more enemy we've made.'

'And a powerful one,' Alfray agreed. 'I wouldn't count on Hobrow letting the star go as easily as that.'

'Which reminds me,' Stryke said. 'Let me see it, Jup.'

The dwarf dug out the instrumentality and handed it over. Stryke compared it to the one he had already had, then slipped both into his pouch.

'I had my doubts about pulling that off,' Alfray admitted.

'It was as much luck as anything,' Jup remarked. He

produced a cloth and began wiping the paste off his face. It was the first chance he'd had to do it.

'Don't undervalue yourself,' Stryke told him. 'You did well back there.'

'The big question now,' Alfray went on, 'is what do we do next.'

'I figured we might have had similar thoughts on that,' Stryke said.

Alfray sighed. 'That's what I was afraid you were going to say. Scratch?'

'There could be another star there.'

'*Could* be. We have no proof of it. All we know for sure is that Hobrow intends going there. Which might not make it the most ideal destination for us.'

'After the blow we've dealt him, I reckon he's not going just yet.'

'Supposing Hobrow's expedition to Scratch doesn't have anything to do with the stars?' Jup suggested. 'What if he's going there as part of his crazy plan to wipe out the elder races?'

'What, to force-feed the trolls poison? I don't think so. There has to be another reason.'

'Slaughtering other races is what humans do, isn't it?'

'When they can let tainted water do it for them? It's too much of a risk. I mean, would you willingly go into that labyrinth unless you had to?'

'But that's exactly what you're asking *us* to do!'

'Like I said, Jup, unless you had to. Let's find a place to camp and at least think about it.'

A little later, when Stryke and Coilla found themselves riding alone at the column's head, he asked her opinion on going to Scratch.

'It's no more mad than most other things we've done lately, though I think we'd face a much more fearsome enemy in the trolls than even Hobrow's fanatics. I'm not keen on the idea of entering that underground hellhole.'

'So you're against it?'

'I didn't say that. Having some kind of mission certainly beats wandering aimlessly. But I'd want to see a well thought-out strategy before we went near the place. Another thing you shouldn't forget, Stryke, is that we've managed to upset just about everybody in the last couple of weeks. We'll have to expect enemies on every side.'

'Which can be a good thing.'

'How do you figure that?'

'It'll keep us on our toes, spur us on.'

'It's going to do *that* all right. Tell me true, how much would going to Scratch be based on logic and how much on clutching at straws?'

'About half and half.'

She smiled. 'At least you're honest about it.'

'Well, I am to you. Don't think I'd be quite so straight with them about it.' He nodded at the band riding behind.

'They have a right to a say, don't they? Particularly as we're now outlaws, and maybe the command structure isn't as strong.'

'Yes, they have a say, and I wouldn't try getting them to do anything they really didn't want to. As for command; like I said before, we have to keep discipline to stand a chance. So unless anybody else puts themselves up for it, I'm staying in charge.'

'I'll go along with that. I'm sure the others do, too. But there's one decision you're going to have to make soon, and it affects all of us. The crystal.'

'Whether it should be divided up or kept as collective band property, you mean? I've been thinking about that. Maybe it's something else we'll have to have a vote on. Not that I'm happy with the idea of voting on every move, mind.'

'No, that could undermine your authority.'

They rode in silence for a few minutes, then she said, 'Course, there is an alternative to going to Scratch.'

'What?'

'Returning to Cairnbarrow and bargaining the two stars for our lives.'

'We know from Delorran what they think of us there. Whatever the rest of you decide, it's not something I'll be doing.'

'Gods, I'm pleased to hear you say that, Stryke.' She beamed at him. 'I'd rather face anything than the reception Jennesta would have waiting for us.'

There was something like a banquet in the grand hall of Jennesta's palace.

But only something like. Although the long, highly polished dining table was set out for a meal, there was no food. There were five guests present, apart from the Queen herself, not to mention twice that number of servants, flunkies and bodyguards. But there was little evidence of gaiety.

Two of Jennesta's guests were orcs; the newly elevated General Mersadion, and Captain Delorran, fresh back from his unsuccessful pursuit of the Wolverines. There was no mistaking their nervousness. But they were not the source of the tension. That had its axis in the three other guests.

They were humans.

Jennesta dealt with humans because of her support for the Mani cause, so seeing members of the race about her palace wasn't in itself that unusual. What was troubling was the nature of these particular humans.

Noticing Mersadion and Delorran's discomfort, Jennesta spoke. 'General, Captain, allow me to introduce Micah Lekmann.' She indicated the tallest of the trio.

A beard would have disguised an old scar that ran from the centre of his stubbled right cheek to the corner of his mouth.

Instead he favoured an unkempt black moustache. His hair was a greasy mop and his skin weather-beaten where it wasn't pockmarked. Lekmann's muscularity and the cut of his clothes spoke of a life of combat. He looked like a man untroubled by notions of gallantry.

'And these are his . . . associates,' Jennesta added. She left hanging an unspoken invitation for him to make the introductions.

Lekmann flashed an unctuous smile and jabbed a lazy thumb at the human on his right. 'Greever Aulay,' he announced.

Where Lekmann was tall, Aulay was the shortest of the three. In contrast to his leader's well-bulked physique, he was lean and slight. He had the face of a baby rat. His hair was sandy blond and his visible eye, the left one, hazel. A black leather patch concealed the other. His wispy goatee beard clung tenuously to a weak chin. Thin lips stretched to reveal bad teeth.

'And this is Jabez Blaan,' Lekmann grated.

The man on his left was the biggest by far in terms of mass. He probably weighed as much as the other two put together, but it was all brawn, not fat. His totally shaved, spherical head seemed to meet his body without the necessity of an intervening neck. The nose had been broken at least once and now impersonated a doorknob. His eyes looked uncannily like twin piss-holes in snow. The pair of ham fists he rested on the table could have been called upon to demolish a stout oak.

Neither spoke nor smiled, contenting themselves with small and perfunctory tilts of the head.

Delorran and Mersadion eyed the trio uneasily.

'They have very special talents to employ on my behalf,' Jennesta explained. 'But more of that later.' The parchment Delorran had brought back lay in front of her. She tapped it with one of her unfeasibly long fingernails. 'Thanks to Captain Delorran, who has just returned from a vitally important mission, we know that my property has been violated. Regrettably, the Captain's efforts did not extend to returning the object itself, or to bringing the thieves to justice.'

Apprehensively, Delorran made a tiny throat-clearing sound. 'Begging your pardon, ma'am, but on that score at least the Wolverines received their just deserts. They were all lost, as I reported.'

'You saw them die?'

'Not . . . as such, Your Majesty. But when I last saw them they had no hope of escape. Their deaths were certain.'

'Not as certain as you think, Captain.'

Delorran gaped at her. 'Ma'am?'

'Reports of their deaths were somewhat exaggerated, shall we say.'

'They survived the battlefield?'

'They did.'

'But—'

'How do I know? Because they were pursued by a dragon patrol after crossing the battlefield, and lived through their attack, too.'

'Your Majesty, I—'

'You would have been well advised to stay a little longer and confirm the Wolverines' destruction, rather than assuming it, would you not, Captain?' Her tone was more chiding than angry, as though she addressed an errant child.

'Yes, Majesty,' he replied meekly.

'You've heard of General Kysthan's . . . demise.' Delorran looked uncomfortable. 'He has paid the price of your failure.'

The Captain had no time to reply before Jennesta snapped her fingers. Elf servants began moving among them, dispensing goblets of wine from silver trays. One was handed to Jennesta with a bow.

'A toast,' she said, raising her glass. 'To the return of that which is mine, and the confounding of my enemies.'

She drank and they all followed suit.

'Which does not mean that there's no price for you to pay as well, Captain,' she added.

Delorran did not immediately get Jennesta's meaning and stared at her in puzzlement. Then the import of her words began to soak in. He looked to the goblet he held, the colour draining from his face.

The glass slipped from his fingers and broke. His jaw dropped and he brought a hand to his throat. 'You . . . *bitch*,' he croaked. He rose clumsily, knocking over his chair.

Jennesta sat impassively, watching him.

Delorran staggered a step or two in her direction, and his shaking hand went to his sword.

She didn't move.

He couldn't co-ordinate himself sufficiently to draw the blade, and was sweating freely now, his face contorted with building agony. A rasping, rattling sound came from his throat and he began choking. Then he buckled and went down. He fell into a jolting, foaming-mouthed fit, spasms running through his body. A trickle of blood seeped from his mouth. His back arched, his legs kicked convulsively. He was still.

Death stamped a dreadful expression on his face.

'Why waste precious magic?' Jennesta asked the silent company. 'Anyway, I wanted to test that particular potion.'

Sapphire the cat appeared and slunk over to the pool of spilt wine. She would have lapped at it if Jennesta hadn't laughingly shooed her away.

The Queen looked up. The three humans were regarding their own half-finished drinks with concern. It rekindled her laughter.

'Don't worry,' she reassured them. 'I've no need to bring in people specially in order to poison them. And you can stop looking at me that way, Mersadion. I would hardly have gone to the trouble of promoting you only to consign you to your grave. Not so soon, anyway.'

It could have been a joke.

She stepped over the corpse and went to sit nearer them. 'Enough of pleasure, now to business. I said that Lekmann and his company have special skills, General. Their particular ability is finding outlaws.'

'There're bounty hunters, you mean?'

Lekmann answered. 'It's what some call us. We prefer to think of ourselves as freelance law enforcers.'

Jennesta laughed again. 'As good a description as any. But don't be modest, Lekmann. Tell the General your speciality.'

Lekmann nodded at Greever Aulay. Aulay produced a sack and dumped it on the table.

'Our business is hunting orcs,' Lekmann said.

Aulay upended the sack. Five or six round yellowy-brown objects bounced across the surface. Mersadion stared at them. Then what they were slowly dawned on him. Shrunken orc heads. An appalled expression crossed his face.

Lekmann gave one of his oily grins. 'We only deal in renegades, you understand.'

'I do hope you're not going to allow any kind of prejudice to colour our dealings with these agents, General,' Jennesta remarked. 'I expect you to give them the fullest co-operation in their work.'

Ambition battled with disgust in Mersadion's features. He began to pull himself together. 'What exactly *is* this work, Your Majesty?' he asked.

'The hunting of the Wolverines, of course, and the recovery of my property. Not instead of the efforts you're making, but in addition to them. I judged the time right to bring in professionals seasoned in this kind of task.'

Mersadion turned to Lekmann. 'There are just the three of you? Or do you have . . . helpers?'

'We can call on others if need be, but usually we work alone. We find it best that way.'

'Where does your allegiance lie?'

'With ourselves.' He glanced at Jennesta. 'And whoever's paying us.'

'They follow neither the Mani or Uni path,' Jennesta said. 'They're irreligious, and simple opportunists. Is that not so, Lekmann?'

The bounty hunter smirked and nodded. Although whether he had any idea what "opportunists" meant, let alone "irreligious", was a moot point.

'Which makes them ideal for my purposes,' the Queen continued, 'unlikely as they are to be swayed by anything other than the reward. Which would be substantial enough to ensure their loyalty.'

Mersadion had put aside any scruples. 'How are we to proceed, ma'am?'

'We know that the last sightings of the Wolverines had them moving in the direction of Trinity. You'll agree that's an odd destination. Unless, as Delorran believed, they've turned traitor and joined the Unis. I find that hard to credit. But if they really are in Trinity, for whatever reason, our friends here are obviously best suited to following them there.'

'What are your orders?' Lekmann enquired.

'The cylinder has absolute priority. If you can slay the band that stole it, their leader in particular, all the better. But not at the expense of gaining that artefact. Employ any methods you see fit.'

'You can rely on us. Er, Your Majesty,' he tacked on, remembering the protocol.

'I hope so. For your sakes.' Her face and voice took on a distinctly chilly aspect. 'For should you think of double-dealing, know that my wrath is limitless.' They all glanced at the body on the floor. 'You'll also learn that no other will pay you as handsomely for the return of what I seek.' Her smile returned. It was possible to mistake it for warm. 'I would leave no stone unturned in the search for this renegade band, so I intend following tradition.'

She beckoned a pair of her orc bodyguards. They moved forward and dragged Delorran's body to a small side door.

Jennesta turned to a servant. 'Let them in.'

The servant went to the dining room's large twin doors and opened them. Two elf elders entered and bowed low.

'I have a proclamation for you,' Jennesta told them. 'Spread these words throughout the realm, and send runners to all parts where such information will be of value.' She waved a hand at the servant by the door. 'Proceed.'

The servant unrolled a parchment and began reading in the characteristically piping elfin lilt. 'Be it known that by order of Her Imperial Highness Queen Jennesta of Cairnbarrow that the orc warband attached to Her Majesty's horde, and known as the Wolverines, are henceforth to be regarded as renegades and outlaws, and are no longer afforded the protection of this realm. Be it further known that a bounty of such precious coin, pellucid or land as may be appropriate will be paid upon production of the heads of the band's officers. To wit, Captain Stryke, sergeants Haskeer and the dwarf Jup, corporals Alfray and Coilla. Furthermore, a reward proportionate to their rank shall be paid for the return, dead or alive, of the band's common troopers, answering to the names Bhose, Breggin, Calthmon, Darig, Eldo, Finje, Gant, Gleadeg, Hystykk, Jad, Kestix, Liffin, Meklun, Nep, Noskaa, Orbon, Prooq, Reafdaw, Seafe, Slettal, Talag, Toche, Vobe, Wrelbyd and Zoda. Be it known that any harbouring said outlaws will be subject to full penalties as laid down by law. By order of Her Majesty Queen Jennesta. All hail the highborn monarch.'

The servant rolled the parchment and handed it to one of the elders.

'Now go and issue it,' Jennesta ordered.

The elders backed out, bowing.

The Queen rose, causing the others to scramble to their feet. She fixed the bounty hunters with a searching gaze. 'You'd best be on your way if you want to beat the opposition,' she said. With a smile, she added, 'Let's see the Wolverines find sanctuary now.'

Then she turned her back on them and swept from the chamber.

21

Jup gently mopped Haskeer's brow with a damp cloth.

From outside the field tent, Stryke, Alfray and a handful of grunts watched the scene with something like amazement.

Incredulous, Alfray slowly shook his head. 'Now I've seen everything.'

'Just goes to show there's nothing as queer as species,' Stryke said.

They went about their business, shooing the troopers away in the process.

Haskeer started to come round. Blinking as though the light was painful for his eyes, he mumbled something incomprehensible. Whether he realised it was Jup tending him, the dwarf wasn't sure. He rinsed the cloth and reapplied it.

'What . . . the . . . fu—' Haskeer slurred.

'That's right,' Jup told him cheerfully. 'You'll soon be back to your old self.'

'Er?'

The befuddlement on Haskeer's face could have been due to his groggy state or finding the dwarf looming over him. Either way, Jup took no notice of it.

'A lot's happened while you've been out of your head,' Jup stated, 'so I thought I'd fill you in.'

'Wha—?'

'I don't care whether you understand me or not, you bastard, I'm going to go through it anyway.'

He proceeded to bring the semi-comatose orc up to date on developments, heedless of the patient's apparent lack of comprehension. But about two-thirds of the way through his story Haskeer's eyes drifted shut again and he immediately began snoring loudly.

Jup got to his feet. 'Don't think you're getting off that easy,' he promised. 'I'll be back.'

He crept out of the tent.

There was dilute sunshine outside. The tinkling drone of fairy swarms could be heard in the distance. He surveyed the landscape. The tracts of land abutting Calyparr Inlet were marshy and inhospitable. They had set up camp on as dry a patch as they could find, but it was still sodden underfoot and pretty miserable.

The band were spread around gathering firewood, grubbing for food and carrying out other mundane but necessary tasks.

Alfray and Coilla wandered over.

'How is he?' Alfray asked.

'Came round for a minute or two.' Jup smiled. 'I think my telling of what's been going on put him out again. He seemed kind of muddled.'

'That's not unusual with some of these human maladies. He should be all right in a while. What surprises me is why you're being so nice to him.'

'Never had anything against him, the way he thinks he does against me. And when all's said and done, he's a comrade.'

'Anybody can look pathetic when they're that ill,' Coilla reminded him. 'Don't go too soft on the awkward bugger.'

'Not much danger of that.'

Alfray took a deep breath. 'You know, it's colder than it should be, and I've been in drier places, but it's not so bad here. This little bit of land in this tiny slice of time is just about the way things must have been in Maras-Dantia before the troubles. If you kind of squint your eyes and use your imagination, that is.'

Coilla was about to have her say on that when they were interrupted by shouts from a nearby glade. They were more raucous than alarming but the officers set off to investigate anyway. As they walked, Stryke joined them.

They were met by a running grunt.

'What's up, Prooq?' Stryke said.

'Bit of bother, sir.'

'What kind?'

'Well . . . best come and see, sir.'

They went a little further and found the rest of the grunts hanging around near the mouth of the glade. A small group of figures were parading themselves in front of them.

'Oh no,' Alfray sighed. 'Bloody pests!'

'What is it?' Jup wanted to know.

'Wood nymphs.'

'And a succubus or two by the looks of it,' Stryke added.

The voluptuous females were dressed in gowns of rustic colours, provocatively low-cut to display maximum cleavage and slashed to the waist, revealing shapely limbs. They cavorted, swung about their autumnal-coloured hair and struck exaggeratedly seductive poses. A keening, wailing, unmelodious screech filled the air.

'What the *hell* is that racket?' Jup said.

'Their siren song,' Alfray explained. 'It's supposed to be alluring and impossible to resist.'

'Not all it's cracked up to be, is it?'

'They're said to be mistresses of deception.'

'They're only deceiving themselves,' Coilla put in grumpily. 'They look like well-worn strumpets to me.'

The nymphs continued adopting crude postures, and were now adding even cruder language to their wailing. Some of the grunts were obviously tempted.

'Look at them!' Coilla seethed. 'I expected better of this band than it should be controlled by a swelling of their fertilising sacs!'

'They're young, they probably haven't come across the like before,' Alfray said. 'They don't know it's an illusion, and that it's likely to kill them.'

'Literally?' Jup asked.

'Given half a chance those whores will suck the life essences from any stupid enough to fall under their spell.'

Jup eyed the fleshy pageant. 'I can think of worse ways to go . . .'

'Jup!' Coilla scolded.

He blushed.

'What are they doing in a place like this anyway?' Stryke wondered. 'It's hardly an ideal spot for luring the unwary.'

'Either they've been driven away from more pleasant parts because they're such a nuisance,' Alfray speculated, 'or they're getting too ravaged for their usual haunts.'

'The latter by the looks of them,' Coilla sniffed.

'They're not particularly dangerous in themselves,' Alfray added. 'They rely on their victims going to them willingly. They have no fighting skills that I'm aware of.'

The grunts were shouting ribald comments back at the nymphs, and several were edging closer to them.

'It's a good thing Haskeer isn't here,' Jup remarked.

Alfray pulled a face. 'Perish the thought.'

'We don't have time for this nonsense,' Stryke decided.

'Just what I was thinking,' Coilla declared, drawing her sword. She strode in the direction of the glade.

'As I said,' Alfray called after her, 'there's no need to fight them!'

She ignored him and kept going. But her target was the grunts. She laid about them with the flat of her sword, singling out their backsides for special attention. Half a dozen whacks and a chorus of yelps later and they were running for the camp.

The would-be nymph seducers jeered in a distinctly unladylike fashion and slunk away.

Coilla marched back to the others. 'There's nothing like a tanned arse to dampen passion,' she proclaimed, re-sheathing her sword. 'Though I'm disgusted that any of our troopers should have been interested in the first place.'

'We've wasted enough time,' Stryke complained. 'We can't kick our heels around here for the rest of our lives. I want a decision on Scratch, and I want us to reach it now.'

They argued the pros and cons, and in the end decided to set out for the trolls' homeland. Once there, they'd reassess the position.

The route they chose followed an ancient trading trail, north towards the Mani settlement of Ladygrove. Before reaching it they would turn north-east to Scratch. It was a journey not without peril, but any movement in the human-infested south had its dangers. All they could do was proceed with caution and stay alert for trouble.

Haskeer had taken no part in the discussion about travelling to Scratch. On his past record, that was unprecedented. They put his taciturn state down to the illness. But he had recovered enough physically to ride unaided. Certainly his stubbornness was sufficiently restored for him to insist he would.

Stryke made a point of riding with him. After an hour or so of virtual silence, he said, 'How you feeling?'

Haskeer stared at him, as though surprised to be asked. Finally he came out with, 'I've never felt better.'

Stryke couldn't fail to pick up the strangely subdued edge to Haskeer's reply, and begged to differ. But he didn't do it aloud, just responded with a neutral 'Good.'

Another wordless moment or two passed before Haskeer said, 'Can I see the stars?'

Stryke was a little taken aback at the request, and hesitated. But then he thought, *Why shouldn't he want to see them? Doesn't he have a right?* It wasn't as if he couldn't handle any problems Haskeer might cause.

Stryke dug into his belt pouch and held the stars out for him to look at.

From the expression on Haskeer's face he was much more interested in them than he had ever appeared to be before. He stretched out his own hand and waited for Stryke to place them in it. Again Stryke hesitated. Then he laid them on the open palm.

Haskeer stared at the objects, fascinated.

The silence went on long enough, as they rode, for Stryke to start feeling a little restive. Something strange, a look Stryke hadn't seen there before, burned in Haskeer's eyes.

At last the sergeant looked up and said, 'They're beautiful.'

It was such an uncharacteristic thing for him to say that Stryke didn't know how to respond. In the event, he didn't have to. A forward scout appeared, galloping hard towards him.

'Tidings from the advance,' Stryke said, holding out his hand. 'Give 'em back.'

Haskeer continued gazing at the artefacts.

'*Haskeer!* The stars.'

'Eh? Oh, yes. Here.'

He passed them over and Stryke returned them to his pouch.

The scout arrived.

'What is it, Talag?'

'Party of humans coming this way, sir. Twenty or thirty of them, about a mile further along.'

'Hostile?'

'I don't think they're a threat, unless it's a trick. They're females, children and babes mostly, with some old of both sexes. Look like they're refugees.'

'Did they see you?'

'Don't think so. They're not a fighting unit, Captain. Most of them can hardly walk.'

'Hold on here, I'll come forward with you.'

Stryke looked at Haskeer. He would have expected him to have something to say about the possibility of an encounter with humans, but he seemed unperturbed. So he ignored him and pulled back to the next rank, where Coilla and Jup were riding abreast.

'Did you hear that?'

They had.

'I'm going ahead. Bring along the column. And, er, keep an eye on things, yes?' He nodded at Haskeer. They got his meaning and nodded back.

'Alfray!' Stryke called. 'Follow me!'

Coilla and Jup assumed the lead as he set off with Talag and Alfray. Spurring their horses, they sped ahead of the column. Rounding a curve or two in the track, they came to the group of humans.

They were as Talag had described; mostly women, some with babes in arms, and children. There was a smattering of hobbling ancient ones. The orcs' arrival sent a ripple of alarm through the ragged company. Children hugged their mothers' legs, old men did their best to stand defensively.

Stryke saw no threat, or any reason to alarm them further. He drew up his horse and, in order to seem less intimidating, dismounted. Alfray and Talag did likewise.

A lone woman stepped forward. She seemed quite young under the grime. Her unwashed waist-length blonde hair was plaited down her back, and her clothing was bedraggled. She was obviously frightened, but faced Stryke with a straight back and proud demeanour.

'We're only women and children,' she said, her voice wavering nervously, 'and a few old ones. We've no ill-intent, nor could we offer you violence if we did. We only want to pass.'

Stryke thought her little speech was delivered bravely. 'We don't make war on females and young ones,' he replied. 'Or on any offering us no threat.'

'I've your word none will be harmed?'

'You have.' He scanned their exhausted, worried faces. 'Where are you from?'

'Ladygrove.'

'So you're Manis?'

'Yes. And you orcs have fought on our side, haven't you?' It was probably said as much to reassure herself as ask a question.

'We have.' Stryke didn't like to tell her that they had had little choice in the matter.

'That's as it should be. You elder races, like us, believe in the pantheon of gods.'

Stryke nodded but said nothing on the subject. There were greater differences between orcs and humans than there were similarities. He saw no point in raising them now. Instead he asked, 'What's happened at Ladygrove that's made you leave it?'

'An onslaught by a Uni army. Most of our menfolk were killed, and we only narrowly escaped.'

'The settlement's fallen?'

'It hadn't when we left. A few were holding out, but in truth they stand next to no chance of avoiding being overrun.' Her glum face brightened a little. 'Are you on your way to help defend it?'

Stryke had been hoping she wouldn't ask that. 'No. We're on . . . another mission. To Scratch. I'm sorry.'

The shadow recast itself over her features. 'I was hoping you were the answer to our prayers.' She put on a bold and unconvincing smile. 'Oh well, the gods will provide.'

'Where are you heading?' Alfray wanted to know.

'Just . . . away. We were hoping to make contact with another of the Mani settlements.'

'Take our advice and don't stray on to the plains. The area around Weaver's Lea is especially perilous at the moment.'

'We'd heard as much.'

'Stick to the inlet,' Stryke added. 'You won't need to be told to avoid Trinity.' He agonised about whether to mention Hobrow's posse. In the event he didn't.

'Our thought was to make for the west-coast settlements,' she explained. 'Hexton, perhaps, or Vermillion. We should have a favourable reception there.'

Stryke took in their pathetic state. 'It's a long march.' *A murderously long march if the truth be known*, he thought.

'With the gods' help we'll prevail.'

He had no reason to be well disposed towards humans, but he wanted to believe she was right.

At that moment the rest of the Wolverines came into view and galloped up to join them. There was another stirring of unease among the refugees.

'Don't be concerned,' Stryke assured them. 'Our band won't hurt you.'

The orcs dismounted and gazed at the raggle-taggle collection of humans facing them.

Most came forward, Coilla and Jup at their head. The sight of a female orc, and a dwarf in orcs' company, drew many curious looks and whispered comments. Haskeer hung back, but Stryke had no time to think about his eccentricities at the moment.

'We left with little more than the clothes on our back,' the woman told them. 'Could you spare us some water?'

'Yes,' Stryke agreed, 'and perhaps some rations. Though not a lot; we're short ourselves.'

'You're kind. Thank you.'

Stryke set a couple of troopers to the task.

A small child, a female of the species, moved hesitantly forward, eyes wide, a thumb planted firmly in her mouth. She clutched the woman's skirt and stared at the orcs. The woman looked down at her and smiled.

'You must forgive her. Forgive us all. Few of us have been in the company of orcs before, for all that your race has fought on our behalf.'

The child, blonde like the woman and sharing her features, let go of the skirt and walked the last few steps to the orcs. Her gaze went from Coilla to Stryke to Alfray to Jup and back again.

She removed her thumb and said, 'What's that?' She pointed at Coilla' face.

Coilla didn't take her meaning. She was puzzled.

The child added, 'Those marks. On your face.'

'Oh, the tattoos. They're emblems of our rank.'

The girl looked blank.

'They let everyone know who's in charge.' Coilla saw a stick by the trail and bent to pick it up. Then she crouched next to a patch of denuded earth. 'Look, I'll show you. Our . . . chief is Stryke here.' She indicated him with the stick, then began drawing a crude picture. 'You see, he has two stripes like this on each cheek.' She scraped ((. 'That means he's a captain. The boss, if you like.' She pointed at Jup. 'He's a sergeant, so the marks make his face look like this.' She drew -(-)-. 'Sergeants are second in command to captains. I'm the next one down, a corporal, and my marks go this way.' She scratched ( ). 'Understand?'

Entranced, the child nodded. She smiled at Coilla and reached for the stick, then began scraping her own meaningless designs.

The grunts returned with the water and some rations.

'They're meagre,' Stryke apologised, 'but you're welcome to them.'

'It's still more than we had before meeting you,' the woman replied. 'May the gods bless you.'

Stryke felt uncomfortable. After all, most of his contacts with humans had been to do with trying to kill as many as he could. At his word, the grunts began moving among the humans and distributing the sparse supplies.

Stryke, Alfray and Jup watched as the troopers were thanked profusely, and at Coilla on her hands and knees with the child.

'The twists fate keeps in store are odd, aren't they?' Jup whispered.

But the woman overheard. 'You find this strange? So do we. But in truth we're not so different to you, or to any of the elder races. At heart, all want peace and despise war.'

'Orcs are born to war,' Stryke replied, a little indignantly. He softened slightly at the look she gave him. 'But it must be just. Destruction for its own sake holds no appeal for us.'

'My race has done you many wrongs.'

He was surprised to hear such an admission from a human, but again held his tongue.

A trooper was passing by the child kneeling with Coilla. He held a water sack. The child reached for it. Removing the stopper, the grunt handed it to her. She was raising it to her lips when her face distorted in a peculiar way. Then a terrible sound issued from her.

'Atishoo!'

Coilla scrambled to her feet. She and the trooper quickly backed off.

To Stryke's horror, the woman smiled. 'Poor little thing. She has a chill.'

'Chill?'

'Just a mild one. She'll be over it in a day or two.' She laid her hand on the child's brow. 'As if she didn't have enough to put up with. I guess we'll all have it before long.'

'This . . . chill,' Coilla said. 'Is it a disease?'

'Disease? Well, yes, I suppose it is. But it's just—'

'Back to the horses, all of you!' Stryke barked.

The band rushed for their mounts, abandoning the water sacks and rations.

The woman was baffled. All the humans were.

'I don't understand. What's wrong? The child has no more than a cold.'

Stryke's fear was that the band would lay into the humans and slay them. He saw no benefit in delay. 'We have to leave. I'm sorry. I wish you . . . well.'

He turned and made for his own horse.

'Wait!' she called. 'Wait! I don't—'

He ignored her, yelled an order and led the band away.

They galloped off at speed, leaving the humans standing in the road looking totally baffled.

As they rode, Jup said, 'That was a near thing.'

'It just goes to show that you can't trust humans,' Alfray remarked. 'Mani *or* Uni.'

As far as Jennesta was concerned, the only good Uni was a dead Uni.

Certainly the Uni corpses half submerged in the bloody water-filled ditch she gazed into had proved useful in providing what she needed. Now, though, she saw it as a mixed blessing.

Jennesta's intention had been to use the pool's gory contents as a medium for farsight. It was a particularly beneficial tool when in the middle of a conflict. Knowing the enemy's deployment gave an obvious advantage. The trouble was that no sooner had she begun scrying than Adpar's smug face appeared in the pool.

At least Sanara's priggish features were absent for once.

Jennesta suffered a moment's barrage of insincere and empty greetings before interrupting. 'This is not the most convenient time for chit-chat,' she snarled.

'Oh dear,' Adpar's likeness replied. *'And there was I thinking you'd be interested in news of those outlaws you've been getting so fussed about.'*

Alarm drums pounded in Jennesta's head. She adopted an air of sham indifference. 'Outlaws? What outlaws?'

'You may come over as a good liar to your underlings, dear, but you could never fool me. So stop the little-girl-lost act, it's sickening. We both know what I'm talking about.'

'Supposing I did. What could you possibly have to say on the matter?'

'Only that those you seek have another of the relics.'

'What?'

'Or perhaps you have no idea what I'm talking about. Again.'

'How did you come by this news?'

'I have my sources.'

'If you had anything to do with this—'

'Me? *And to do with what, exactly?'*

'It would be just like you to try to scupper my plans, Adpar.'

'So you have plans, do you? Perhaps I will take an interest after all.'

'Stay out of this, Adpar! If you so much as—'

'Ma'am!' someone called from nearby.

Jennesta looked up, glaring. General Mersadion was standing several paces away, looking like a child who'd come to announce he'd fouled himself.

'What is it?' she snapped.

'You told me to let you know when we reached the point of—'

'Yes, yes! I'll be there!'

He backed off, humbly.

Jennesta turned back to Adpar's grimacing visage. 'You've

not heard the last of this!' Then she slashed her hand through the icy, bloodied water, banishing the image.

She got to her feet and strode to the bowing general.

They were on a hill overlooking a battlefield. The battle about to start was not particularly large, having perhaps a thousand combatants on either side, but it was to be fought over a point of strategic importance.

The Queen's side consisted of Manis, dwarves and orcs, the latter, as ever, forming the backbone. The other side was almost entirely composed of Unis, with a smattering of dwarves.

'I'm ready,' she told Mersadion. 'Prepare the protection.'

He swiped down his hand and a row of orc buglers further along the hill turned their backs on the battlefield and sounded a shrill blast. Mersadion covered his eyes.

Down below, Jennesta's army, hearing the signal, did the same thing. Much to the mystification of the Unis.

She raised her hands and wove a magical conjuration. Next she reached inside her cloak and produced an object resembling an extraordinarily large gem. The multi-faceted fist-sized jewel shimmered, its interior swirling with a myriad of colours. She tossed it into the air.

Jennesta exerted no more than casual force, yet the bizarrely sized gem travelled up and up as though it were a feather caught by the wind. Many of the opposing army below saw it, glinting in the weak sunlight, and followed its climb with fascination. She noticed that a few of the enemy warriors aped her force and covered their eyes. There were always one or two smarter than the rest. But never enough.

The jewel rose lazily, turning slowly end on end, a glittering pinpoint of concentrated illumination.

Then it detonated with a silent flash of light that would have shamed a hundred thunderbolts.

The intense explosion of radiance lasted barely a second. It had hardly faded when the screaming started own below. The enemy were staggering in panic, pawing at their eyes, dropping their weapons, colliding with each other.

There was another blast from the bugles. Her army uncovered their eyes and rushed in for the slaughter.

Mersadion was at the Queen's side.

'A useful addition to our armoury,' she said, 'optical munitions.'

The screams of the helplessly blind were drifting up to them.

'We can't use it too often, though,' she added. 'They'll be wise to it. And it is dreadfully draining.' She patted at her forehead with a lace handkerchief. 'Bring me my horse.'

The General ran off to obey her order.

On the battlefield, the butchery reached a pitch. It was gratifying, but not her immediate concern.

Her mind was on the Wolverines.

22

The following days passed more or less uneventfully for the Wolverines.

Only Haskeer's mood caused them concern. He swung between periods of elation and depression, and often said things they found difficult to understand. Alfray assured the band that their comrade was still recovering from an illness most elder race members were lucky to survive, and that he should soon be on the mend. Stryke wasn't alone in wondering when that would happen.

But this was put to the back of everyone's mind when they arrived at Scratch on the evening of the third day.

The trolls' homeland was in the centre of the great plains, as near as damn, but the terrain couldn't have been more different to its lush surroundings. Rolling grassland gave way to shrub. In short order the shrub itself blended into shale, and the shale gave way to a landscape more rock than soil.

Scratch proper was heralded by a collection of what seemed to be ragged hills. Closer inspection revealed them to be rock. It was as though mountains had somehow been covered by earth to ninety per cent of their height, leaving only their rugged peaks exposed.

What the orcs knew, as everybody did, was that the action of water, aided by troll mining, had honeycombed the porous ground beneath with a labyrinth of tunnels and chambers. What they held was a mystery. Few if any of those bold enough to enter had ever returned to tell their tale.

'How long has it been since anybody mounted an armed attack on this place?' Stryke wondered.

'I don't know,' Coilla admitted. 'Though it's a good bet they were of greater strength than a depleted warband.'

'Kimball Hobrow seems to think he can do it.'

'He's unlikely to go in with anything less than a small army. We're not much more than a score.'

'We're small in number, yes; but experienced, well armed, determined—'

'You don't have to sell it to me, Stryke.' She smiled. 'Not that I'm overly keen on anything that takes me away from the open air.' She glanced around the rocky terrain they were creeping through. 'But none of this means a thing unless we can find a way in.'

'There're said to be secret ways. We don't have much hope of stumbling on any of those. But a main entrance is spoken of as well. That'd be a start.'

'Wouldn't they hide a main entrance too?'

'They might not need to. They'd probably have it well guarded, and perhaps more importantly, the reputation Scratch has is enough to keep most away.'

'Right on cue. Look.'

She pointed at a massive outcropping of rock. The face it turned to them was a pool of blackness, much darker than any of the other jutting slabs around it. Staring hard, Stryke realised it was an opening.

They approached it warily.

It was a cave-like aperture, but not very big; the size perhaps of a modestly proportioned farmhouse. The interior seemed empty, though they couldn't be entirely sure as it was so dark inside.

'Just a minute,' Coilla said. 'This should help.'

She took a flint from her belt, and one of the cloths she used to polish her knives. Making fire, she ignited the twisted rag, producing just enough light for them to see a few steps ahead. They edged in.

'I'm beginning to think this is just a hollowed rock,' Stryke commented.

Coilla happened to glance down. *'Stop!'* she hissed, grabbing his arm. Her voice echoed. 'Look.'

No more than three paces ahead of them was a cavernous hole in the ground. They crept to it and peered over, but couldn't make out anything in its inky depths. Coilla dropped the burning cloth. They watched as it became a minute pinpoint of light, then vanished.

'Could be bottomless,' Coilla speculated.

'I doubt it. Anyway, unless the other search parties come up with anything better, this might be our only way in. Let's get back.'

Greever Aulay fingered his eye-patch.

'It always hurts when those bastards are around,' he complained.

Lekmann gave a derisive laugh.

Aulay scowled. 'You can mock. But it was paining like hell when we were in Jennesta's palace with all those damn orcs about the place.'

'What do you think, Jabez?' Lekmann said. 'Reckon the boy's got an orc sniffer in that empty socket of his?'

'Nah,' Blaan replied. 'Reckon *he* does though, ever since one of 'em took his eye.'

'You don't know what you're talking about, the pair of you,' Aulay grumbled. 'And don't call me *boy*, Micah.'

Trinity was well behind them now. Their search hadn't taken them into the Uni settlement. They wouldn't be so foolhardy. But they knew from speaking to women working in the fields, to whom they presented themselves as good, upright Uni gentlemen, that the Wolverines had been there.

There had apparently been some kind of a fuss. But when Lekmann tried to find out exactly what, the women clammed up. All they could find out was that the orcs had done something bad enough that it warranted half the township chasing them clear over to Calyparr Inlet. Which seemed to point to the warband not being in league with the Unis. The bounty hunters didn't care about that. All that concerned them was getting the relic, and as many renegade heads as they could carry back for the reward.

So they headed for Calyparr too, in the hope of picking up the trail. But they had wandered along the water's edge for nearly a day now without seeing hide nor hair of the outlaws.

'I think we ain't going to find them in these parts,' Blaan declared.

'You leave the thinking to me, big man,' Lekmann advised him. 'It never was your strong point.'

'Maybe he's right, Micah,' Aulay said. 'If they were ever here, they've long gone.'

'Oh, so your eye ain't that reliable after all,' Lekmann mocked.

Their exchange was cut short as they rounded a knot of trees.

Lekmann's eyes widened. 'Now what we got here?'

By the side of the trail was a pitiable makeshift camp. It was populated by a motley crew of human women, children and oldsters. They looked all but done in.

'Don't see no men,' Aulay remarked. 'None likely to trouble us at any rate.'

The humans, seeing the approaching riders, began to stir.

A woman detached herself from the rest and came forward.

Her garb was grubby and her lengthy blonde hair was bound in a single strand. Lekmann thought there was a certain haughtiness about her.

She looked at the oddly matched trio. The tall, skinny one with the scar. The short, hard-faced one with the eye-patch. The one with no hair and built like a brick shit-house.

Lekmann gave her a leering smile. 'Good day.'

'Who are you?' she asked suspiciously. 'What do you want?'

'You got nothing to worry about, ma'am. We're just going about our business.' He looked the crowd over. 'In fact we got a lot in common.'

'You're Manis too?'

That was what he wanted. 'Yes, ma'am. We're just good gods-fearing folk like yourselves.'

She seemed relieved at that, but not much.

Lekmann slipped a foot from its stirrup. 'Mind if we dismount?'

'I can't stop you.'

He climbed off his horse, keeping his movements slow and deliberate so as not to spook them. Aulay and Blaan did the same.

Lekmann stretched. 'Been riding a long time. It's good to take a break.'

'Don't think we're being unneighbourly,' the woman told him, 'but we've no food nor water to share.'

'No matter. I can see you're down on your luck. Been on the road long?'

'Feels like forever.'

'Where you from?'

'Ladygrove. There's trouble in those parts.'

'There's trouble in all parts, ma'am. These are tormented times and that's a fact.'

She eyed Blaan and Aulay. 'Your friends don't say much.'

'Men of few words. More doers than talkers, you might say.

But let's not waste words ourselves. We stopped because we were hoping you could help us.'

'Like I said, we don't have any—'

'No, not that way. It's just that we're looking for . . . certain parties, and as you've been travelling a while we thought you might have seen 'em.'

'We've seen precious few people on our journey.'

'I'm not talking people. I'm referring to a bunch of elder racers.'

What could have been a cloud of renewed suspicion passed across her face. 'What race might that be?'

'Orcs.'

He thought the word hit some kind of target. The shutters seemed to come down behind her eyes. 'We'll, I don't—'

'Yes we did, Mummy!'

The bounty hunters turned and saw a girl child skipping forward. 'Those funny men with the marks on their faces,' she said. Her voice was nasal, as though she had a cold. 'You remember!'

Lekmann knew they'd struck gold.

'Oh yes.' The woman strained to sound casual. 'We did run into a group of them, couple of days back. Did no more than pass the time really. They seemed in a hurry.'

Lekmann was about to put another question when the child came up to him.

'Are you their friends?' she asked, sniffily.

'Not now!' he snapped, irritated at the interruption.

The girl backed off, frightened, and ran for her mother's protection. Lekmann's reaction made the woman even warier. A look of defiance came to her face. The other Manis were stiffening with tension too, but he saw little to worry about there and paid them no heed.

He dropped the friendly manner. 'You know where these orcs went?'

'How should I?'

Now she'd got her back up. That was a shame.

'Anyway, why do you want to find them?' she added.

'It's to do with some unfinished business.'

'You sure you aren't Unis?'

He grinned like a latrine rat. 'We're not Unis, that's for sure.'

Aulay and Blaan laughed. Unpleasantly.

The woman was growing alarmed. 'Who *are* you?'

'Just travellers who want to be on our way once we've got some information.' He looked around slyly. 'Maybe your menfolk would know where the orcs went?'

'They're . . . they're out hunting for food.'

'Don't think they are, ma'am. I don't think you've got any menfolk.' He glanced at her companions. 'At least none young and fit. One or two would have stayed with you if you had.'

'They're nearby, and they'll be back any time now.' A note of desperation crept into her voice. 'If you don't want trouble—'

'You're a bad liar, ma'am.' He stared pointedly at the child. 'Now let's keep this nice and friendly, shall we? Where did those orcs go?'

She saw what was in his eyes and visibly gave up. 'All right. They did mention something about heading for Scratch.'

'The trolls' place? Now why would they be doing that?'

'How should I know?'

'It don't add up. You sure they didn't tell you anything else?'

'No, they didn't.' The child tugged at her skirt and started to cry. 'It's all right, darling,' the woman soothed. 'Everything's fine.'

'Don't believe you're telling me all you know,' Lekmann said menacingly. 'Maybe they ain't even heading for Scratch at all.'

'I've told you all I know. There's no more.'

'Well, ma'am, you'll appreciate I have to be sure of that.'

He nodded at Blaan and Aulay. The three of them moved forward, fanning out.

By the time they left, he knew she had been telling the truth.

The way Stryke saw it, circumstances dictated a straightforward plan.

'We've got just one chance, and I say we have no choice but a direct assault. We go in, do the job, get out.'

'That sounds fair enough,' Coilla said. 'But think about the difficulties. First, going in. The only possible way we've found is that shaft in the cave. It might not lead into the trolls' labyrinth. Or even if it does, it could be incredibly deep.'

'We've got plenty of rope. If we need more we can find some vines and make it.'

'All right. Then you say we'll do the job. A lot easier said than done, Stryke. We don't know how many miles of tunnels there are down there. If they have a star, which is only a maybe at best, we have to find the thing. Don't forget that for all we know, it's going to be pitch black down there. The trolls have eyesight that copes with the dark. We don't.'

'We'll take torches.'

'And really make ourselves obvious. We'll be on their ground and at a disadvantage.'

'Not as far as our blades go we won't.'

'Finally, getting out,' she ploughed on. 'Well, that speaks for itself, doesn't it? You're assuming we could.'

'We've taken on long odds before, Coilla. I'm not going to let that stand in my way.'

She gave a resigned sigh. 'You're not, are you? You're determined to go through with this.'

'You know I am. But I'll not take any with me who don't want to go.'

'That's not the point. It's *how* we do it that concerns me. Just charging in isn't always the solution, you know.'

'Sometimes it is. Unless you can see a better way.'

'That's just it, damn you, I can't.'

'I know you're worried there's so much that could go wrong. So am I. So we'll take a little time getting this right.'

'Not too much,' Alfray interjected. 'What about Hobrow?'

'We bloodied his nose. I don't think he'll be here for a while yet, if at all.'

'It isn't only Hobrow. For all we know, everybody's out for us. And moving targets are the hardest to hit.'

'Granted. But targets that hit back tend to get left alone too.'

'Not when the whole damn country's after their heads.'

'What did you mean about taking time, Stryke?' Coilla asked. 'How much?'

He glanced up at the gathering twilight. 'The light's nearly gone. We could spend tomorrow searching for another way in. A really thorough search, with the area sectioned out. If we find a better way in, we'll use it. Otherwise we'll go for the entrance we know.'

'Or what we think is an entrance,' Coilla corrected him.

'Stryke, I don't want to put a damper on things,' Jup said, 'but *if* there's a star here and *if* we can get it . . . what then?'

'I was hoping nobody would ask that question.'

Alfray backed Jup. 'It has to be asked, Stryke. Else why go on here?'

'We go on because . . . well, because what else is there for us to do? We're orcs. We need a purpose. You know that.'

'If we carry on as we have, if we're being logical, and assuming we get out of Scratch in one piece, then we need a plan to find out where the other stars are,' Coilla reckoned.

'We've been lucky so far,' Jup said. 'It won't hold forever.'

'We make our own luck,' Stryke maintained.

Coilla had an idea. 'I was thinking that if trading the star, or stars, with Jennesta is out—'

'Which is it,' Stryke interrupted, 'as far as I'm concerned.'

'If that's not an option, perhaps we could trade them with somebody else.'

'Who?'

'I don't know! I'm clutching at straws here, Stryke, like the rest of you. I'm just thinking that if we can't find all five stars then the others aren't of any use to us. Whereas a good hoard of coin might make our lives easier.'

'The stars mean power. A power that could maybe do a lot of good for orcs and all the other elder races. I won't let that go easily. As for coin, you're forgetting the pellucid. Even a small amount would bring a good price.'

'What about the crystal, by the way?' Alfray asked. 'Have you thought of how it should be distributed?'

'I reckon that for now we keep it as communal property, for the benefit of the band in general. Any of you object?'

None did.

Haskeer, who had been standing at a distance and taking no part in the conversation, wandered over to them. He wore the vacant expression they'd almost got used to.

'What's happening?' he said.

'We're talking about how to get into Scratch,' Coilla told him.

Haskeer's face lit up as a notion hit him. 'Why don't we talk to the trolls?'

They laughed. Then it dawned on them that he wasn't trying to be funny.

'What do you mean, talk?' Alfray said.

'Think how much better things would be if the trolls were our friends.'

Alfray's jaw dropped. 'What?'

'Well, they could be, couldn't they? All our enemies could if we talked rather than fought them all the time.'

'I can't believe you're saying this, Haskeer,' Coilla confessed.

'Does it seem wrong?'

'Er, it just seems not . . . *you*.'

He considered the proposition. 'Oh. All right. Let's kill them then.'

'That's kind of what we thought we'd do, if we have to.'

Haskeer beamed. 'Good. Let me know when you need me. I'll be feeding my horse.'

He turned and walked away.

Jup said, 'What the *hell*?'

Coilla shook her head. 'He's seriously dippy these days.'

'Do you still say it's something he'll get over, Alfray?' Stryke asked.

'He's taking his time about it, I'll admit. But I've seen something similar to this before when troopers were recovering from heavy fevers. Or when they get ague of the lungs; you know, water in 'em. Quite often they spend days afterwards in a sort of daze, and it's not unknown for them to behave out of character.'

'Out of character!' Coilla exclaimed. 'He's about as far from his character as he can get.'

'I don't know whether to be worried or to thank the gods for the mood he's in,' Jup confessed.

'At least it's giving you a break from his bullying, and all of us a rest from his constant grumbling.'

'You're assuming he's this way because of the illness, Alfray,' Stryke said. 'Is it possible there's another reason? Could he have taken a blow to the head we don't know about?'

'There's no sign of that. He might have, I suppose, but you'd expect to see some marks of it. I'm no great expert on head injuries, Stryke, I just know, like you, that they can cause an orc to do and say odd things.'

'Well, he seems harmless enough, but keep an eye on him, all of you.'

'You can't let him take part in the mission, can you?' Coilla wanted to know.

'No, he'd be a burden. He'll stay behind, along with a grunt or two to guard the camp and horses. Not to mention the crystal. I thought you might like to stay with them, Coilla.'

She flared her nostrils. 'You're not saying *I'd* be a burden?'

'Course not. But you're not keen on enclosed places, you've made that clear more than once, and I need to leave somebody I can rely on. Because I'm not taking the stars with me. That's too much of a risk. You could look after them until we get back.' He noticed her expression. 'All right, it had crossed my mind that *if* we don't get back you could carry on the work, so to speak.'

'All by myself?'

Jup grinned. 'You'd have Haskeer.'

She glared at him. '*Very* funny.'

They all looked in Haskeer's direction.

He was patting his horse's head and feeding it from the palm of his hand.

23

It was the Lord's wrath in action. Kimball Hobrow had no doubt of it.

His search for the ungodly, the thieving non-humans that had taken what was his, had led him to range the shores of Calyparr, a group of followers ten score and more at his back. Now, as night fell, they had come upon a charnel scene. The bodies of some two dozen humans, mostly women and children, littered a stretch of land beside the merchants' trail.

Hobrow recognised their dress. It was immodest and self-indulgent, its bright colours pandering to vanity. He knew their kind; blasphemers, deviators from the path of righteousness. Wretched adherents of the Manifold spoor.

He walked among the slaughtered, a clutch of custodians in his wake. If the signs of butchery, of mangled limbs and rendered flesh, had any effect on the preacher he didn't show it.

'Take heed,' he intoned. 'These souls digressed from the true and only way. They embraced the obscene paganism of the impure races, and the Lord punished them for it. And the irony, brethren, was that He used non-humans as His tool, the instrument of His revenge. They lay down with the serpent and the serpent devoured them. It is fitting.'

He continued his inspection, studying the faces of the dead, the severity of their wounds.

'The arm of the Almighty is long and His ire knows no limit,' he thundered. 'He strikes down the unrighteous as surely as He rewards His chosen.'

A custodian called out to him from the other side of the killing ground. He strode to the man.

'What is it, Calvert?'

'This one's still alive, master.' He pointed to a woman.

She had a braid of long blonde hair. Her breast was bloody, her breathing shallow. She was near her end.

Hobrow knelt beside her. She seemed dimly aware of him and tried to say something, but no words came from her quivering lips.

He leaned closer. 'Speak, child. Confess your sins and unburden yourself.'

'They . . . they . . .'

'Who?'

'They came . . . and . . .'

'They? The orcs, you mean?'

'Orcs.' Her glazed eyes focused for a second. *'Yes . . . orcs.'*

'They did this to you?'

'Orcs . . . came . . .'

The custodians had gathered around. Hobrow addressed them. 'You see? No humans are safe from the accursed inhuman races, even those foolish enough to take their part.' He turned back to the dying woman. 'Where did they go?'

'Orcs . . .'

'Yes, the orcs.' He spoke slowly and deliberately. 'Do you know where they went?'

She made no reply. He grasped her hand and squeezed it. 'Where did they go?' he repeated.

'Scr . . . Scratch . . .'

'My God.' He let go of her and stood. Her hand reached for his and, unnoticed, feebly dropped back.

'To your horses!' he boomed, messianic passion burning in his eyes. 'The vermin we seek are in league with others of their kind. We embark upon a crusade, brethren!'

They dashed for their mounts, infected with his fervour.

'We'll have our revenge!' he vowed. 'The Lord will guide us and protect us!'

The Wolverines spent the entire day searching for another way into Scratch. If such existed, it was too well hidden for them to find. But they didn't encounter any trolls either, as they had feared they might, and that at least was a stroke of luck.

Stryke decided they would enter the labyrinth by the main entrance, as they'd come to call it, first thing in the morning. Now that night had fallen, all they could do was wait for the dawn. As some held that trolls came to the surface in the dark, double guards were posted, and all kept their arms near to hand.

Alfray suggested that a little pellucid be shared out. Stryke had no objection, providing they kept to a small quantity and none was allowed the guards. He didn't use any himself, but instead laid out a blanket at the edge of the camp and settled down to think and plan.

The last thing he was aware of as he drifted into sleep was the crystal's pungent odour.

Stars were beginning to show through in the gathering twilight. They were as sharp and clear as he had ever seen them.

He stood on a cliff's edge.

A good spear throw away a corresponding wall of sheer rock faced him. He saw trees on the other side, tall and straight. The space between was a deep canyon. Far below roared a white-foamed river, throwing up clouds of vaporous mist as it pounded at boulders in its path. The channel of rock extended for as far as he could see on either side.

The cliffs were spanned by a gently swaying suspension bridge built from stout rope and woven twine, with wooden slats to walk on.

For no other reason than that it was there, he set his foot upon it and began to cross.

Away from the shelter of the rock face, a stiff breeze tempered the pleasant warmth of the maturing evening. It carried a fine spray of droplets from the torrent beneath, cooling his skin. He walked slowly, savouring the magnificence of the scenery and breathing deep of the crystal air.

He was perhaps a third of the way across when he became aware of someone walking towards him from the other side. He couldn't make out their features, but saw that they moved with a purposeful step and easy confidence. He kept on and didn't slow his pace. Soon the other traveller was near enough to be properly seen.

It was the orc female he had met here before. Wherever here *might be.*

She wore her head-dress of flaming scarlet war feathers, and her sword was strapped to her back, its hilt visible above the left shoulder. One of her hands lightly touched the guide rope at her side.

Recognising each other at the same time, she smiled. He smiled too.

They came together midway.

'Our paths cross again,' she said. 'Well met.'

He felt the same strange tug at his feelings that he had in his previous encounters with her.

'Well met,' he returned.

'You're truly an orc of passing strangeness,' she told him.

'How so?'

'Your comings and goings are veiled in mystery.'

'I might say the same of you.'

'Not so. I'm always here. You appear and disappear like the haze bred by the river. Where are you going?'

'Nowhere. That is, I . . . explore, I suppose. And you?'

'I move as my life dictates.'

'Yet you carry your sword where it can't be quickly drawn.'

She glanced at his blade, hanging in its belt sheath. 'And you don't. My way is better.'

'Your way used to be the custom in my land, at least when travelling in safe parts. But that was long ago.'

'I offer none a threat and travel as I please without danger. It's not so where you come from?'

'No.'

'Then your land must be grim indeed. I offer it no offence in saying that.'

'I take none. You speak the truth.'

'Perhaps you should come here and make your camp.'

He wasn't sure if it was some kind of invitation. 'That would be pleasant,' he replied. 'I wish I could.'

'Something stops you?'

'I don't know how to reach this land.'

She laughed. 'You can always be counted on for riddles. How can you say that when you're here now?'

'It makes no more sense to me than it does to you.' He turned from her and looked down at the thundering water. 'I understand my coming here no more than the river understands where it flows. Less so, for the river has always flowed to the ocean, and is timeless.'

The female moved closer to him. 'We are timeless too. We flow with the river of life.' She reached into her pouch and took out two small pebbles, round and smooth. 'I took these from the river's bank.' She let them slip from her hand and they fell away. 'Now they're one with the river again, as you and I are one with the river of time. Don't you see how apt it is that we should meet on a bridge?'

'I don't know if I understand your meaning.'

'Don't you?'

'I mean, I feel there's truth in what you say, but it's just beyond my grasp.'

'Then reach further and you'll understand.'

'How would I do that?'

'By not trying.'

'Now who's talking in riddles?'

'The truth is simple, it's we who choose to see it as a riddle. Understanding will come to you.'

'When?'

'It begins by asking that question. Be patient, stranger.' She smiled. 'I still call you stranger. I don't know your name.'

'Nor I yours.'

'What are *you called?'*

'Stryke.'

'Stryke. It's a strong name. It serves you well. Yes . . . Stryke,' she repeated, as though relishing it. 'Stryke.'

'Stryke. Stryke! *Stryke!*'

He was being shaken.

'Uh? Uhm . . . Wha . . . what's *your* name?'

'It's me, Coilla. Who did you think it was? Snap out of it, Stryke!'

He blinked and took in his surroundings. Realisation returned. It was daybreak. They were at Scratch.

'You look strange, Stryke. You all right?'

'Yes . . . yes. Just a . . . a dream.'

'Seems to me you've been having a lot of those lately. Nightmare, was it?'

'No. It was far from being a nightmare. It was only a dream.'

Jennesta dreamt of blood and burning, of death and destruction, suffering and despair. She dreamt of the principles of lust, and the enlightenment to be gained thereof.

As was her wont.

She woke up in her inner sanctum. The mangled body of a

human male, barely into manhood, lay on the crimson altar amid the detritus of the previous night's ritual. She ignored it, rose and wrapped her nakedness in a cloak of furs. A pair of high leather boots completed her wardrobe.

It was first light and she had business to attend to.

As she left the chamber the orc guards outside stiffened to attention. 'Come,' she ordered briskly.

They fell in behind her. She led them through a maze of corridors, up flights of stone-slab stairs and finally into the open air, emerging on to a parade ground in front of the palace.

Several hundred members of her orc army were there, standing in well-ordered ranks. The audience, for that was what it amounted to, had been made up of representatives from each regiment. It was an efficient way of ensuring that word of what they were about to witness would spread quickly through the whole of Jennesta's horde.

The troops faced a stout wooden stake the height of a small tree. An orc soldier was lashed to it. There were bundles of faggots and kindling stacked almost to his waist.

General Mersadion met Jennesta with a bow. 'We're ready to proceed, Your Majesty.'

'Let the verdict be known.'

Mersadion nodded at an orc captain. He stepped forward and raised a parchment. In a booming voice, the attribute that had landed him his unpopular task, he began to read.

'By order of Her Imperial Majesty Queen Jennesta, let all note the findings of a military tribunal in the case of Krekner, sergeant ordinary of the Imperial Horde.'

All eyes were on the man at the stake.

'The charges laid against said Krekner were, one, that he knowingly disobeyed an order issued by a superior officer and, two, that in disobeying that order he did show cowardice in the face of the enemy. The tribunal's findings were that he be judged guilty on both counts and should be condemned to suffer such penalty as the above charges carry.'

The Captain lowered the parchment. It was deathly silent in the square.

Mersadion addressed the prisoner. 'You have the right of final appeal to the Queen. Will you exercise it?'

'I will,' Krekner replied. His voice was even and loud. He was bearing the ordeal with dignity.

'Proceed,' Mersadion said.

The sergeant turned his head to Jennesta. 'I meant no disrespect as far as my orders went, ma'am. Only we were told to re-engage when there were comrades lying wounded that we could have helped. I held back just long enough to stem a fellow orc's flow of blood, and believe I saved his life by doing it. Then I obeyed the order to advance. It was a delay, not disobedience, and I plead compassion as the cause. I feel that my sentence is unjust on that count.'

It was probably the longest, and certainly the most important speech he had ever made. He looked to the Queen expectantly.

She kept him, and all of them, waiting for a full half-minute before speaking. It pleased her that they might think she was considering mercy.

'Orders are given to be obeyed,' she announced. 'There are no exceptions, and certainly not in the name of . . . *compassion.*' She mouthed the word as though it were distasteful to her. 'Appeal denied. The sentence will be carried out. Let your fate be an example to all.'

She lifted a hand, muttering the while an incantation. The condemned orc braced himself.

A slither of concentrated light spurted from her fingertips, arced through the air and bathed the kindling at his feet. The fuel ignited immediately. Orange-yellow flames erupted and instantly began to climb.

The orc sergeant faced his death courageously, but in the end he could not hold back the screams. Jennesta looked on impassively as he writhed in the blaze.

In her mind's eye, the victim was Stryke of the Wolverines.

The Wolverines were ready to set out.

Stryke thought that Haskeer would object to not being included in the mission. He was wrong. His sergeant accepted the news without complaint. In a way, that was more troubling than one of the rants they'd become accustomed to.

Taking aside Coilla, Alfray and Jup, Stryke outlined his plan.

'As agreed, Coilla, you'll stay here at base camp with Haskeer,' he said. 'I've assigned Reafdaw to stay too.'

'What about the pellucid?' she asked.

'Rather than leave it divided up in individual saddlebags, I've ordered it to be pooled.' He pointed at a bundle of sacks stacked near the tethered horses. 'You might like to load it on to a couple of mounts. That way, if you need to make a quick getaway, without the rest of us, you'll save time.'

'I understand. What about the stars?'

Stryke reached into his pouch. 'Here. What you do with them if we don't get out is up to you.'

She studied the strange objects for a second, then slipped them into her own belt bag. 'In the event, I hope it'll be something you'd approve of.' They exchanged smiles. 'But what *are* the contingency plans if you don't come back?'

'None that involves you coming in after us. Is that understood?'

'Yes.' It was a reluctant reply.

'It's an order. I'd say that if we're not out by this time tomorrow, we won't be out at all. In which case get yourselves away from here. You might use the time to think about where to go.'

'The gods know where that'll be. But we'll think of something if we must. Just don't give us cause to, right?'

'We'll do our best. And it goes without saying that if any trolls turn up above ground before the deadline's reached, that's likely to mean only one thing. In which case get out of here anyway.'

She nodded.

'What's the plan for us once we get down there, Stryke?' Alfray said.

'Flexible. Has to be. We don't know what we'll find, or even if what we think is an entrance will turn out to be one.'

'A blind mission. Not ideal.'

'No, but we've been on them before.'

'What worries me is that we'll be literally blind down there if anything goes wrong,' Jup confessed.

'The trolls have the advantage in terms of the darkness, it's true. But we're taking plenty of torches. As long as we have them, we should be a match for any opposition. And don't underestimate the element of surprise.'

'It's still a hell of a risk.'

'Taking risks is what we're trained for, and I'd wager we have more experience in it than the cave dwellers below.'

'Let's hope so. Shouldn't we be going?'

'Yes. Muster the grunts. Gather the ropes and torches.'

Jup and Alfray went off to do it.

'I want to come as far as the entrance with you,' Coilla stated. 'All right?'

'Come. But don't linger there. I want you back here helping to guard base camp and that pellucid.'

The band left Haskeer with Reafdaw and marched to the entrance.

Daylight made the interior of the cave look even darker, and they entered with caution. At the edge of the shaft they ignited torches.

'Toss over some light,' Stryke ordered in a hushed tone.

A pair of grunts dropped two brands each. They watched them plummet. This time, unlike the burning rag Coilla had dropped, they didn't disappear from sight. They landed on something solid, but it was a long way down.

'At least it doesn't look too deep for the amount of rope we have,' Alfray judged.

The guttering torches threw out a circle of light, though not enough for the band to make out any details of what lay below. At least nothing seemed to be moving down there.

Several grunts were given the job of firmly securing the ends of three ropes around rocks and trees outside the cave.

'Just in case there's some kind of trap waiting to be sprung below,' Stryke told them all, 'we go down quickly and in force.'

The band formed three lines by the ropes. More torches were lit and passed out to them. Some band members clutched knives in their teeth.

Coilla wished them luck and backed off.

Stryke nodded. 'Let's go,' he said, clasping a rope.

He went over the edge first. The rest of the band quickly spilled into the pit after him.

24

Stryke let go of the rope and dropped the last ten feet or so.

He quickly drew his sword. Jup landed beside him and likewise plucked free his blade. The rest of the band landed in short order and looked around.

They were in a roughly circular chamber that opened out to about three times the diameter of the shaft they had just climbed down. Two tunnels ran from it, the larger directly ahead, a smaller one to their left.

The place was as quiet as the grave and there was no sign of inhabitants. It smelt unpleasantly earthy.

'What now?' Jup whispered.

'First we secure our bridgehead.' Stryke motioned over a couple of grunts. 'Liffin, Bhose. You'll stay here and guard the exit. Don't move from this spot until we come back or the deadline expires.'

They nodded and took up position.

'The question now is which way to go,' Alfray said, eyeing the tunnels.

'Do you think we should split into two groups, Captain?' Jup asked.

'No, that's something I definitely want to avoid. Our force is small enough as it is.'

'What, then? Toss a coin?'

'My feeling is that a large tunnel leads to something important. I'm drawn that way. But we should check the smaller one first, just in case it holds any unpleasant surprises.'

He sent Kestix and Jad to stand guard at the larger tunnel's mouth. Then he called over Hystykk, Noskaa, Calthmon and Breggin. He hefted a coil of rope and tossed it into the latter's hand. 'I want you four to walk that tunnel to the extent of this rope. If it looks as though it leads anywhere interesting, one of you can come back and let us know. But take no risks. At the first sign of trouble, head home.'

Jup took hold of one end of their rope. Breggin looped the other about his wrist, lifted his torch and led the others into the tunnel.

The band waited tensely as the rope played out. After a few minutes it went taut.

'What if they run into something they can't handle?' Alfray wondered. 'Do we go in after them?'

'That's a headache we could do without,' Stryke said. 'Let's see what happens.'

They didn't have long to wait. The troopers soon returned.

'Well?'

'Nothing to tell really, sir,' Breggin reported. 'The tunnel just went on and on; much further than the rope. There weren't any side passages or anything.'

'All right, we'll concentrate on the other tunnel. And we'll lay a rope trail along that one too, though I doubt the rope's going to go very far.'

'Won't that be a giveaway to any troll coming across it?' Jup put in.

'I think a warband tramping around with flaming torches is enough of a giveaway by itself, don't you?' He addressed them all. 'If we meet any defenders, strike first, ask questions later. We can't afford to give quarter. Stay together and keep noise to a minimum.'

With a final reminder to Liffin and Bhose to remain alert, he led the band into the main tunnel. Alfray walked beside him, holding a torch.

The tunnel ran arrow-straight, although it sloped downward at a gentle gradient. As they walked, Stryke became aware of a drop in temperature, and his nostrils were assailed by a disagreeably stale odour. They kept up an even pace for what Stryke judged to be around five minutes, but he suspected his time sense was distorted in this dark, silent world. Then they came to a side tunnel.

It was narrow, not much more than the width of an average doorway, and the entrance was low. The walls were damp and slimy. When they threw light into it they saw that the floor inclined to almost vertical. A rope around his waist and clutching a torch, one of the grunts edged down for a look.

When they tugged him back up, he said, 'It ends in a narrow shaft, like a well.'

'I reckon it's a storm channel,' Alfray speculated. 'To siphon off water if there's a flood.'

Stryke was impressed. 'Clever.'

'They've had a long time to build in such touches, Stryke. The trolls may be savage but they're not necessarily ignorant barbarians. We'd do well to remember that.'

They resumed their exploration of the main tunnel, which now dipped a little more sharply. Twenty or thirty paces later, the guide rope ran out. They left it and carried on. Another five minutes passed, in Stryke's quite possibly skewed estimation, and the tunnel began to widen. A little further on it opened out into another chamber. They paused.

As it seemed empty, and there were no sounds to be heard, they went in.

Barely had they entered when shapes suddenly disgorged from the shadows and rushed at them.

Their antagonists only half visible in the light of the flickering torches, the band laid into them. Fights broke out all around, near silently save for the clashing of blades, grunts of effort as weapons were swung, and occasional yells.

A fast-moving, dimly perceived figure came at Stryke and he lashed out at it. The blow was countered. He slashed again and missed. By sheer chance he caught sight of the glint off a blade aimed at his neck. He ducked and heard steel whistle above his head.

Stryke lunged forward, sword at arm's length. It impacted soft flesh and his foe went down. He turned to engage another shadowy attacker.

Beside him, Alfray and Jup were slugging it out with their own opponents. The dwarf battered open a skull. Alfray thrust his burning brand into a troll's face, inspiring a horrible screech. He cut it short with a follow-on from his blade.

Then there were no more of the enemy to fight. The skirmish had been brief and brutal, with the Wolverines prevailing despite the trolls' vision advantage.

Stryke looked around. He saw there was another passageway set in the far wall of the chamber.

'Guard that tunnel!' he barked.

Several grunts ran to stand by it, peering into its mouth, their swords at the ready.

'Anybody down?' he said. 'Any hurt?'

None had taken more than minor wounds.

'We were lucky,' Alfray panted.

'Yes, but only because we outnumbered them, I think. It could easily have gone the other way. Let's see what we've got here.' Stryke took Alfray's torch and held it over one of the bodies littering the ground.

The troll was short, very muscular and covered in shaggy

grey fur. It had the kind of physique, and wan complexion, to be expected of a subterranean race. The barrel chest had developed from living in rarefied air at lower depths. There were disproportionately long arms and legs. The hands were powerful, with long, thick taloned fingers, due to burrowing.

Though dead, its eyes were still open. They'd adapted to a lack of light by evolving to a much larger size than most races', with enormous black orbs. There was something pig-like about them. The nose was bulbous and soft like a dog's. In contrast to the washed-out appearance of the fur and beard, the creature's head was topped by a shock of almost primary-coloured hair. As far as they could tell in the uncertain light, it was a rusty orange.

'Not the sort of thing you'd like to bump into in the dark, is it?' Jup remarked wryly.

'Let's keep moving,' Stryke said.

They went into the new tunnel with renewed caution.

This passageway soon curved sharply to the right before straightening again. They passed a couple of side chambers, which proved small and empty. Then the tunnel narrowed to such an extent that they had to walk single-file. Perhaps a hundred feet further along they came to a stretch where the walls and ceiling were shored up with tree trunks and propped with wooden joists.

Stryke and Alfray were walking a little way ahead of the others. They reached a thick, jutting beam, and Alfray was first to start edging past, holding his torch aloft.

He was through before he realised the strut hid a blind tunnel.

By then it was too late.

A troll leapt at him from the shadows. The impact of its loathsomely hairy body sent Alfray flying and the torch was knocked from his hand.

Stryke moved in fast, slashing at the attacker, which danced back a step or two to avoid his blade. Springing forward again, it unleashed a torrent of blows that Stryke was hard put to hold at bay.

The space was so confined that the rest of the band couldn't get near enough to aid him. They were forced to watch helplessly as orc and troll exchanged hefty blows.

Stryke aimed a swing at the creature's chest. It jumped aside with amazing speed and his sword thudded deep into a wooden upright. A drizzle of dust descended.

The precious second it took Stryke to dislodge the blade almost cost him his life. Growling ferociously, the troll came at him, swiping the air madly.

But the creature hadn't counted on Alfray. On his hands and knees now, recovering from the initial clash, he reached out and grabbed the troll's legs. It wasn't sufficient to bring down the attacker but it distracted it long enough for Stryke to land a hit. His stroke cleaved into the troll's side. It wailed and fell back, smashing with force into the already half-severed upright.

The joist cracked with an echoing report.

An ominous rumbling came from above. Earth and stones began showering down. The troll let out a hideous, despairing scream.

Stryke snatched Alfray's jerkin and dragged him clear. He caught a fleeting glimpse of Jup and the rest of the band, behind them on the other side of the propped section.

There was a sound like a thunderclap. Then the ceiling crashed down on the blundering troll, crushing it instantly under masses of rocks and rubble. A shockwave like a mini-earthquake threw Alfray and Stryke to the ground. Clouds of choking dust swept over them.

They lay there with their hands over their heads, not daring to move, for what seemed like an eternity as the after-shocks reverberated.

Finally the cacophony died away, the avalanche subsided, the dust started to settle. Coughing and gasping for breath, they climbed to their feet.

At their rear the tunnel was completely blocked from floor to ceiling. Several huge boulders were among the debris. Alfray snatched up the still burning torch, their only source of light, and they scrambled to investigate.

It was instantly obvious that they couldn't hope to shift the downfall.

'Not a chance,' Alfray said, pushing uselessly at the immovable barrier. 'It must weigh tons.'

'You're right, we're not going to get through it.'

'You don't think it caught any of the band, do you?'

'No, I'm sure they were clear. But I can't see them being able to shift any of this from their side either. *Fuck it!*'

Alfray expelled a long breath. 'Well, if there was any doubt the trolls didn't know about us, that settles it. Unless they're all deaf.'

'We can't go back, and we can't stay here in case there's another fall. That only leaves one choice.'

'Let's hope the rest of the band find a way round this mess.'

'Or we find a way to them. But I wouldn't count on it, Alfray.'

'Two against the troll kingdom. Not very good odds, is it?'

'Let's hope we don't have to find out.'

They took a last look at the blocked tunnel, then turned and headed into the unknown.

Coilla reflected that while it had never exactly been fun to be in Haskeer's presence, at least it used to be a lot livelier when he was his old self.

She glanced at him, sitting opposite. He was using a saddle for a seat, hands hanging to either side, staring vacantly at nothing in particular.

Reafdaw was carrying out her orders and loading the sacks of pellucid on to a pair of the stronger horses. Just in case. Apart from that, there wasn't a lot they could do except wait. Certainly conversation with Haskeer was a dismal prospect. She'd already asked him how he felt half a dozen times and received the same unconvincing assurances of good health. That left few other topics of discussion, and the silence was uncomfortable.

So she experienced a mixture of relief and some apprehension when Haskeer looked up, seemed to see her properly for the first time, and said, 'Do you have the stars?'

'Yes, I do.'

'Can I look at them?'

Innocence seemed a wildly inappropriate word to apply to Haskeer at the best of times, but the way he made the request brought it to mind.

'Why not?' she replied.

She was aware of him watching her closely as she dug into her belt pouch. When the instrumentalities were produced, he held out his hand to take them. She thought that was where to draw the line.

'I think it'd be best if you looked but didn't touch,' she told him. 'No offence,' she added hurriedly, 'but Stryke ordered me not to let anybody else handle them. Nobody, not even you.'

It was a lie, but she knew Stryke would have intended that. She waited for Haskeer's blustery protest. It didn't come. This new Haskeer seemed infuriatingly reasonable. She wondered how long it would last.

Coilla sat there facing him with the stars sitting in her outstretched palm, and he stared. He seemed transfixed by the strange relics in the way a hatchling might be enchanted by a particularly shiny toy.

After a couple of minutes of Haskeer regarding their booty with an unbroken gaze, Coilla started to feel uncomfortable again. She could easily imagine this going on for hours, and she had better things to do. Actually, she didn't. But she was damned if she was going to sit there pretending to be a pedestal for the rest of the day.

'I reckon that's enough for now,' she announced, closing her fist on the stars. She returned them to her pouch.

Again, she was conscious of him watching her every move, the expression on his face mingling fascination and disappointment.

Another pall of silence descended. It was getting too oppressive for her.

'I'm just going over to the lookout point,' she said. 'They might be on their way back.' She didn't really think they would be; it was far too soon for that. But it gave her something to do.

Haskeer said nothing, just watched her walk away.

Coilla passed Reafdaw at the horses and called out to tell him what she was doing. He nodded and carried on working.

Their observation point wasn't far. It was an elevated slab of rock in sight of the camp, and from which the entrance to Scratch could just be seen. She walked to it unhurriedly, more intent on killing time than expecting to see her returning comrades.

Having climbed to the rock's flat plateau, she looked back. There was no sign of Reafdaw. She assumed he'd finished the chore and was with Haskeer. Good. Let somebody else share the boredom.

She turned around and concentrated on the distant cave-like entrance to the troll underworld. It wasn't a particularly sunny day, as was usual of late, but she still had to shield her eyes to make out any details.

There was no movement. That wasn't a surprise. She didn't expect any results yet.

Anything was better than going back to the tedium below, so she decided to kill a few more minutes up there.

She got to wondering whether Stryke hadn't bitten off more than he could chew this time. With a shudder, her mind went to that pit of darkness her fellow warriors had climbed into.

Then something heavy smashed into the back of her head and she fell into a black pit of her own.

Coilla returned to consciousness and a sea of pain.

There was the most gods-awful ache running from the back of her head and down her neck. She gingerly reached for the source of agony and her fingers came away bloody.

Realisation hit. She quickly sat up. Too quickly. She gasped, her head throbbed and spun.

There must have been an attack. The trolls! She got unsteadily to her feet and surveyed the surroundings. There was no sign of anybody in any direction, and their base camp looked deserted.

Groaning with the effort, she scrambled down from the rock and headed back as fast as she could. It crossed her mind to wonder how long she'd been lying on the rock. It could have been hours, though a glance at the sky indicated that was unlikely. She dabbed at the back of her head again. It was still bleeding but not profusely. She'd been lucky.

At that point it occurred to her that if her attacker had been a troll she wouldn't be alive now. That led to a second, far more dreadful thought. Her hand went to her belt pouch.

It was open. The stars were gone.

She cursed aloud and started running, the pain be damned.

When she reached camp there was no sign of Haskeer or Reafdaw. She called out their names. Nothing.

She called again. This time she was answered by groans coming from the direction of the horses. She sped that way.

Reafdaw was spread out on the ground, dangerously near the tethered mounts. Which explained why she hadn't seen him earlier. She knelt at his side. He too had a bloodied head. His complexion was chalky white.

'Reafdaw!' she said, shaking him violently.

He groaned again.

'Reafdaw!' Her shaking grew even more insistent. 'What happened?'

I . . . he . . .'

'Where's Haskeer? What's going on?'

The grunt seemed to gather a little strength. *'Haskeer. Bastard . . .'*

'What do you mean?' She was afraid she already knew the answer to that.

'Just . . . just after you left he came . . . over to . . . me. Didn't say . . . much. Then he went . . . berserk. Near . . . near stove my head . . . in.'

'He did the same to me, the swine.' She looked at the trooper's wound. 'It could be a lot worse,' she told him. 'Reafdaw, I know you feel like shit, but this is important. What happened then? Where did he go?'

The grunt swallowed, the pain clear in his eyes. 'He went . . . off. I was out . . . for a . . . while. Came round. He was back. Thought . . . thought he was going to finish . . . me. But no. Took . . . a horse.'

'*Damn!* He got the stars.'

'Gods,' Reafdaw responded weakly.

'Which way? Did you see which way he went?'

'North. I think . . . it was . . . north.'

She had to make a decision, and fast.

'I've got to go after him. You'll have to look to yourself until the others get back. Can you do that?'

'Yes . . . Go.'

'You'll be all right.' She got up, her head blazing, and snatched a water sack from the nearest horse. She laid it in his hands. 'Here. I'm sorry, Reafdaw, I have to do this.'

She staggered to the fastest-looking horse and unhitched it. Clambering on to its back, she spurred it hard.

And headed north.

25

Jup and the remainder of the band hadn't been able to dig through to Stryke and Alfray. They weren't even sure if they'd escaped the collapse of the tunnel roof.

The only thing they could do was turn around and head back the way they'd come.

Having rendezvoused with Liffin and Bhose, standing guard beneath the shaft, they had their first disappointment. The slim hope that Stryke and Alfray might have found a way round the blocked tunnel and back to the entrance was dashed.

Jup's next thought was to try to reach them another way. The only possibility was the smaller of the two tunnels. He led the band into it. But after a long and uneventful walk, during which they found only empty side chambers and cul-de-sacs, they reached its end.

With heavy hearts they returned to the starting point.

There seemed little point in waiting. The only remaining hope was that the pair might have discovered another way out of the labyrinth and to the surface. Jup ordered a retreat. They all climbed back up the shaft and headed for camp at speed.

On arrival, the further crushing disappointment of not

finding their comrades had returned was overlaid with disaster when they came across Reafdaw.

He'd managed to rise to a sitting position, and nursed his head as they stood around him, horrified at the tale he had to tell.

'So that was it,' the grunt concluded. 'Haskeer attacked me and Coilla like a madman and he got the stars. She went haring after him. That's all I can tell you.'

Jup ordered that his injuries be dressed.

The band set up a clamour about what they should do.

'Shut up!' the dwarf yelled, and they quietened. 'Trying to get Stryke and Alfray out of that labyrinth should be the priority. We know they're living on borrowed time down there. On the other hand, we can't let Haskeer get away with the stars, and it sounds as though Coilla might not be in a fit state to stop him.'

'Why not split the band and try both?' somebody shouted.

'We'd be slicing our forces too finely. A rescue bid down below needs all we've got, and more. Scouring the countryside for Haskeer could easily take all of us.'

Another voice was raised. 'So what *are* we going to do?' it demanded. Then added 'Sergeant' as a far from respectful afterthought.

There was an unmistakable edge of hostility in the question, and on more than one of the anxious faces surrounding him. The simmering resentment some felt about his race and rank was in danger of breaking surface.

But he didn't know what to say. He had to make a choice and make it now, and it would be so easy to get it wrong.

He stared at them, saw the expectation in their eyes, and in a few, something more menacing.

Jup had always been ambitious for command. But not this way.

*

Coilla had a stroke of luck about half an hour after setting out on her search.

She was beginning to think she'd never find him, and have to return in shame, when she caught a glimpse of a distant rider, galloping across the skyline along a ridge of hills further north.

She wasn't certain, but it looked like Haskeer.

Digging in her heels, she urged her mount to greater effort.

The horse was foaming by the time she made the hills, and she allowed it no rest in climbing. Once at the top she paused, raising herself in the saddle to scan the land in the direction of distant Taklakameer. She couldn't see the rider. But it was a mixed terrain and there were endless places that might conceal him. Having no other option, she galloped onward.

The route she followed took her into a shallow, verdant valley, with clumps of trees on either side and others scattered in her path. She didn't allow that to slow her speed, though now she began to fear that the horse wouldn't be able to sustain the pace much longer.

Then she caught another glimpse of the rider, far off at the valley's end. She bore down and rode like fury.

Suddenly she wasn't alone.

Two riders came in from the trees at her right, another appeared on her left. They seemed to be humans.

She was so taken by surprise that when the one on her left quickly moved in and side-swiped her mount with a leather whip, she lost control. The reins flew from her hands. Her horse stumbled and went down. The world tilted at a crazy angle.

Coilla thudded into the ground, rolled several times and came to a stop, the wind knocked out of her.

Head swimming, she tried to rise, but only got as far as her knees.

The trio of humans had pulled up and dismounted. She looked at them, her vision clearing.

One was tall and guileful-eyed. He had a mean, pinched face disfigured by a scar. The second was short and lithe. He worried at a black eye-patch and grimaced at her through rotten teeth. The last had the build of a mountain bear and it was all muscle. He was completely hairless and had an oft-broken nose.

The tall one grinned and it wasn't friendly. 'Now what do we have here?' he said, his voice oily and laden with menace.

Coilla shook her head, trying to clear the pain away. She wanted to stand but couldn't manage it.

The three humans moved forward, reaching for their weapons.

For something like an hour, Stryke and Alfray walked the tunnel they had no choice but to follow. They were no side-shoots or chambers leading off from it, and it altered only in descending at an ever-increasing rate.

Finally they came to another chamber, by far the biggest they'd seen so far. They knew it to be untenanted because, unlike the others, it was brightly lit by scores of flaming brands. Its jagged ceiling was far overhead, prickling with stalactites, and at least six tunnels ran off from it in different directions.

The chamber housed just one object; a vast block of fashioned stone resembling a lidded sarcophagus. Mysterious symbols were carved on its sides and top.

They walked to it, their footsteps echoing in the great hollow space.

'What do you suppose this might be?' Alfray wondered.

'Who can say?' Stryke replied. 'It's said these denizens of the lower world worship dark and terrible gods. This has the look of ritual about it.' He laid his hand on the time-smoothed surface. 'We'll probably never know.'

'You are wrong!'

They spun to the source of the voice.

A troll, clothed in robes of spun gold and with a silver crown upon his head, had entered the chamber unseen behind them. He was of mightier build than any they had slain, and he held an ornate crook almost equal to his height.

Stryke and Alfray brought up their swords, ready to take on the unexpected visitation. But as they did so, a multitude of trolls poured into the chamber from all the other tunnels. They numbered scores, and all were armed, many with spears bearing barbed tips.

The orcs glanced at each other.

'I'm for taking as many as we can,' Stryke hissed.

'Well said,' Alfray agreed.

'That would be foolish indeed,' the troll boomed, sending forward his troops with a flick of his hand.

A forest of spears were aimed at the orcs, and now they saw that the second ranks bore notched bows with arrows aimed at them. They couldn't reach their foes, let alone set about killing them.

'Lay down your arms,' the troll demanded.

'That's not something an orc's used to doing,' Stryke told him contemptuously.

'The choice is yours,' the creature returned. 'Surrender them or die.'

The mass of spears edged closer. The archers' strings were made more taut.

Alfray and Stryke exchanged a look. An unspoken agreement passed between them.

They threw down their swords.

The trolls rushed forward and seized them. But if the orcs expected instant death, they were wrong.

'I am Tannar,' the troll headman informed them, 'king of the inner realm. Monarch and high priest in one, servant of the gods that protect our domain from such as you.'

Neither orc replied, but showed him a proud demeanour.

'You'll pay for your intrusion,' Tannar went on, 'and pay for it in a way most beneficial to our gods.'

The trolls soldiers forced Stryke and Alfray back to the stone slab. And then they knew beyond a doubt what function it served.

It was a sacrificial altar.

Rough hands bound them. The troll army parted to allow their king through.

As he slowly approached, he produced something from the folds of his cloak. The vile keenness of its curved steel caught glints of light. Deep and sinister, the assembled trolls began to chant in an outlandish tongue.

Moving towards the orcs at a funereal pace, Tannar raised the sacrificial blade.

'The knife,' Alfray whispered. 'Stryke, *the knife*!'

Stryke looked at it and understood.

To have tasted freedom and then have it snatched away like this was as cruel a jest as any the darkest gods could devise. That all had come to nought was bad enough. But what Stryke saw was the bitterest blow imaginable.

The richly ornamented knife the troll king held aloft was further decorated with a very particular addition. Attached to its hilt was an instantly recognisable object.

They had found the star they sought.